She felt her pulse skip.

"Jeff."

Familiarity filled his eyes. "Marsha." He strode toward her, his arms open in greeting.

She rose and walked into his embrace.

"It's been a long time," he said.

She drew back and studied his deep blue eyes. "Too long," she agreed.

Good-looking and always so nice. She realized how much she'd missed him. Seeing him on the island seemed so right. So real.

His gaze swept her face. "I wondered how I'd entertain myself while I'm here, and here you are."

Books by Gail Gaymer Martin

Love Inspired

Upon a Midnight Clear #117
Secrets of the Heart #147
A Love for Safekeeping #161
*Loving Treasures #177
*Loving Hearts #199
Easter Blessings #202
 "The Butterfly Garden"
The Harvest #223
 "All Good Gifts"

*Loving Ways #231
*Loving Care #239
Adam's Promise #259
*Loving Promises #291
*Loving Feelings #303
*Loving Tenderness #323
In His Eyes #361
With Christmas in His Heart #373
In His Dreams #407

Steeple Hill Books

*Loving

The Christmas Kite
Finding Christmas
That Christmas Feeling
 "Christmas Moon"

GAIL GAYMER MARTIN

says when friends talk about things that happen to them, they often stop short and ask, "Will this be in your next novel?" Sometimes it is. Gail is amazed that God has blessed her with a writing career. She loves the privilege of writing stories that touch people's hearts and share God's promises.

Gail is a multipublished author in non-fiction and fiction with over one million books in print. Her novels have received numerous awards: A Booksellers Best Award in 2005 and 2006, a Holt Medallion in 2001 and 2003, a Texas Winter Rose 2003, an American Christians Romance Writers 2002 Book of the Year Award and the *Romantic Times BOOKreviews* Reviewers Choice as best Love Inspired Novel of 2002.

Gail lives in Michigan with her husband, Bob, her dearest friend and greatest fan. When not behind her computer, she enjoys a busy life—traveling; presenting workshops at conferences; speaking at churches, business groups and civic centers; and singing as a soloist and member of her church choir. She is also involved in playing handbells and handchimes and she sings with the renowned Detroit Lutheran Singers.

Gail enjoys hearing from readers. Write to her at P.O. Box 760063, Lathrup Village, MI 48076 or at authorgailmartin@aol.com. Visit her Web site at www.gailmartin.com.

In His Dreams
Gail Gaymer Martin

Steeple
Hill®

Published by Steeple Hill Books™

STEEPLE HILL BOOKS

Steeple
Hill®

ISBN-13: 978-0-373-87443-9
ISBN-10:   0-373-87443-X

IN HIS DREAMS

www.SteepleHill.com

Printed in U.S.A.

Be joyful in hope,
patient in affliction,
faithful in prayer.
—*Romans* 12:12

For my stepdaughter Brenda whose faith, determination and courage have made a difference in my life.

Blessings to the residents of Beaver Island whose lives have been touched by this amazing island filled with so much history and beauty. Thanks particularly to Steve West from the Chamber of Commerce, Editor Elaine West of *Northern Islander,* Jane Bailey of East Wind Day Spa, Phyllis Moore, librarian of Beaver Island Public Library, and Louise King of Beaver Boat-tique who all answered my tons of questions.

Chapter One

"Change…just accept it, Marsha. The only thing permanent is death." Marsha Sullivan muttered her thoughts aloud.

Her mind filled with equal parts nostalgia and frustration as she leaned against the chalet's deck railing and gazed beyond the Lake Michigan beach to the glistening water. The cottage brought back too many memories. She had feared this would happen. It had once before.

She smacked her fist against the wooden rail and turned her back to the rolling waves. "Barb," she called to her sister inside the summer cottage, "let's go into town for a while and pick up groceries."

Straining to hear her sister's response, she waited a moment before calling again. "Barb? Did you hear me?"

"What?" Her sister's voice bounded through the screen.

"Let's take a ride into town for groceries."

The screen door slid open, and Barb stepped through the doorway with a frown darkening her face. "We just got here. We should have shopped when we got off the ferry."

Marsha's shoulders tensed. "We came here first because I thought you'd like to put away your clothes and unpack the car."

Barb's frame blocked the doorway, her cheeks flushing with color. "Don't think for me. Please. You're always doing that."

You're always doing that. Marsha sank onto the picnic-table bench and leaned against the rough wood. "I'm sorry, Barb. I'm not trying to control you." Tension tightened the muscles in her back. She'd heard the criticism before, even from her husband, Don, before Lou Gehrig's disease had taken his life four years earlier. "I thought we could go into town and look around a little. Enjoy ourselves."

"I am enjoying myself. I'm in the middle of a novel." Barb swished a strand of hair from her forehead, her move-ment showing her irritation. She stepped back and slid the screen closed.

"Sorry I asked," Marsha mumbled, then immediately re-gretted her tone. She pulled her back from the hard table edge and pressed her fingers against her forehead. Finally, she stood, paused to calm herself, then pushed the screen along the track and entered the living room. "Okay. I'm going into town for a while. Enjoy your novel."

"Have a nice time," Barb said, her eyes glued to the pa-perback.

Marsha grabbed her purse from the kitchenette counter and strode to the back porch, not stopping the screen from slamming. She stood a moment outside, longing to bridge the distance that separated her and her sister, but she couldn't. She should be used to her sister's detachment by now. Barb had been like that for years.

Marsha wished she hadn't slammed the door. She knew her sister's ways and she understood. No, she didn't understand, but she wanted to. Her sister was only forty, two years younger than Marsha and her life had seemed to stall. Marsha had often pondered when Barb had changed so much and why.

When she was younger, Barb had been thin and quite pretty, but in her teen years, she'd changed. She'd let her social life slide and sat around the house avoiding exercise. She seemed to let food become her friend. How could two people raised in the same home be so different? The question was moot. Barb seemed happy with her life. It was Marsha who guessed that, deep inside, she actually wasn't. Marsha never asked why Barb had changed, and she figured her sister would never discuss it with her, anyway.

Marsha drew in a lengthy breath of clean island air and headed for her car parked on the gravel driveway. A pebble slipped into her sandal, and she stopped a moment, leaning her hip against the car, to remove a pea-sized stone. Amazing what tiny things could cause such irritation, she thought, then realized that seemed to be a truth for much of life.

As she stepped from beneath the shade of a cedar tree, the warm sun fell on her arms. She opened the car door and slid onto the hot seat cushion, raising her legs and wishing she'd worn slacks instead of shorts. Back home, she'd never think of wearing shorts in public, but here, no one knew her and she enjoyed the freedom.

Instead of using the air conditioner, Marsha rolled down the window and let the wind whip through her hair. Much time had passed since she'd felt this kind of liberation. "Thanks for buying this cottage, Don," she said, a bittersweetness welling inside her. She pushed away the feeling and kept her thoughts focused on her trip to town.

She followed the narrow road and, through the passenger window, Font Lake flashed between the evergreens. She and Don had rented a boat one summer and paddled around the lake, watching the turtles sun themselves on the lily pads. She recalled one day when they'd run into Don's brother, Jeff, and his wife rowing toward them on the lake. They'd teased back and forth, singing "There's a Hole in the Bottom of the Sea," each taking turns to add another line. Jeff's pleasant voice still rang in her head. He was such a handsome man, and Marsha wondered if she'd met him first what might have happened.

Guilt nudged at her for the thought, and she let it slip and filled her mind with the silly song. "There's a frog on the bump of the log in the hole in the bottom of the sea." She sang into the wind.

Marsha threw her head back, enjoying the memory. She wondered if Jeff remembered that day. Regret rolled over her. She hadn't seen Jeff in so long. Too long. She and Jeff spent so much time together, but after Don's death, she'd drifted away from the entire family. It was wrong. Jeff probably could have used her support when his wife had died so suddenly in that tragic car accident. She should have offered Jeff some help instead of clinging to her own loss for so long. Being the single parent of their disabled young daughter, Bonnie, couldn't be easy for him.

As the last view of the lake flashed past, Marsha pulled herself from her doldrums and breathed in renewed vigor. Maybe she'd rent a boat one afternoon, even if she had to rent it alone. Perhaps she could even convince Barb to go.

She shrugged off her melancholy emotions and enjoyed the scenery. The thick woods gave way to buildings as she drove into St. James, the island's only town. Nearing Main

Street, Daddy Frank's caught her eye, a small gray-and-white building with a blue awning. In front, two white open-air tents had been erected for customers to sit beneath at picnic benches and enjoy their famous waffle ice-cream cones.

As if her car suddenly had a mind of its own, Marsha found herself veering to the right and put her foot on the brake. Ice cream. It could raise the most downcast spirit. She exited the car and went inside to order a double dip of peanut-butter cup.

She strolled outside and slid onto one of the picnic benches, licking the creamy dessert and convincing herself to ignore her disappointment with Barb and enjoy herself.

The afternoon sunlight blinded her, and she dug into her purse for sunglasses. Apparently, she'd left them back at the cottage when she had made her dramatic exit. She shook her head at the thought. *I need patience, Lord,* she thought as she shifted farther beneath the covering to avoid the direct rays. When she looked up, a man and young girl were climbing from a car parked beside hers. She felt her pulse skip, realizing it was her brother-in-law.

"Jeff."

He turned and stared at her a moment as if he didn't recognize her. Then familiarity filled his eyes. "Marsha." He strode toward her, his arms open in greeting.

She rose and walked into his embrace. Her gaze shifted from his warm smile to the full head of dark hair that framed his classic features. Good-looking and always so nice. She realized how much she'd missed him. "I was thinking about you when I passed the lake."

A grin flickered on his lips for a moment. "The boat rides and that silly song."

She nodded. "You remember."

He grinned and gave her another squeeze.

Marsha searched his face, unable to get her fill of him. Seeing him on the island seemed so right. So real. It took her back to the good times years earlier.

His gaze swept her face. "I wondered how I'd entertain myself while I'm here, and here you are."

"That would be fun."

"And look at Bonnie. You're getting more grown up every day." Her niece had her mother's light brown eyes, her dad's slightly turned nose and those darling dimples, but the child's maturing form gave Marsha pause.

Bonnie gave her a shy look but moved closer and focused on the creamy treat in Marsha's hand. "We're getting ice cream, too." She motioned to Marsha's cone.

Marsha gave the ice cream another lick. "It's really good."

Bonnie looked at the treat a minute and dragged her tongue over her lips before tugging on her father's arm. "Let's go, Daddy."

"In a minute, Bonnie."

"I want to go now." Her voice rose to a piercing whine.

Jeff cringed, then sent Marsha a look that was probably supposed to be an apologetic grin. "We'll be back." He took Bonnie's hand and led her toward the building.

Marsha understood his look. She recalled that Bonnie tended to go into a tizzy when she didn't get what she wanted, and Jeff apparently had difficulty dealing with it. Having a disabled child was difficult enough for two parents. One parent having to do it all seemed an unfair task.

As strong as her faith had always been, Marsha wondered sometimes what God had been thinking when He'd taken the life of a major caregiver like Marilou. She'd been a gentle woman, so patient and understanding with Bonnie, while Jeff seemed to use avoidance as his method of coping.

Coping. In recent years, Marsha had learned to cope with difficulties and sadness as part of her daily life. Yet, she knew that God was good and He had a purpose for everything. She only wished the Lord would give her a hint sometimes. Maybe then she'd be more patient.

She turned away from the hot sun to face the door, her mind on Jeff's unexpected arrival. She really shouldn't have been surprised. They both owned summer homes on the island. Well, *home* hardly described her A-frame chalet, but Jeff's ranch was a real home, filled with all the loving touches that his and Don's parents had added over so many years.

Jeff's image settled into her mind as she watched the door for him and Bonnie. Jeff would probably be considered more handsome than Don, but Jeff lacked the deep smile lines that she loved about her husband's features. The brothers had the same trim muscular builds, about six feet tall and, when Jeff had given her a welcoming hug, she'd felt comfortable and almost whole again in his friendly embrace.

The restaurant door swung open, and Bonnie came through followed by Jeff. She held a double-dip waffle cone whose contents had already left a spot on her T-shirt. The girl looked a bit disheveled, as if needing a mother's touch.

Bonnie slid across the bench from her, the cone leaning precariously toward the ground, and Marsha shifted forward as if hoping to stop the ice cream from falling, but Jeff saw her concern and straightened Bonnie's hold.

"Be careful, Bonnie, or you'll be crying because you lost one of your dips. Push your hair out of your eyes, too, honey."

She looked at the cone and then at her dad. "I'm eating it. It's called bubble gum." She giggled. "But it won't blow bubbles. Look." She stuck out her tongue and blew a spray of ice cream into the air while it dripped down her face.

Jeff looked disconcerted and grabbed a napkin to clean up the mess. "It's ice cream. Bubble gum is just the name of it. Please don't do that again, Bonnie."

Bonnie scowled and lowered her head as if irked at her father's reproach.

Marsha wanted to say something to ease the tense situation, but Jeff's voice stopped her thoughts.

"I'm sorry I didn't get in touch for so long, Marsha. After Marilou's—" He faltered and eyed Bonnie.

"I understand." Marsha's chest tightened. "I've missed seeing you. I—" She paused, not wanting to mention Marilou again. "How long are you staying?"

He shrugged. "Maybe a month if we don't get too bored." He gave a toss of his head toward Bonnie. "How about you?"

His gaze unsettled her. His look seemed to probe so deeply into her eyes that she thought he was trying to read her mind. "About the same. I've only been here twice since…"

She caught herself again and wished their conversation didn't hinge on the past, not only for Bonnie, but for herself. She'd lived too long in the shadow of Don's death and the sadness that had followed, and she was certain Jeff had struggled with the same grief over Marilou. "I've thought about selling the place. It's too lonely."

"I know." He glanced away. When the sun hit his face, he squinted, then slid farther along the bench into the shade. "And you figure you can handle it now?"

"Handle it?"

"The loneliness." The word came out softly and faded into nothingness.

She didn't want to talk about loneliness. "Barb's with me."

He glanced toward her car. "Here?"

"She stayed back at the cottage." Marsha drew in a ragged breath, then stopped herself from complaining about her sister. "I suppose you have a schedule of activities while you're here."

"We have no particular plans." He gave her a questioning look, and the silence stretched awkwardly until his attention turned to Bonnie. He handed her another napkin to catch the leak at the bottom of the cone where she'd bitten off the end. "I'm just taking it day by day, so if you have any ideas let me know."

Plans? Marsha had been taking life day by day. She'd been alone for four years—never dated and couldn't imagine herself doing so, but plans with Jeff might be good for both of them.

Marsha eyed his handsome face. "Are you seeing any—" She cringed hearing the question she'd almost asked. "What do you do for fun, Jeff?"

His neck stiffened and he looked surprised. "Fun?" His eyes searched hers. "I—" He shrugged and appeared to chew the inside of his bottom lip for a moment. "Bonnie keeps me busy."

Sorry she'd made him uncomfortable, Marsha shifted her attention to her niece. "She's almost a young lady."

"I know."

Jeff seemed at a loss for words. Sadness filled his eyes. The look wrenched Marsha's chest. Bonnie was growing up, but living an independent life some day seemed far out of the girl's reach.

"How old are you now, Bonnie?" Marsha asked, leaning closer to her niece.

Bonnie's head popped up and she grinned an ice-cream smile. "Eleven."

"Eleven. Wow! That's amazing. I can remember the day you were born."

The girl gave her a questioning look. "You can?"

"Sure do." Marsha let her comment slide. Jeff and Marilou had been ecstatic, but years passed and then troubles begun when Bonnie'd had learning problems and displays of tantrums. She wished things had been different for them.

"I suppose we'd better go," Jeff said, mopping up more of Bonnie's ice-cream drippings.

"Already?" Marsha asked, then wished she'd been more discreet about her feelings. Seeing Jeff reminded her of the good days when life had seemed to have purpose. "Any plans tonight?"

"No. None. How about you?" His inquiring look grew to a playful grin. "Any suggestions?"

"How about coming over later for a swim and then staying for dinner?" Heat rose in her cheeks and the sensation embarrassed her. She and Jeff without Marilou and Don seemed strange.

"Would you like that, Bonnie?" she added to dissuade her anxious feeling.

Jeff glanced at Bonnie, who didn't respond, and his cheery look faded. "She's shy. I don't think—"

"Are you having hot dogs?" Bonnie asked without looking up.

Marsha laughed and her discomfort faded. "How about spaghetti?"

"I love spaghetti."

Marsha grinned at Jeff. "What do you say?"

Jeff appeared to ponder her question before turning to Bonnie. "Do you want to go to Aunt Marsha's for dinner?"

"And swimming." Bonnie grinned and nodded.

"Great. Then we'll see you about four. Swim first."

"Swim and dinner," Bonnie said as her cone tipped and slipped from her fingers.

Jeff made a grab, but it was too late. The ice cream drizzled down her pants and fell to the ground.

"My ice cream," Bonnie whimpered as her hands coiled into fists.

Jeff bent to retrieve the dirty cone. "It's gone, but you've had enough ice cream, anyway."

Bonnie swung back and struck Jeff's shoulder.

He wrapped his hand around her fist and held her still. "Bonnie, the ice cream was almost gone. If you can behave, we'll go to Aunt Marsha's. If you can't, we'll stay home. It's your choice."

Tears rolled down her cheeks until her shoulders finally sagged and she lifted her head. "Aunt Marsha's."

"Good choice." Relief spread across his face and he gave Marsha a grateful look.

She released a stalled breath that had nearly burst from her lungs. Although Jeff·had handled Bonnie well this time, the situation broke her heart as she imagined his need for patience.

Marsha opened the car's backseat door and pulled out her two bags of groceries. Now that Jeff and Bonnie had agreed to come for dinner, she'd added a few treats to her shopping list.

She hit the remote lock, then chuckled to herself. Who'd steal her car? Crime was nearly nonexistent on Beaver Island.

Hoisting the two bags in her arms, Marsha headed for the house and maneuvered through the doorway. She plopped the bags on the kitchen counter, noticing her sister sitting on the same sofa and in the same spot she'd been when Marsha left.

"Guess who I saw in town?" Marsha asked.

Barb lifted her head and lowered her novel. "I have no idea."

"Jeff and Bonnie."

Barb's eyes narrowed. "Who?"

"Don's brother, Jeff Sullivan, and his daughter. You remember them."

She nodded. "It's been a long time." She refocused on the novel.

"They're coming over later for a swim and joining us for dinner."

Marsha watched the book inch downward as Barb peered at her from over the pages. "Dinner? I thought we were here to relax and——"

"Dinner's nothing fancy, Barb. Spaghetti with jar sauce. I'm not cooking a five-course meal."

Barb drew in a lengthy breath. "I guess you can do what you want." She lifted the book, then lowered it again and gave Marsha an apologetic look. "I'm sorry. You know I'm not always comfortable with small talk."

Small talk. Marsha had to clamp her mouth shut from saying something hurtful like *Lately you're not one for any talk.* She lifted her shoulders without comment and pulled groceries from the sacks. As she folded the paper bags, Marsha tried again. "Have you been outside? It's a beautiful day."

"Too many bugs. I went out for a minute."

Marsha grabbed a magazine from a table and headed toward the sliding door to the deck. "I'm going out. You can join me if you'd like." She stepped outside, glanced back in at Barb, who didn't budge, then slid the door closed.

Disappointment settled over her. She sat on the wooden steps leading toward the sandy path to the beach and gazed at the blue-green water lapping against the sand. White foam rose on the waves, then dissipated. Marsha bowed her head. *Lord, give me an idea what to do. Ignore Barb? Don't take it personally? What should I do?*

She flung open the cover of her magazine, then added an *amen* as if she'd forgotten her talk with God had been a prayer. What did people do who needed someone to talk with and didn't have the Lord? She couldn't imagine.

An article on healthy eating caught her attention and, the next time she looked at her watch, Marsha realized her company would arrive in less than half an hour.

Pushing herself up from the hard plank, she stepped onto the deck and went inside. Barb had left the sofa and stood in the kitchen, rummaging through the groceries. Barb opened a cellophane package and took out a handful of cookies. "What time are you eating?"

"About six." She watched her sister and wondered what she was thinking. "Jeff and Bonnie will be here soon if you'd like to swim."

"No thanks, but I'll help with dinner."

Pleased with her offer, Marsha patted Barb's arm. "Thanks."

Barb jerked as if startled. "You're welcome." She pulled a cookie from the wrapper and popped it into her mouth.

Marsha hesitated a moment, addled by Barb's wavering

attitude—standoffish one minute and cooperative the next. She longed to make things better between them. Not knowing what else to do or say, other than the thanks she'd already said, she headed into her bedroom and opened a dresser drawer. She stared into it, pondering which swimsuit to wear.

Barb's bedroom door thudded closed, and Marsha figured she'd hibernate there until Jeff and Bonnie had gone down to the beach. Again, her thoughts darkened. What could she do to make life different for Barb? They were so opposite. Barb's life seemed to stagnate while hers... What? It had been stagnating, too, hadn't it, these past years?

Jeff rose in her mind. He hadn't said much about himself, except when it related to Bonnie. Yet one admission had slipped out. He'd said he felt lonely. Loneliness did strange things to people. She nearly became a bear with her hibernation—except hers was year round. She let so many things slip past since Don had died.

Marsha shook her head to get rid of the dark thoughts. Today, she wanted to enjoy herself and not dwell on the past. The past just held people back from the future.

She chose her pale blue swimsuit, dressed and, as she tugged a beach cover over her head, a car door thudded in the driveway. Her pulse skipped and she paused, trying to make sense of her excitement. It was only Jeff and Bonnie, but the company pleased her.

Jeff's tap sounded on the door, and she grabbed a beach towel from her bed, then opened the door. "Come in," she called down the short hallway. She shut the bedroom door and hurried to greet them.

Jeff stood outside dressed in khaki shorts with a navy

T-shirt on top and a towel draped around his broad shoulders. His skin already showed a rich tan. Marsha gazed down at her white legs and grimaced. Maybe a few sunny days could change that. Maybe a few sunny days could change a lot of things.

Jeff held the door open, waiting for Bonnie. She ambled in, and he glanced at Marsha with a look that sent her pulse skipping.

What was *that?* The sensation startled her. She drew her eyes away from his and forced herself to focus on her niece, though her gaze kept shifting to Jeff's tall frame. "Ready for a swim?" she asked Bonnie, trying to sound normal.

"Ready," Bonnie said, dragging her beach towel along the linoleum.

"Ready." He shifted beside her and rested his hand on her shoulder. The warmth ran down her arm.

"Everyone's ready then," she said, amazed at the feelings that were beginning to weave through her.

Jeff gave her a smile.

She smiled back, yet wondered how ready she really was.

Chapter Two

"Please pick up your towel before you trip over it," Jeff said, touching Bonnie's shoulder as they followed Marsha toward the sliding door.

Marsha gestured for him to go ahead, and he did, wondering if coming here had been a mistake. He felt strange accepting an invitation to his brother's cottage without his brother being there. He'd always been fond of Marsha. They had a great bond when Don was alive, and he always found her attractive and charming, but now things had changed. He had changed. They had changed.

Bonnie bounded down the deck stairs, her towel once again sweeping along the sand. He let the matter go. Instead, he studied Bonnie, pondering Marsha's comment at Daddy Frank's earlier that day. He gave a shudder. Bonnie was no longer a little girl. Her behavior seemed to have stood still, but her body had turned into a young woman's. The situation scared him. How could he explain life to her as her body matured but her behavior didn't? How could he be both father and mother to a teenage daughter?

Marsha stood beside him as he scanned the bay, watching the water's slow, sun-tipped ripples. A sweet scent wrapped around him like spring rain in a flower garden. He drew in the pleasant aroma, remembering the familiar fragrance that Marsha always wore. They had been a foursome—Marsha and Don, he and Marilou. The memory wrenched his heart. Today, they were two, standing by the same rolling water on the same beach—but without so much of what they'd had before.

His thoughts meandered away from the past to the present. The sun's rays glinted on Marsha's red hair. It fell in long curling waves below her shoulders, so heavy and full he wondered what it weighed. He flinched, wondering why he was calculating the weight of her hair like a sheep farmer selling wool. The preoccupation filled him with discomfort. Marsha wasn't just anyone. She was his brother's wife—his deceased brother's wife. His stomach tightened as a flood of guilt washed over him.

He turned away and found a patch of wild grass mingled with wildflowers and dropped his towel. He drew in another breath. Maybe it was the wildflowers he'd smelled earlier, but the aroma had faded where he stood.

"Bonnie, put your towel here," he called, then realized it was too late. She'd already pulled it into the surf undulating along the beach.

As Marsha dropped her belongings beside his, the sweet fragrance returned, twisting his emotions. He hurried away toward Bonnie, took her towel and gave it a toss onto the dry sand.

When Marsha neared, her eyes captivated him, a metallic-blue that deepened as he studied them, enhanced by the color she wore.

He realized she'd noticed him gazing at her and heat rose up his neck. He stepped into the water and shivered as the cold water hit him, trying to recover from his embarrassment.

She sent him a warm smile that could take the iciness out of even the coldest lake.

Rubbing her arms, Marsha waded into the chilly water. The deeper the water, the faster she rubbed, as if the friction might warm the water rising up her legs.

Jeff fought to keep his gaze from Marsha as she forged into the deep water. He garnered courage and dived beneath the frigid waves. When he shot up, he let out a howl, then laughed.

Marsha followed suit and dived beneath the ripples. When she bobbed up, she let out a yell mingled with a laugh.

Shifting his gaze to Bonnie, Jeff felt guilty he'd nearly forgotten to keep an eye on her. She trudged toward him deeper into the lake, and his concern rose, knowing she wasn't a good swimmer. "Careful," he called. "Wait for me."

"I can do it myself," Bonnie said.

When he reached her, he took her arm. "Let me help you."

Bonnie jerked away. "No."

He swallowed his frustration. "Bonnie."

"No. I can swim by myself."

He feared a tantrum. They erupted at unexpected times, and she'd been well behaved for so long he knew the cork would blow soon. He hated for Marsha to witness it again. She'd seen too much already at Daddy Frank's. He reached toward Bonnie. "Let's swim together. Okay?"

Bonnie pushed away from him and tried to run, but she stumbled and slipped beneath the water, her arms flailing above her head.

Jeff reached for her and pulled her, coughing and sputtering, to the surface. He wanted to say *I told you so,* but he knew that would solve nothing. "Deep water can be dangerous. Right?"

She nodded and coughed again.

"Take my hand," he said.

"No," she cried, swinging away from him.

In frustration, he glanced toward Marsha and saw her bouncing in the water toward them. Bonnie spotted her and, her tantrum forgotten, she laughed at Marsha's antics.

"We'll go out toward Aunt Marsha. Take my hand," he said, reaching toward her.

She took it, and his heart lifted, hearing Bonnie's giggle and realizing Marsha had caused a well-needed distraction and had, perhaps without knowing it, prevented a scene.

Jeff studied Marsha again, her face brightened by the sun and her smile just as warm. Her wet hair now clung to her face and the sunlight highlighted the copper streaks in her red hair. He realized she'd missed out on something important to so many women—being a mother. Was the decision by choice? The topic had never been discussed, but seeing her today with Bonnie made him curious.

While Marsha played in the water with Bonnie, he decided to join in, but Bonnie hardly seemed to notice him. Her attention seemed glued to Marsha. Jeff felt touched by Marsha's understanding and playfulness. He felt better than he had in a long time.

He stood aside, enjoying their laughter reverberating over the water. He hadn't sought a woman's company since Marilou had died, but now he recalled how pleasant it was to hear a woman's laugh. Everyone needed adult companionship and communication. He'd neglected himself in trying to be devoted to Bonnie. He'd probably done them both a disservice. Today, he sensed how much he missed a woman in his life.

Marsha shivered and rubbed her gooseflesh-covered arms. "I'm heading in."

When Jeff glanced at Bonnie to see her reaction, her lips had turned a bluish tint. "Want to go back to the beach?"

"You can make a sand castle," Marsha called over her shoulder as she bounded toward the shore. "I've had enough ice-cube water for one day."

"There's no ice cubes in here," Bonnie said, waving her arms through the water as if trying to find some.

Jeff tousled her wet hair. "Aunt Marsha's teasing, but let's make a sand castle. That's a good idea."

With no argument from Bonnie, they headed back to the beach. When they reached the shore, he and Bonnie sank into the damp sand while Marsha dashed across the sand. Jeff watched her grasp a towel and dry her limbs before placing the terry cloth on the grassy knoll. She slid her arms into her beach robe and settled onto the towel, then stretched her legs into the sun and tilted her face upward, eyes closed.

She looked lovely and relaxed. Jeff recalled so many times he'd gone to his brother's to give Marsha a hand, and she'd looked so tired, but now...

He struggled to keep his mind on helping Bonnie build the castle. Searching in the sand, Jeff found a shell and used it to scoop sand as Bonnie mounded it into a tower. Finally, Bonnie lost interest in the castle and searched in the sand for seashells. Jeff took advantage of her occupation and returned to where Marsha was seated. He sank onto his towel, remembering how lonely he had been for the past two years and wondering how long it would take to feel whole again.

"She's having fun," he said, giving a nod toward Bonnie.

"You're a good dad, Jeff."

"I wasn't always and, most of the time, I feel helpless. I left most everything up to Marilou."

"But you're doing fine now."

He wondered about that. "I'm trying," was all he could say.

She shifted her hand to his and gave him a pat. Her fingers felt warm against his flesh. He leaned away on the towel, wondering how wise it had been for him to agree to join her today.

Marsha's gaze followed Bonnie while he struggled to find conversation. "I thought Barb was here with you," he said finally.

"She is. She was in the bedroom when you came." She turned and glanced back toward the chalet. "She's working on dinner, and I suppose I should get up there and help her."

When he opened his mouth to apologize for intruding on their meal, Jeff stopped himself, recognizing the old feeling-sorry-for-himself syndrome. He needed to take a long vacation and give himself a breath of fresh air. "I appreciate your invitation. This is really great."

Marsha leaned over to slip on her sandals. "You're welcome. It's nice to have company."

He stood and brushed off the sand from his damp swimsuit. "I'd better get Bonnie thinking about changing clothes." He reached out and extended his hand to help Marsha rise.

She grasped it and stood, then gathered her towel. "I'll see you inside."

He watched her bound up the incline, still feeling the pressure of her small hand in his.

* * *

Marsha gathered the dirty plates from the table, eyeing Bonnie's T-shirt spotted with spaghetti sauce. Another smear clung to her cheek. She was nearly a teenager, yet so far from it.

"Thanks again. This was delicious," Jeff said.

His comment pulled Marsha from her thoughts. "You're welcome anytime."

"It's nice eating a home-cooked meal made by someone else, for a change." He slid back his chair and rose. "Thanks, Barb, for all your work."

"No problem," she said from the living room. She'd taken flight to the sofa immediately after dinner.

Jeff leaned back and tugged at the waistband of his shorts.

"Need some exercise? How about a walk on the beach?" Marsha asked as she gathered the dessert dishes into the kitchen and slipped them into the sink.

He didn't answer but wandered to the screen door and gazed toward the lake.

With no response, Marsha decided to wait a moment before breaking into his thoughts. She returned to the living room and lowered the wings of the drop-leaf table they'd used for dinner, then slid the furniture against the wall. "It's still daylight, and maybe we can catch the beginning of a sunset on our way back."

"Sounds good," he said, then turned his attention to Bonnie. "Want to go for a walk, Bon?"

Focused on a coloring book, she curled up her nose. "I don't want to walk."

"It's good exercise."

Bonnie frowned and turned away from him.

Jeff lifted his shoulders with a sigh and gave Marsha a

hopeless look. "Not worth the battle. I guess we'll forget that idea."

Barb stirred, closing her magazine. "I'll stay here with Bonnie."

To Marsha's amazement, Barb smiled at Bonnie with a playful wink.

"We can color." Bonnie sent Barb a pleading look from the floor and wagged the coloring book at her.

Barb slid off the sofa and settled beside Bonnie, then grasped a crayon. "We'll be fine."

Marsha didn't know what to say. She gaped at her sister spread out on the carpet beside Bonnie. Being willing to stay back wasn't the surprise. Agreeing to color with Bonnie was.

"Thanks. We won't be long." Jeff knelt beside Bonnie. "Okay, Bon?"

She nodded while focusing on the crayons.

Marsha slid open the screen and stepped onto the deck as a warm breeze wrapped around her and she descended the three steps to the sand. As she ambled down the path to the lake, her gaze drifted to the tall grass and the myriad wildflowers—oxeye daisies, orange hawkweed and bladder campion—that flanked her trek to the beach. The bright colors stood out among the spikes of timothy, wild oats and oxtail. Sometimes amid life's weeds, she'd found a few bright spots in her life. Today seemed to be one of them.

Jeff strode behind her and, when they reached the beach, he motioned to the left. "Let's head that way."

She nodded, slipped off her sandals, tossed them on the grass and walked beside him, feeling his arm brush against hers while they struggled to keep their balance as their feet sank into the shifting sand.

Spending time with Jeff seemed strange yet familiar. It

took her back to years earlier when life had still held wonderful promises. In her mind, she could hear Don and Jeff tossing barbs back and forth as brothers seemed to do, and the memory swept her with a bittersweet feeling.

They walked in silence except for the sound of the gentle waves lapping against the shore and the occasional caw of a seagull.

"You're quiet," Jeff said after they'd traveled a distance.

"Enjoying the walk. It's nice to have someone to spend time with."

"You have Barb."

A stab of guilt shot through her. "Yes, that's true. I meant someone different." She managed a grin while another thought struck her. "Did I tell you Barb is living with me?"

He gave her a questioning look. "You mean—"

"At home in Sterling Heights."

Surprise registered on his face. "Really? How did that happen?"

How did that happen? "I don't know exactly. I suggested it. She was living in an apartment, and I had the big house. No kids. Alone. Double expenses for both of us. It seemed like a good idea." I was lonely. The truth smacked her in the chest.

Jeff slowed, then stopped. "And now?"

She paused beside him and dug her feet into the sand, then watched it spread across her arch and between her toes. It took her a moment to remember his question. "We're working on it."

He rested his hand on her shoulder. "Problems?"

"It's an adjustment."

His hand dropped and he began walking again. "You're not going to change Barb."

"Why do you say that?" She heard an edge in her voice.

"I sense you're unhappy with her. It's not what you say, but your tone of voice. A look on your face."

"I'm not trying to change her. I only wish she'd be more—"

"I realize I haven't seen you in a couple of years, but I know your traits…your character. I can sense you want to take care of Barb, and I don't think she wants to be taken care of."

Marsha flinched with his comment. "I—"

He captured her arm and stopped her. "I watched you with Don all those years. I know you're a tremendous care-giver."

"Thanks. I got a lot of practice."

"I meant that as a compliment." His hand slipped from her arm, and he looked across the water.

"I know you did," she said, sorry that she'd been sarcastic.

He shoved his hands into his pockets and stared at the sand. "It was a long time to practice. I know it was awful, Marsha."

"I don't regret it. Not one minute. Don was a wonderful husband. You and Marilou helped so much. I only wish I could have done more for him."

Jeff slid his arm around her shoulder and gave her a gentle hug. "You did all you could. I can never thank you enough for sticking by him during those years."

"For better or worse, Jeff. I made that vow to Don and to God. You got the short end of the stick, too, with Marilou. You're raising a daughter alone. That's not easy."

He leaned over and picked up a stone, slid his finger back and forth over the flat surface, then gave it a fling into the lake. The pebble skipped four times, leaving a row of concentric circles—neat and precise—as life should be, but wasn't.

"I manage," he said finally, then found another flat stone and skipped it across the water. He nodded toward the precise circular pattern on the ripples. "Wouldn't life be great if it was that perfect?"

Her heart skipped hearing him say the words that had just filled her mind.

"Let me ask you a question," he said, tucking his hands back into his pockets and striding on again. "How did you keep your faith so strong during all that time?"

His question surprised her and she found herself fumbling through her thoughts for an answer. Finally, she shook her head. "I guess I trusted God. I know each of us has a purpose, and God can see the big picture, so I had to accept that the Lord knew what He was doing."

"That takes powerful faith, Marsha. I give you credit."

"Don't give me credit. I probably can't remember the precise verse, but the Bible says something like hope doesn't disappoint us, because God has filled our hearts with His love through the Holy Spirit."

"And you believe God is with you in all of this?"

Marsha's chest tightened, hearing his disbelieving voice. "Absolutely. Do you ever dream about things being better?"

"Sure. Everyone does."

"Dreams. Hopes. They're the same, but when our dreams—our hopes—are backed by God's promise, we can feel confident. *Be joyful in hope, patient in affliction, faithful in prayer.* That's a verse from Romans 12. I've memorized it. I needed to say it every day." She gave him a wry grin.

He didn't smile, but seemed to ponder the verse. "Joyful in hope and patience." He shook his head. "That's a tall order."

His comment upset her. She drew back and her ankle

turned in the uneven sand. As she stumbled sideways, Jeff grasped her by the waist and pulled her against him.

Their eyes met, and an overwhelming sensation washed over her, the desire to be close to him. Troubled by the longing, she bolted away. "Thanks. I need to be more careful."

"I'm sorry, Marsha." He held up his hands. "I upset you."

"Upset me? No. I feel stupid that I almost fell." She tried to laugh, but it sounded false in her ears. She could see he didn't believe her.

He motioned to the quack grass ridged along the sand. "Let's sit a minute." He headed toward the raised area.

Marsha wanted to erase the past minutes. She'd set them both on edge with her reaction to his embrace. Being honest with herself, it wasn't Jeff coming to her aid that bothered her. It was her own longing that seeped from the recesses of her memory. She could smell the warm sun on his skin. She felt small and protected beside him. Those sensations had preoccupied her all day.

She sank beside him.

"Let's be honest. I feel like you do, Marsha."

"What are you talking about?"

"Uncomfortable. Uneasy in a way."

Hearing his comment, she winced. "I don't feel—"

"Yes, you do. For years, we spent time together with each other and our spouses. You were my brother's wife. Now, Marilou and Don are gone and it's different. We feel guilty."

"Guilty? But we're not doing anything wrong."

"No, but we're alive and they aren't."

Marsha lowered her head, understanding what he meant. "You're right."

"I know, so let's get rid of the guilt stuff. We're alive. Life goes on."

With her heart in her throat, she nodded. "It's good to talk and it's nice being with you, Jeff. You were always a good friend."

"And there's no reason why we can't be good friends, is there?"

Marsha felt her heart give a kick. "No."

"Okay, then," he said, resting his hand on her shoulder.

She felt the warmth of his touch emanate through her chest as she looked across the water at the beginning of the setting sun spreading across the horizon—gold and coral dappled with swirls of cerulean-blue. The hues glinted on the water, rippling into a kaleidoscope of patterns as the waves rolled to the shore.

"It's beautiful," she said, motioning toward the skyline.

Jeff looked toward the horizon. "Red sky at night, sailor's delight." He dug his toe into the ground and kicked a spray of sand toward the water.

She hesitated. "Sunsets promise smooth sailing the next day."

"It's just an old wives' tale."

"I think there's truth to the statement. The sailors learned from experience, just as I have."

He gave her a questioning look, and she couldn't stop herself.

"Sunsets remind me God is faithful to His promises. I remember a verse about satisfying us in the morning with His unfailing love. I see that in sunsets."

He sat in silence, his head hanging, his hands knotted between his knees. "We'd better get back," he said, rising.

Marsha sat a moment, then let the subject drop, but

the concern stayed in her head as they walked back to the cottage. Jeff needed to find faith again, not only for himself but for Bonnie. She deserved to know Jesus. How could anyone survive without faith and trust?

Chapter Three

Jeff stared at the breakfast dishes and rubbed his temples. His nerves had felt on edge since he'd woken, aware that he'd dreamed of Marsha. Marsha. His brother's wife. The dream had been innocent enough, but she'd seemed so real. She'd worn a dress the same color as the bathing suit she'd worn two days earlier, and he recalled trying to speak with her while being mesmerized by her eyes. What had come over him?

His head pounded and he lowered it and rotated his fingers against his temples. A headache seemed to hang on the fringes of his senses, and he wanted to ward it off. Bonnie had been throwing one fit after another about nearly everything. She talked about Marsha incessantly, and he wondered whether spending time with Marsha had been a good idea.

He'd managed as a single parent, not well, he admitted, but he'd tried to do his best. He met Bonnie's needs as well as he could, ran his business with an experienced hand and his employees respected him. At least, he thought they did.

What did he do for himself? Not much, but then there wasn't much time for that.

Jeff hoisted himself from the table, happy that Bonnie had gotten distracted by some TV cartoons. He carried the dirty dishes to the sink, turned on the tap and rinsed the plates and silverware, then slid them into the dishwasher. Marilou had insisted on the dishwasher, saying the summer home was her vacation, too. Now he understood what she meant.

Thinking of Marilou, a flash of guilt pierced him. What would she think of him dreaming about another woman? He shook his head. She would have laughed. Marilou hadn't had a jealous bone in her body. And dreams weren't much to get upset over, anyway. So why was he rattled by it?

He chewed the inside of his bottom lip, wanting to push the memory aside. He grabbed the frying pan from the stovetop, jerking when the telephone rang. That was a sound he rarely heard on the island, but he kept the phone for emergencies.

Jeff set the pan in the sink and grabbed the receiver, surprised to hear Marsha's voice. The image of her dressed in the blue dress of his dream rose in his mind.

"I'm thinking about renting a rowboat and taking a ride on Font Lake. Lots of turtles. Would you and Bonnie like to come along?"

His heart beat a little faster, and he swallowed. Her eager voice made his decision difficult. "This isn't a good day for us," he said. "Bonnie's watching TV right now and she's been in a bad mood. I'd hate to inflict that on you."

"I wouldn't mind. Maybe getting out would distract her."

Jeff drew in a breath and forced the words out of his throat. "I think not, but thanks for asking."

"I'm sorry you can't come. Maybe some other time."

Disappointment filled her voice, but he kept his guard up and didn't let her quiet response sway him. "Have fun."

"Thanks," she said, and, when she'd hung up, he dropped the phone in the cradle feeling like an ogre. He'd had a nice time with Marsha on Monday, but he was confused. She'd been Don's wife, and he almost felt as if he was betraying his brother.

Jeff had to admit he found Marsha attractive and, though he'd given her the "no guilt" talk, he still felt guilty. Marsha wasn't only good-looking; she was amazing. Her devotion and patience with Don still moved him, and he saw the same manner with Bonnie. She'd been gentle and loving despite the years of stress. Naturally, he admired her.

He'd wanted to tell her how he really felt when they had talked on the beach, but it seemed inappropriate. They'd only had dinner, a swim and a walk, nothing that could be construed as anything more. They were in-laws and that was it. He stopped his mental struggle. Marsha had let him know she felt the same when she'd jerked away from him on the beach.

Jeff returned his focus to Bonnie, He knew she'd soon be tired of the TV and she'd be back to her boredom, her whining and misbehavior. Maybe he should accept Marsha's invitation for Bonnie's sake. It could be a good distraction, as Marsha had suggested.

Besides the dream upsetting him, he realized what other stress he felt. Her discussion about Barb gave him concern. Marsha had a way of wanting to take care of everyone. She'd taken care of Don, for years, and now it appeared she had her eye on changing Barb. After their discussion about faith, logical reasoning led him to think that Marsha would also like to take him under her wing. Even the thought triggered unbridled tension.

For years, he'd believed he'd been under God's wing, and now he felt differently. Since his wife's death, he'd been determined to be under no one's wing but his own. He'd make his own choices, his own decisions. He wasn't sure he was ready to trust again—in Marsha or God.

He looked across the room at Bonnie. She looked unkempt, her clothes mismatched, her hair straggly and in need of a good washing. He knew he should talk to her about grooming and clothing, but what did he know about girls' styles? Frustration flooded him.

"Bonnie, you need to take a shower."

"No."

He took a step forward. "Then take a bath. What if we wanted to go somewhere and you weren't ready?"

"Where are we going?"

"Nowhere, but what if we were?"

Jeff realized she'd been sitting there tearing out the pages of a new magazine he'd picked up in town. He grabbed it away from her. "Why are you doing this?"

She jammed her fists against her ears and screamed.

He lowered his head, trying to hold on to his patience. "Bonnie, I'm sorry, but this magazine is new." *Was* new. "When it's old, you can tear out the pages."

She flung herself against the sofa cushions, then beat her fists and screeched.

Jeff felt like doing the same thing.

"Aunt Marsha called." The words flew from his mouth.

Bonnie's scream slowed, then stopped, and she lifted her head.

"She asked us to go for a boat ride on Font Lake. It's filled with turtles."

"Are we going?" Her fists uncurled and she straightened.

"You're not ready. Should I call her and tell her you can get ready?"

Bonnie nodded. "I am ready."

"You need a shower and some clean clothes and your hair combed."

Her eyes narrowed, and he waited for another fit of temper. Instead, the look became thoughtful. "I need a shower to go to Aunt Marsha's?"

"Yes."

She pondered that a moment. "Okay."

Relieved, Jeff spun around and headed for the phone. He may not be ready to trust again, but a boat ride with an old friend might be good for him and Bonnie.

"Be careful, Bonnie," Marsha said, extending her arm toward her niece, who was strapped into a life jacket. "Take my hand."

Jeff held the boat against the dock while Bonnie hesitated with one foot on the pier and one in the rowboat. "Get in with both feet, please."

Bonnie stretched for Marsha and clasped her hand with a trembling grip, her legs wobbling and fear written on her face. When she had both feet in the dinghy, Marsha helped her make her way to the bench seat in the bow. Bonnie let out a nervous laugh. "I did it."

"Good for you," Marsha said, helping her ease onto the bench, then she went to the back of the dinghy, scooted the lifesaver cushions to the side and sat.

The tension in Jeff's face relaxed, and he put one foot into the boat, then gave a push away from the dock and sat on the middle bench. "We're off," he said, grasping the oars and guiding them away from shore.

Marsha watched Jeff as he pulled the oars. His skin had browned to a warm copper and he looked healthy and relaxed. His dark hair tousled in the breeze and a small cowlick stood at the back of his part. She longed to brush it down just to feel the texture of his thick hair. The thought unsettled her and she turned her gaze away.

She'd been surprised but happy when Jeff called back just as she was heading out the door. Renting a rowboat alone hadn't seemed like great entertainment, but she felt determined to have fun.

The shore grew more distant as Jeff directed the rowboat toward a small grassy island. The area wasn't big enough to dock a boat, but she could see the lily pads with their white blossoms surrounding the dot of land, and she remembered from her past trip seeing turtles lolling there in the sunlight.

The sun glimmered off the water and heated her arms. She stretched her legs outward, hoping to pick up a little tan before she returned home. Glad she caught her hair in a ponytail, Marsha tilted her head back to let the sun hit her face, hoping for some color there, too. She hoped to look a little healthier with some relaxation.

When Marsha finally lowered her head and viewed Bonnie, she held her breath. Her niece was leaning far over the boat edge, dragging her fingers in the water. Jeff had his back to Bonnie and couldn't see what she was doing. Marsha wanted to warn her to be careful, but she was hesitant to issue a directive.

"Watch out for snapping turtles, Bonnie," she said. "There might be some in the water and they'll think your fingers are food."

Jeff glanced over his shoulder as Bonnie pulled her

hand from the lake, eyeing her fingers as if counting to make sure they were all there.

"Please keep your hands inside the boat, Bon. What would I do if you fell in?"

Bonnie peered at the expanse of water as a questioning look settled on her face. Then her face brightened. "Can we go to that island?" She pointed ahead of her.

"That's where we're headed," Jeff said.

"Can I get out of the boat?"

"It's not solid ground. You'd sink into the water, and it's filled with frogs and turtles and probably snakes."

Though disappointment replaced her questioning look, the reference to snakes must have settled the possibility in her mind. "I don't want to get out."

"Smart girl," Jeff said, giving Marsha a grin.

Jeff's expression looked wonderful to Marsha. Earlier, when she'd studied him without him knowing, his face had seemed lined with tension. Now, when he smiled, it lifted her and made her smile back. At that moment, he looked absolutely handsome—like Pierce Brosnan.

Marsha pulled her focus back to the boat ride. Lily pads spotted the water, and, the nearer the rowboat came to the oasis of grass, the thicker the lily pads became.

"Look at the water lilies, Bonnie," Marsha said. "And look right there." She pointed. "What do you see?"

"Turtles," Bonnie yelled, her excitement causing her to nearly rise, but when the boat swayed, she thought better of it and lowered herself to the bench.

Marsha released a relieved breath.

Jeff paddled them around the island while Bonnie clapped her hands and let out yells when she saw the turtles balancing on lily pads or stacked two and three on a log.

As they headed away from the island, Marsha and Jeff's conversation drifted back and forth easily. Marsha even told him about her thoughts to return to teaching, and he listened without influencing her one way or the other. She wished she could be more like Jeff instead of being so opinionated.

When they fell into silence, Marsha watched Bonnie's excitement. Though her hair still straggled along her face, it looked clean and shiny. Her outfit was color coordinated, and Marsha guessed she'd had a little help from Jeff today.

Marsha longed to talk with Jeff about Bonnie. Her niece needed a woman in her life. She cringed as the thought struck her. Not me, she added as if dissuading herself, but Bonnie needed so much, especially her first bra and some information about growing up. She hoped Jeff wouldn't take offense. Marsha cared about Bonnie. Becoming a woman was scary enough for any child, but one with disabilities could face even more challenges. She wondered if Jeff had talked with her, or if he even realized it was time.

The hot sun prickled against Marsha's skin and she glanced into the clear, sunny sky. "I'm afraid I'm going to burn," she said, hating to ruin their outing. "You know us redheads."

Jeff gave a nod and, once they turned around, he veered the nose of the boat toward the shore. As they, again, approached the stand of lily pads, Marsha studied Bonnie to see which way she was looking and, when she knew the girl wasn't watching, she reached into the water, plucked a water lily and tucked it behind her.

Jeff paddled, his firm stroke drawing them closer to shore. Marsha watched the muscles in his chest and arms ripple against his T-shirt, reminding her he was a single man now. Finally, the dinghy bumped against the dock, and Jeff caught the pier and pulled the boat against the planks. He climbed out, tied the rope to a piling, then helped Bonnie. With her safely deposited, he reached for Marsha's hand. His strong fingers wrapped around hers and he assisted her onto the dock.

He gave her hand a squeeze. "Thanks for inviting us." His eyes looked sincere and his mouth curved to a tender smile.

"You're welcome. This was much more fun with you doing all the work."

"Good exercise," he said, grinning and flexing his arm.

She moved forward and pressed her fingers against the hard knot of his bicep, feeling the warmth of his skin and the ripple of his strength. "Not bad," she said, trying to sound playful, but suddenly she felt breathless. The intimacy overwhelmed her. Feeling the lily in her other hand, Marsha stepped back and held it out toward Bonnie. "Look what I have for you."

"A flower." Bonnie reached toward it, a smile brightening her eyes.

Marsha pulled a bobby pin from beneath her ponytail. "Let's put this in your hair."

Bonnie's eyes widened. "In my hair?"

Marsha tucked the girl's hair behind one ear and used the hairpin to anchor the flower. "You look beautiful."

She turned to Jeff with a huge smile. "I look beautiful."

"You do, Bon, just like a Hawaiian princess."

But Bonnie was already distracted by a frog hopping in the grass and she trotted off to chase it.

"Thanks," Jeff said, resting his arm on Marsha's shoulder, "that was thoughtful."

Marsha felt a tug in her chest. "Women like flowers."

"And thanks again for everything. Besides the exercise and the scenery, just plain ol' talking felt good." He drew her toward him and gave her a hug.

Marsha's pulse escalated at the feel of his arms around her shoulders. He drew back, and she couldn't look into his eyes, afraid he'd see the thoughts that swirled through her mind. She drew in a breath. "I thought maybe I'd bored you."

He shook his head, an intense look in his eyes. "You know how it feels to be really hungry? I've been hungry for conversation."

The confession touched her, and she pressed her hand against his cheek, feeling the roughness of his beard just breaking through. Her intimate action surprised her, and she dropped her hand. "I'm often hungry for that, myself."

"I'm hungry," Bonnie said.

Marsha swung around, surprised that Bonnie had returned to their sides without a sound. She and Jeff laughed while Bonnie's forehead wrinkled questioningly.

"We'll eat in a while," Jeff said, giving Marsha a telling look. "Big ears," he whispered as Bonnie skipped off again, distracted by a butterfly.

Marsha drew up her courage. "I'm worried about her, Jeff." She tilted her head toward Bonnie.

"Worried?"

She nodded. "If you haven't already, you need to have an adult conversation with her very soon. She's right on the verge of—"

"Marsha, I know."

His voice startled her, but she couldn't let go now. "Why not hire some help for her? A woman who can help with—"

"Marsha!"

She stared at him while the words died in her throat. "I'm sorry. I only thought—"

"It's been difficult, but I'm taking care of Bonnie's needs. I'm not perfect, but I'm her father and I can do this. I've been doing it for the past two years."

"Jeff, I know. You're doing a great job. I didn't mean—"

He held up his hand. "It's your way. I understand. You took care of Don, for years, and now you're transferring that need to Bonnie. You want to fix everyone, but…"

His voice trailed off, leaving Marsha's spirits sinking. She meant well. She really meant well.

Chapter Four

Y ou want to fix everyone. The words rang in Marsha's head as they had for the past two days. She wanted to kick herself for ruining the pleasant afternoon. She'd put her nose into Jeff's business with Bonnie.

She needed to kick herself for her overzealous imagination. Jeff was becoming special to her, and it was foolishness. He resented her meddling with Bonnie, which made their friendship rocky. If she valued his friendship, Marsha needed to control her romantic notions.

Realizing what she'd been doing, she dropped the magazine on the love seat. She'd been staring at the pages without focusing, her mind too tangled in her situation to concentrate. She pushed herself from the cushion and pressed her fists into her lower back, then stretched upward to relax the tightness.

"What's wrong with you?"

Marsha stared at her sister reclining in her favorite spot on the sofa. "What do you mean?" She lowered her fists and took a deep breath. "Nothing's wrong."

Barb shook her head. "Look at your face in the mirror."

Marsha didn't need to look in a mirror. She felt the tension in her neck and on her face.

She watched Barb's curious expression follow her as she made her way into the kitchen. She finally gave up pretending and plopped her elbows against the counter that divided the kitchen area from the living room. "I'm upset, I suppose."

"At me?"

"No. At myself."

Barb fluffed the pillow beside her and rested her arm on the cushion. "What happened? Something with Jeff?"

"I nagged Jeff about Bonnie, and he's overly sensitive. I need to learn to keep my mouth shut."

A laugh flew from Barb until she stifled the sound. "Sorry." She shook her head and gave Marsha a telling grin. "Keeping your mouth shut is a challenge, Marsha. I don't mean to be rude, but you need to be in charge and it doesn't always set well with people. I've told you that a million times."

Marsha rubbed the tension in her neck, then shifted her fingers to her temples and rotated them to ease the ache. "I care about Bonnie." The statement brought her up short. She cared about Bonnie *and* Jeff.

"Jeff cares, too."

Heat rose up Marsha's neck until she realized Barb meant Jeff cared about Bonnie.

Barb placed a bookmark between the pages and closed the cover. "So do I."

Pushing aside her guilty thoughts, Marsha gave Barb a long look. Her sister's admission touched her. She'd watched Barb reach out to Bonnie, and it warmed her heart.

Getting herself under control, Marsha slipped from

behind the counter and settled onto the love seat again. "I don't know what to do to let go of my concerns."

Barb rose, crossed the room to the love seat and stood there a moment. "I don't know, either. It's who you are, I guess." She rested her hand against Marsha's shoulder and gave it a squeeze. "You can't change who you are, but you can monitor your behavior."

When she looked up, Marsha studied Barb's face. She saw a tenderness she hadn't expected, and it warmed her. "I don't want to be this way. I don't seem to know the difference between helping and meddling."

Barb let her hand drop to the arm of the love seat. "It's a fine line."

Marsha's thoughts drifted to her sister's silent struggle, and she fought her desire to ask what caused her to be so distant. Yet, today, the distance had narrowed. A fine line.

"Are you worried because Bonnie's maturing so fast?" Barb opened the refrigerator and pulled out a soft drink. "Want one?"

"An orange pop. Thanks."

Barb flipped open the tabs and carried the cans back into the living room. She handed Marsha the orange pop, then settled onto her usual spot on the sofa and took a long drink. "Is that your problem, not knowing the difference between helping and meddling, as you called it?"

"That and so much more."

Barb gazed at her without a response, and Marsha longed to know what she was thinking. She watched her sister's expression go from concern to acceptance. Finally, she shook her head. "Tell me about you and Jeff."

Marsha's heart tripped at Barb's blunt question. "Tell you what?"

"You've been mooning like a hound dog."

"Mooning?" Why deny it? She had been. "I told you that I'm sure Jeff's upset with me. He hasn't called me, and I hate to call him."

"Why? You've been spending a lot of time together."

The tone of her voice made Marsha wince. "Too much, do you think?" She glanced at her sister but saw no response. "It's like old times. Jeff and Marilou were always good friends." But it hadn't been like old times. These feelings were new, so unexpected and felt so inappropriate.

"I'm not judging you. It's nice to hear you laugh and focus on something else, for a change."

Marsha winced again before grasping her good humor. "You mean, focus on someone other than you."

Barb lifted an eyebrow along with a crooked grin. "You said it."

Her tone and expression made Marsha chuckle. "I need to work on that."

"You're enjoying Jeff's company, right?"

Marsha's pulse tripped. "Right. And I care about my niece. Bonnie's not a problem for me. We get along fine."

"Then why try to change things? Just let it go. Subtlety works better than forcing your will on someone, even if you're offering them good advice."

"You're right, Barb. Jeff is Bonnie's father, and I can see how tough it is to be a single parent. He's trying to be mother and father and he knows he can't be both. Maybe he'll ask for help."

"And, when he does, you'll be there. If you alienate him by pushing, you've lost a friend."

A friend. Barb was right. Jeff had always been a friend,

and being single now should make no difference. Friendships were precious and good ones were rare. "Thanks. You said some things I needed to hear." She rose and looped her arm around Barb's shoulder in a one-armed hug.

Barb didn't flinch this time and squeezed her back with her free hand. "You're welcome."

Marsha straightened and turned toward the glass door to the lake. "So what do I do now? Give him time."

"You've been complaining about fixing a few things around here. That'll keep you busy for a few hours." Barb chuckled.

"Hours?" She rolled her eyes at her sister. "Days. Weeks."

"Then you'll stay out of trouble and let me read my novels." She tossed her book on the lamp table with a laugh.

"Words of wisdom," Marsha said, accepting Barb's humor.

"You know I'm teasing, but something else is bothering you, and you should get it out in the open."

Marsha had to bite back the words that flew to her throat. What about you? "I suppose you should know."

Barb's smile shriveled. "Some things are meant to be private, Marsha, and some things aren't. You're upset with Jeff, and that's something you can fix."

Some things are meant to be private. A cold anxiety seeped down Marsha's limbs, and she fought back her curiosity. Not now. Not when Barb was really talking. "I guess you're right."

Marsha wandered from the doorway into the kitchen and pulled off the lid of a peanut can. She eyed the calories on the label and knew she was eating out of frustration, but that didn't stop her. She stuffed a handful into her mouth.

"Let's go somewhere," Barb said.

"Whaff?" she asked, trying to dislodge the nuts from her throat.

Barb chuckled at her sister's predicament.

She forced the peanuts down with a swig of pop. "What did you say?"

"I finished my novel." She waved the book above her head. "Let's do some of that sightseeing you're always talking about."

Marsha staggered backward and plastered her hand over her heart. "Are you my sister or some imposter?" Her playful drama was good-natured, but she realized it could be hurtful, and this wasn't the time to turn a positive moment into a negative one.

Barb's smile faded. "I know. I haven't been good company. Sometimes I don't control my bad moods, either."

Now Marsha understood. Apparently, she'd been in a bad mood, too. "Touché."

Barb grasped the paperback and patted it. "This novel lifted my spirit." She sent Marsha another questioning look. "How about it? We could drop a couple of books off at the library, first. Then do whatever." She swung her hand toward the door. "I could use some fresh air."

Watching the book wave in her hand, Marsha was amazed that a novel made a difference. "I could use some air, too." Or anything to cheer me, she thought, anxious to get rid of her doldrums.

Marsha scanned the room for her car keys. Though she didn't understand her sister's sudden change in mood, Marsha had no inclination to question Barb's willingness to have fun. She'd been thinking of Jeff for the past days, and Barb's advice had sparked her desire to talk with him.

Friends. Good friends. Old friends. Why let a good thing fall apart because of a misunderstanding?

Jeff rose and brushed the dirt from his knees. Trying to keep the weeds from encroaching on his few perennials seemed impossible when he made so few trips to the island. He picked up his carton of weed killer and sprinkled the pellets over the freshly tilled flower beds.

After he set the carton beside his feet, Jeff arched his back to relieve the ache. He wished he could arch his conscience and relax the tension there. He missed Marsha's company, but he felt convicted by her concern for Bonnie and her obvious faith.

He scoffed at himself. He didn't need anyone. In his heart he knew God looked down on him, but it was a God he didn't like anymore. How could he pray to a God who didn't listen and didn't seem to care about a little girl who needed her mother?

Guilt rolled in with his thoughts. Marilou had been a good mother, and he'd become a miserable father at times…like lately. His thoughts had been wound around Marsha.

He tried to focus. Bonnie was bored out of her mind, and, for the past two days, he'd tried to entertain her with games and coloring, walks on the beach, but nothing stopped her frustration and temper. Maybe he'd been wrong to give up on hiring help for Bonnie. He'd had consultations at school, and she was holding her own in her class—very slow but learning. Apparently, he was the failure.

Last semester, Bonnie's teacher had been a woman. She gave Bonnie a feminine touch that he couldn't. He observed that Bonnie seemed to connect with Marsha, too, in a way that he couldn't.

Had he made a mistake with Marsha? Now that he thought about it, she was only trying to mother Bonnie. It was natural, but as close as he felt to Marsha, when she mothered Bonnie it felt as if she was taking Marilou's place. Now matter how he denied it, no matter what his heart said, it seemed wrong. Then it seemed right. He didn't know his own mind.

His gaze drifted to the beach where he'd let Bonnie play with the shells she'd collected. Unable to see her now, he took a step forward, then pulled off his garden gloves and threw them on the ground as he hurried down the hillside to the water's edge.

As he neared the shore, his eyes shifted to scan the beach, but she wasn't there.

"Bonnie!"

His heart hammered as he searched the rolling waves. She promised she'd stay away from the water. She knew the dangers, and he trusted her.

"Bonnie!"

His feet dug into the beach as he forced his legs to run in the slipping sand. "Bonnie!" A long stretch of beach spread in front of him, and he pivoted and headed the other way, his mind spiraling with fear and his lungs soon bursting from lack of oxygen.

"Bonnie!"

Ahead, he saw a man sitting in a beach chair. He called again and waved his arms, but the tide rolling in seemed to block his words. Nearer, he called again. "Bonnie!"

Finally, the man looked his way and rose. "Looking for a girl?" he asked, his hand motioning up the rise toward his cottage.

"Yes," Jeff panted, trying to catch his breath. "Have you seen her?"

"She's playing with my son in the back. He's only six, and I thought—"

"Bonnie's eleven but she's—" the words caught in his throat and he cleared it "—she's emotionally impaired."

The man drew back, his eyes as wide as a full moon. "I figured something was wrong." His gaze darted up the hill. "She won't hurt him, will she?"

Jeff stiffened, then monitored his emotion. "No. She wouldn't hurt anyone." He thought of the many times she'd struck out at him, but he felt grateful she never smacked anyone else.

"Whew!" The man let out a blast of air from his lungs. "She seemed harmless enough and a sweet little thing. Billy took to her so I figured they'd be okay."

Jeff nodded, then motioned up the hill with a blend of frustration and relief. "I'd better check on her." He bounded in the direction the man had indicated. "Bonnie!"

When he passed the edge of the house, he saw her sitting in a sandbox with the young boy, surrounded with shells and miniature dump trucks.

"I'm babysitting, and we're playing," she said when she saw him, looking as if she had no idea she'd wandered too far from home.

"I'm not a baby," the boy said.

Jeff strode to Bonnie's side and gazed down at her sand-covered hair and arms. "You shouldn't leave the property without asking me." He reached toward her, and she jerked her arm away.

"I want to play."

"You have to come home now." He feared a tantrum if he didn't think of some way to tempt her to leave. He leaned over and rested his hand on her shoulder. "You look like a sand lady. You need to—"

"No, I don't. Go away. I'm babysitting Billy."

The boy put his hand on his hip. "I'm not a baby. I'm six."

"Bonnie." Jeff counted to eleven, hoping her age was the special number to keep him calm. "We have some things to do."

"What?" Her eyes widened. "See Aunt Marsha?"

He swallowed and bit the inside of his lip. Bonnie's eyes were filled with eager hope, and, he had to admit, he wanted to see Marsha as badly as Bonnie. He was being stubborn and, at the moment, it seemed silly. "We'll call her and see if she's busy."

Bonnie jumped up and stepped from the box, her arms and legs glittering with grains of sand. "We'll see Marsha," she said, darting down the hill before he could get his bearings.

He chased after her and caught her on the beach. "Bonnie, why did you leave the house without telling me?"

"I'm going to see Aunt Marsha." She pulled her arm from his grasp.

He stopped and drew her into his embrace. "Bonnie, you know you're not supposed to go anywhere without asking first."

Anger flashed in her eyes, but then she must have thought better of it, realizing going to Aunt Marsha's hinged on her behavior. "I forgot."

"You can't keep forgetting things. You could fall in the water and drown or—" He struggled, thinking of a million ways she could be hurt.

"I found shells. See." She dug into the pocket of her pants and pulled out a handful of shells—snail shells and clams, some broken, some whole. She lifted them up for him to see.

"They're pretty, but you must listen."

"The man said I was pretty."

Worry pricked him. "What man?"

"Billy's daddy. He patted my head and said I was a pretty girl."

Pretty girl. Bonnie wasn't anyone's pretty girl except his, especially not a stranger's. He grasped Bonnie's hand and marched up the incline and into the house, his stomach knotting with dawning awareness. She was growing up. Marsha'd said it, and she was right.

"Wash off the sand," Jeff said, steering her toward the bathroom.

"Call Aunt Marsha," she said as she walked down the hallway.

Marsha filled his mind. Her gentle touch, her kind eyes, her thoughtfulness stirred his emotions. She'd tried to tell him, but he hadn't listened. Mothering Bonnie—or taking care of him? Was that his fear? Or was it just guilt?

He sank into the chair beside the phone and bowed his head. *Lord, take care of*— He stopped himself. What was the point? God did what He wanted to do, and not what Jeff needed. As Bonnie's father, Jeff needed to be watchful of Bonnie every minute.

Why did he have to insist on doing it all alone? The answer was clear. Who else did he have? He'd trusted

God to keep Marilou safe. She died. Bitterness pushed against his heart. He pushed his mind away from the memory. Two years had passed. He should be getting over it by now. His life needed to go on, and he shouldn't feel guilty about his friendship with Marsha.

Jeff grasped the telephone receiver and punched in Marsha's phone number. Two rings. Three rings. Four.

His shoulders drooped as he dropped the receiver onto the cradle. He'd never felt so lonely.

Marsha turned the key in the ignition. "Library first, then where do you want to go?"

"One of the lighthouses. Anywhere's fine with me."

"I've got an idea. Let's check out the junk art on Donegal Bay Road first. I haven't been there yet this year."

"Junk art?"

Marsha gave a double take. "You must have seen it. This guy creates those silly displays using junk—wire, machine parts, buckets, pots and pans. You name it and the man makes something from it."

"You know who'd get a kick out of that," Barb said, sliding into the passenger seat. "Bonnie."

Bonnie. Marsha shifted into Reverse. "Are you suggesting we drive by and ask them to join us?"

"Sounds like a plan."

Marsha let her sister's agreeable tone settle into her thoughts. People could change. Barb was living proof. Marsha wondered if she could ever change. A quick prayer sailed to heaven as she backed out of the driveway.

After the library, she headed toward Donegal Bay Road. Though nervous about seeing Jeff, she also felt like a kid on the way to the circus. She clipped along the rugged road and she felt the wheels pounding beneath her feet.

Barb glanced at her with a questioning look. "In a hurry?"

She took the hint and lifted her foot from the accelerator, avoiding the brake. No way was she admitting her excitement, but heat flooded her cheeks and she feared that would give her away, anyway.

Why was she so excited? Visiting a friend didn't seem to deserve that kind of exuberance, but then, Jeff wasn't just a friend. He was part of her past, part of her life when she'd felt whole and fulfilled. She loved the feeling, and Jeff seemed to give her back what had been drained from her by time and sadness.

"We're almost there," Marsha said, seeing Jeff's ranch in the distance. She grinned at Barb, who still gave her a curious look, but then turned away and looked down the road toward Jeff's. She felt like a pendulum, her emotions swaying back and forth from pleasure to guilt and back.

When she pulled into the driveway, Marsha noticed the weeded flower beds. Jeff apparently had used their time apart for something worthwhile, unlike she had. He hadn't missed her one iota, she guessed, and the thought dampened her spirits.

She turned off the ignition and opened the door. Barb followed more slowly as if she now wondered why she'd asked to come along.

As Marsha headed for the back door, she heard a whoop inside the house and, in an instant, Bonnie came bounding through the doorway, her arms open for a hug. Marsha took her into her arms, smelling soap yet feeling grit above her elbows. The combination made her smile.

"We called, and you're not home," Bonnie said, her eyes searching Marsha's.

"No, I'm here so I couldn't be home." *We called.* The words lightened her heart. With Bonnie still nestled by her side, she lifted her gaze and saw Jeff standing behind the screen door. When their eyes met, a grin slid across his generous mouth. He pushed open the door and stepped outside, his jaw darkened by a growth of whiskers.

"Hi." He ambled closer with a look of question and apology.

"Hi," she said back, releasing Bonnie's hold on her. "We're taking a ride to look at the junk art, and Barb and I thought Bonnie might enjoy it."

He tucked his hands into his pockets and greeted Barb with a nod. "I hear the artist died. I wonder if it's still there?"

"I think so. I flew past a little of it yesterday."

"We haven't been there for a long time. I doubt if Bonnie remembers."

Bonnie wrinkled her nose. "What's junk art?"

"You'll see," Marsha said, noticing more sand sprinkled in her hair. "You were on the beach?" She brushed the grit from her niece's hair with a chuckle.

Bonnie glanced at her dad, then back at Marsha and nodded. "I found shells." She dug into her pocket but drew out her empty hand. She waved toward the doorway. "They're in the house. I forgot."

"I'll see them later."

Bonnie grabbed Barb's hand. "Come on. I'll show you."

As Barb followed behind Bonnie, Marsha faced Jeff.

He gazed at her without speaking, his hands tucked into his pockets as if they were safer there.

She accepted his unspoken apology but felt at a loss for words with her conflicting emotions.

"Bonnie missed you."

His soft voice wove through her senses. "I—"

"I missed you, too, Marsha."

His honesty sent a wave of emotion surging through her. "We're like two old shoes, aren't we?"

He shook his head. "I don't think so. We're brand new shoes that might fit but still cause blisters."

She couldn't help but smile. "That's pretty poetic."

He gave her an embarrassed look. "I've been feeling poetic lately." His gaze probed hers as if asking if she understood.

She did understand, and her heart fluttered with the response that settled in her. "I know, Jeff. It's been—"

"Here they are," Bonnie called, bounding toward Marsha with a host of shells cupped in both hands.

"Wow!" Marsha said, sending a fleeting what-can-we-do look to Jeff.

"They're pretty," she said, then twirled with a giggle. "A man said I was pretty, too."

Marsha's flutter turned to a skipping pulse. Her eyes shifted toward Jeff's. "A man?"

Jeff rested his hands on Bonnie's shoulders. "A neighbor. She wandered down the beach—" he leaned over her shoulder to look into Bonnie's eyes "—without permission. She scared me to death."

The whole idea scared Marsha, but she didn't know what to say. Today, she harnessed her words as she'd promised herself she would do. Barb had said it. If Jeff needed her, he would ask. "We always need permission to go for a walk."

Bonnie frowned as if trying to weigh Marsha's words, but the thought was fleeting, and she twirled again. "Junk art."

"Would you like to come along?" Marsha gazed into Jeff's searching eyes.

"Bonnie would love it," he said, cupping Marsha's elbow in his hand. "And so would I."

Suddenly, Marsha was again filled with confusion. She needed help, and she lifted her eyes heavenward. If anyone needed God's intervention, she did. How could she make sense out of anything when her head was vying with her heart?

Chapter Five

◝✦◜

Before Jeff could slip out of the backseat, Bonnie had tumbled from the car and darted to the junk-art character riding a bicycle. She darted around it, looking at the details, letting out a screech that scared birds in the evergreens nearby. They fluttered upward, their wings a muted thunder beneath Bonnie's piercing scream.

"Bonnie." Jeff darted to her side and placed his hand against her cheek. "Calm down." He pointed along the roadside. "Look down there."

"More people," she yelled.

"But we won't be able to stay if you're so noisy, so please quiet down, okay?"

She bit at her lip as if trying to harness her exuberance with her teeth. "What is this one? A boy on a bicycle?"

"That's what it looks like." A worn red bicycle had been decked with a bulging body covered by a green T-shirt and pipe arms that clung to the handlebars. The figure wore brown pants with green-and-white-striped socks beneath a pair of old sneakers. The face had been painted on an oval board—red hair, wide blue eyes and a pleasant grin.

"Can I ride the bike?" Bonnie asked, touching the handlebars.

"This bike belongs to the make-believe boy." He grinned at Marsha, amazed how his stomach tightened when he looked into her smiling face.

"Check that one out." She pointed down the row. "There's a man made from coiled wire...or Slinkys." She chuckled at Bonnie, who darted from her father's hold and raced to view the strange character.

"This one's even better," Barb said. She grasped Bonnie's hand and hurried her ahead, seeming to have as much fun as Bonnie. Her enthusiasm surprised Jeff. Today her usual aloofness seemed long gone.

Jeff fell into step with Marsha and put his arm around her shoulders. "We need to finish our conversation. Alone."

"You mean, the we're-new-shoes talk?"

"Sort of." He gave her shoulder a squeeze, enjoying the feeling of the trim woman at his side. Her fresh scent drifted into his senses, filling him with nostalgia.

She looked at him, her eyes smiling, yet something behind the smile looked—he couldn't name it—uneasy or questioning. He didn't let that stop him. He hugged her again, then slipped his arm from her shoulder as they joined the others, knowing they didn't have enough time to get things out in the open right now.

At the next display, Bonnie crouched in front of a wagon adorned with a colorful beach umbrella. Inside the wagon sat a papier-mâché baby with stuffed animals nestled at its side.

"Look at the mother," Bonnie said, giggling at the tank vacuum-cleaner body with suction-tube arms and metal legs. The head had been created from a black frypan with a painted face.

Bonnie bounded off, and Barb called out after her. Barb's voice drifted back to Jeff. "Wait for me."

After Barb caught up with her, Bonnie turned around with her hand on her hip. "You can't tell me what to do."

"Oh, yes, I can," Barb said, grasping her hand and giving her a hug. "We need to watch for cars."

Jeff winced at Bonnie's behavior, but Barb's response gave him hope. Bonnie's belligerence ended as quickly as it happened, and she seemed to behave with Barb's reprimand. Marsha had the same effect. "Good for Barb," he said to Marsha as he heaved a sigh.

Marsha rested her hand on his shoulder. "We understand Bonnie."

Her tenderness touched him. "You do far more than that." He watched Barb and Bonnie continue down the road's edge as if nothing had happened, but Jeff held back, hoping now was the time to be honest. He'd already apologized for his behavior the other day, and she'd accepted it, he knew, from her invitation today to join them. Her forgiving nature had been a lesson.

Jeff caught her hand and turned her toward him. "I'm being serious when I say I've missed you."

Her eyes sought his, and he sensed she was searching for a response. Sadness poured through him for the mess they were making of an amazing friendship. They'd always had a good relationship, and now he was letting guilt push him away. "I'm not happy with how things are going."

As her mouth curved downward at the edges, her forehead wrinkled. "I don't understand, Jeff."

"Yes, you do."

"With Bonnie or me?"

He lifted her hand and squeezed it. "With *you* and me."

She gave him a quizzical look.

"What's going on with us?"

As if surprised by his question, Marsha's hand went limp in his, but her eyes said something more, and he wasn't ready to give up.

"I'm serious about this, Marsha. How can two old friends fall apart in a few days without at least discussing the problem? We can apologize over and over, but let's get down to the real issues."

Marsha squeezed his hand back. "That's the problem." She lowered her gaze and kicked at a few pebbles on the dirt shoulder. "I don't know what the problem is."

Jeff felt his head jerk back. "You don't? Let's be real, Marsha. You know as well as I do."

She lifted her gaze. "I suppose you're upset with my pushiness."

Her pushiness? That was nothing new. He'd begun to accept that. He managed to control his frustration. "No, our relationship. Let's talk about that."

"I'll ruin it if I'm always on your back about Bonnie."

Was she playing games, or did she really not get it? "Forget the pushiness. It's my reaction as much as what you say."

"I just worry about her, that's all."

Jeff drew in a lengthy breath. Marsha thought the whole problem was Bonnie when it was so much more—it was about her strong faith, his lack of it and, most importantly, his strong feelings for her. They had happened so quickly he hadn't had time to process them.

Marsha touched his arm. "I've made a promise to myself that I won't bug you, anymore." Her eyes searched his as if doubting he would believe her. "Really."

He didn't know what to say. His gut ached with

conversation—each of them talking about something different. "Thanks, but the problem is more about us. Our relationship."

She looked away as if thinking. "We've already agreed to be friends, Jeff, and now I promise to stop meddling. You're Bonnie's dad, and I need to remember that."

Seeing the pleading look in her eyes, he leaned forward and kissed her cheek, wishing he could say more, but grateful he'd said a little.

"Let's enjoy our time together. I don't like having the stress between us." She threw her arms around his shoulders and gave him a bear hug, and he reeled backward with her unexpected reaction.

If he knew what he wanted, he would be more direct, but telling her what riled his heart seemed too ridiculous. Too amazing. He needed time to make sense out of the past few days. Things had happened so fast. He didn't want to make a fool of himself, and he had no idea what was on Marsha's mind. He could only hope.

"Daddy." Bonnie called, "aren't you looking at the funny people?"

Marsha laughed and it sounded like music. "We are, Bonnie." She nudged his arm and began to walk. "We're two funny people, don't you think?"

Funny? Mixed up was the way he saw it.

"That was fun," Barb said, searching beside the sofa and coming up with a novel in her hand.

Marsha watched her settle back into her usual spot, but, instead of feeling irked, she let it slide. Barb had been outgoing today. She seemed to relate to Bonnie, and Marsha chalked it up to compassion. As distant as Barb had been as a teenager with adults, she'd always liked children. Marsha felt a pang of sorrow that Barb had never married and had the opportunity to be a mother.

Unbidden, the thought jolted her. Though she'd been married, she'd never had a child, either. Marsha settled onto the love seat and tilted back her head, thinking about how that had happened.

Like so many newly married couples, she and Don had decided to wait a while before they started a family. Three children was what they'd wanted. They'd figured it would give them three chances to have at least one boy and one girl. Silly idea, now that she thought about it.

And college. She'd gotten a late start, hating to give up the full-time job she'd had since her graduation from high school. Later, Don had encouraged her to get a degree, and she'd had a year and half of college to complete before becoming a teacher.

Then things had happened. Don had become ill, and the rest was history. Her college days had ended to be a caregiver, a time she never resented. Not for one minute. The only lingering sadness had been the children they never got to have. When Don had died, she had been left with no one. Nothing that was both part of him and part of her. She'd become single—no longer a family. One lone person in a world that seemed to be filled with married couples.

"Bonnie's a little character, isn't she?"

Marsha jolted from her reverie and took a moment to find words. "She reminds me of the wire-and-kitchen-tool characters we saw earlier today. You never know what she'll be made of next. One minute she's an angel, the next minute totally out of control, but I love her anyway. Her problems are great, but her own world is so simple. Too bad we can't all be like that."

"You're being very philosophical today."

"I've been doing some serious thinking. And praying."

"Me, too." She patted the novel on her lap. "I know you think I'm wasting my time with these books, but they give me something that's difficult to explain."

That piqued Marsha's curiosity.

"Do you ever read?"

Marsha faltered, needing to think. "I do occasionally. I used to read more years ago, but when Don was sick I wanted to spend every minute with him. After he died, somehow the stories seemed like fairy tales."

"Not these. I read Christian fiction. Good stories, lots of emotion, no graphic sex or swearing and a faith message, to boot."

Marsha crossed the room and took the book from Barb's hand. "Are these what you usually read?"

She nodded. "They're entertaining, but they also give me something to think about."

Marsha turned the book over and scanned the back. "What do they give you to think about?"

Barb tilted her head as if she thought Marsha was kidding.

"I'm serious. This looks like a romance. How does this help you think?"

"Look at the Bible verse in the front."

Marsha opened the first pages and spotted the verse. "'If any one of you is without sin, let him be the first to throw a stone at her.' John 8:7-8. I take it the book's about a woman who commits adultery."

"No, but the verse fits the story as well as our lives. It

reminds me that we're all sinners and no one has the right to judge someone else without first looking at his own sin."

The lesson smacked Marsha between the eyes. She always figured women without romance in their lives read romance books. She'd been judging without knowing the truth, and she knew that was a sin. But Christian fiction? She knew there was such a thing, but Christian romance seemed a misnomer.

Marsha felt ashamed as she admitted to herself that she'd thought Barb was wasting her time on novels. She always seemed buried in the books as if her only life was through the characters, but, in reality, the stories and characters gave her support. "That's something we should all think about before judging others." She pressed her palm against the cover of the book and sent up a prayer, asking the Lord to bring that verse back to mind when she butted her nose in other people's business.

"The books always give me more than the one verse. Every story deals with real human issues. They remind me of God's promises. They give me hope."

Hope? Hope to get married someday? Hope for what? She handed the book back to her sister while questions rattled in her mind.

Barb rubbed the cover, a longing look in her eyes. "I'd like to write one."

"Write a novel?" Marsha's eyebrows flew upward before she could control them.

"Don't look surprised. I have stories in my head, but I don't have the slightest idea what to do with them."

Marsha felt her mouth sag, amazed at her sister's revelation. "Why not give it a try? Start writing with paper and pen. That's the way they did it before computers. Once you're home, you can use my computer."

She uttered the words, but the idea amazed her. Barb, a novelist? What about emotion and plot? Her life seemed so empty.

If any one of you is without sin, let him be the first to throw a stone at her. Marsha cringed as the verse filled her mind.

From the porch swing, Jeff heard Bonnie crying. He hoisted himself from the seat, not wanting to pull his mind from his thoughts. After they'd talked, Marsha had been wonderful yesterday—just like old times, except with the stress of Don's illness gone. He pictured her face in the sunlight. All the worry lines had vanished, and she had looked younger than she had four years ago.

The memory of his brother's long struggle saddened him. Yet, Don had been a Christian, and Jeff assumed God rewarded those who stuck by Him through life's trials. Don was in heaven. Why couldn't Jeff have the same faith for himself?

Don had been stronger, he guessed. Jeff shook his head to loosen the thoughts as he heard Bonnie. He hurried into the house, following her muffled sobs.

He found her stretched across her bed, her face buried in her pillow, her hands pressing the top of her head.

"What's wrong, sweetie?"

She shook her head, burying her face deeper into the pillow.

"Bonnie. Tell me what's wrong."

A ragged sob tore from her throat. "Go away."

"I'm not going away." He sat on the edge of the bed. Her mother had gone away, but he wouldn't, God willing. God willing. He was sounding like Marsha. "Do you have a headache?"

He rubbed her back in circles with one hand while he touched her cheek with the other. She felt slightly warm, but nothing serious. "Do you have a headache?"

"No!"

"Bonnie," he said, lowering his voice to a near whisper. "Are you upset? Tell Daddy what's wrong."

"I don't know," she moaned, turning her hands into fists and slamming them against the bed.

"Come here." He pushed his arm beneath her and drew her closer. He wished he could sing like Marilou had. When Bonnie was upset, Marilou had sung her songs and soon she'd quieted. He began to hum a random tune.

Bonnie's body relaxed beneath his arm. She turned her head and nestled it against his shoulder.

His disoriented tune slipped into a familiar melody, and Jeff heard "Amazing Grace" coming from his lips. Amazing grace? That was what he needed. Something amazing in his life. Something to calm his child and help him meet her needs.

She had no friends on the island. At least, at school she had people she related to and, at home, a seven-year-old neighbor girl came over to play house or to color. Barb had colored with her, and she seemed to like that. Bonnie needed a friend. She needed something to do instead of moping.

"Want to do something?"

She didn't stir.

"Would you like to go somewhere?"

"To Aunt Marsha's?"

Marsha again. Bonnie was becoming dependent on her. He needed to do something about it, but what? When they returned home, she wouldn't have Marsha as she did now—not at her beck and call. Ignoring Marsha hadn't been the answer. He needed her, too. She seemed to brighten his day and, now that they'd talked, Jeff had hopes they could continue the old friendship they'd enjoyed for so many years. Maybe it would even blossom into more.

"I'll give her a call," he said, as much for himself as for Bonnie.

"Well, now, look who's here."

Marsha spun around, whacking Jeff's elbow with a caulking tube. She couldn't help but grin at her accidental attack on his arm and even more the coincidence that they were both at the hardware store. "Sorry. A caulking gun in my hands can be a dangerous weapon."

He raised his hands over his head and grinned. "I'm unarmed."

"You have arms, Daddy," Bonnie said, hanging on to Marsha's basket and looking at the items she'd tossed into it. "Are you fixing your house?"

"Trying," she said, making a silly face for Bonnie.

She laughed at Marsha's goofy look, then eyed Jeff as if to make sure he laughed, too.

"I have to see this."

"Me, too," Bonnie said.

Marsha dropped the caulk into the basket. "What are you doing here?"

"Looking for you."

"Looking for me?"

"I called, and Barb said you were here." He picked up a package of screws and a light-fixture cover. "Remodeling?" he gave her a wink as he waved the packages at her.

She couldn't help but chuckle at his silly expression. "Not quite. I've let things go, and I either need to do it myself or hire someone to do it for me."

"Good idea. I know just the man."

She gazed at the basket as relief flooded her. "Really? Do you have his card?"

"No, I can do better than that. He's in the store."

"Great. Introduce me."

He slipped his hand into hers. "Marsha, I'd like you to meet Jeff Sullivan." He gave her hand a firm shake.

"You?" She shook her head that she'd been so naive. "That's one thing I've always loved about you, Jeff." The word *love* nudged her consciousness. She managed to ignore the feeling. "You were always playful, while Don was more serious." Don. Jeff. Why did she keep comparing them? "I was more serious then, too."

"You had reason to be."

"I suppose, but I loved the laughter you brought into the house."

"I figured you needed a little lightheartedness." He rested his hand against her arm, offering her a gentle smile. "Now, getting back to the home improvement." His smile turned to a playful grin. "I'd be happy to help if you can give me a hand in return."

Curiosity pulled at her face. "Sure, if I can."

He clasped his hands on Bonnie's shoulders and turned her toward Marsha. "Here's your challenge."

Bonnie grinned at her, waving a screwdriver like a magician's wand over the edge of the basket.

"No challenge. I'd be happy to accept your offer."

"How could I do it without you?"

"Very well, I'm sure," she said, going along with the joke.

He slipped an arm around her shoulder and grasped the handle of the basket with the other hand.

As they ambled up and down the aisles finding what she needed, her spirits dimmed. She was concerned about Jeff's attitude toward God. She prayed for him, and since he'd known the Lord once, she asked the Holy Spirit to lead him back to his faith. How could a man so good and so kind not understand that God didn't always say yes? According to His will and purpose, He sometimes said no, and no one knew that better than Marsha. It shouldn't change their faith in Him.

Bonnie tugged at the side of the basket as they walked, making it wiggle. She laughed when he asked her to stop until finally she became bored and grasped Marsha's hand as they headed to the checkout counter.

Earlier Marsha had thought about asking Jeff to help with the repairs, but she knew he had his hands full with Bonnie and, to be honest with herself, she felt confused spending so much time with him. It seemed too comfortable and she feared she'd miss his company when she returned home. The city was different than an island. Things happened. Jobs and responsibility got in the way. People drifted.

His teasing question, How could I do it without you? filled her thoughts. Yet, that wasn't the real question. What would she do without him?

Chapter Six

Marsha leaned her shoulder against the bathroom door frame and watched Jeff as he straddled the bathtub and dug into the old caulking. The discolored curls of putty broke and dropped into the tub as he pried it loose so he could recaulk.

Jeff's broad shoulders flexed beneath his shirt, and Marsha let her gaze slip to the muscles that knotted beneath the pressure of the scraper. Jeff's lean build disguised his strength. Marsha couldn't help but admire his physique.

"How's it going?" she asked, wondering if he realized she'd been watching him. She leaned against the sink counter as he brushed perspiration from his forehead.

"Slow going, but I'm getting there." He swung his leg over the tub edge and rested both feet on the floor. "What's up?"

She gave her head a toss toward the doorway. "I'm running to McDonough's Market and thought I'd take Bonnie. Okay?"

Jeff's shoulders raised as he took a deep breath. "Are you sure you can handle it?"

"I only need a couple of things. It'll give her something to do."

Jeff didn't respond for a moment. "You know, she can be a handful."

"I can handle her."

He rose and tilted her chin upward. "You're an amazing woman."

She had never been called *amazing,* and she stretched upward and kissed his cheek. "You're even more amazing."

A tender look filled his eyes, and warmth swept through her. "I need to go." She pulled away, afraid of the intimacy she felt standing beside him. She needed to keep her distance. In-laws weren't supposed to be that affectionate. As the concern bolted into her mind, she asked herself, why not? Friends showed affection. It was natural.

Hoping she hadn't made a mistake with her decision to take Bonnie along, she grabbed her grocery list and her shoulder bag. Bonnie charged from the porch into the kitchen and nearly tripped over Marsha as she headed out the door. Marsha wished she could harness that kind of energy.

For some reason, getting Bonnie into a seat belt felt like trying to lasso a wild boar. "I don't need a seat belt," she said, folding her arms across her chest.

Marsha sat behind the wheel, counting and asking God to keep her calm.

"Let's go. Let's go," Bonnie yelled, slapping at the steering wheel.

"We can't go anywhere, Bonnie," Marsha said, keeping her voice as controlled as she could under the circumstances.

"Yes, you can." She gave the wheel another wallop.

"It's against the law. I'd be in jail for letting you ride without a seat belt."

Bonnie threw herself against the seat cushion, but, in

a moment, she fumbled with the buckle and strapped herself in.

"Thank you," Marsha said, sending up a prayer for patience.

During the short trip to town, Bonnie returned to her more pleasant self, and Marsha's confidence grew. So did her admiration for Jeff. She'd been critical of him, but today, she had second thoughts. Not that she didn't worry about Bonnie needing to understand how her body was growing, but she realized the difficulty in explaining this to the mentally immature girl.

Only a few cars were parked in front of the market. Marsha pulled into a slot and turned off the ignition.

"Can I push the basket?" Bonnie asked as she slipped from the car.

Marsha weighed the request and agreed. Though Bonnie darted too quickly through the doorway and whacked the cart against the glass, she slowed when she reached the aisles.

Marsha tossed items into the cart and, before long, Bonnie left her position behind the handle and wandered to a cookie display. Sugar was one thing her niece didn't need, but Bonnie snatched a package off the shelf and knocked a few to the floor.

"We have some at the cottage, already," Marsha said, picking up the fallen boxes and returning them to the shelf. She held out her hand for the package.

Bonnie tucked them behind her back. "They're mine. You can't have them."

"They're not yours until you pay for them."

"They're mine," she screamed. "You're not in charge of me."

"Right now I am."

A mixture of embarrassment and frustration sent heat up her neck. Marsha took a step forward as Bonnie took one backward. "You're not a child, any longer, Bonnie. You're growing up, and you need to act—"

"You're not my mother. Don't tell me what to do."

"Please, Bonnie," Marsha said, extending her hand toward Bonnie as she backed away.

Her mind twisted with solutions. She could buy the cookies, but what did that teach Bonnie? If she pulled them away, she knew a major tantrum could result.

"I can do things myself," Bonnie said, continuing to back away until she came to the end of the aisle. When Bonnie saw where she'd ended, she darted around the corner.

Marsha stood paralyzed and waited for the crash. She refused to chase her. Yet Jeff had told her the kind of damage Bonnie could do. Her heart felt heavy as her hopes sank. *Lord, what should I do?*

She grasped the cart to steady herself and took a long deep breath.

"They're mine!"

She heard Bonnie's voice soar from the next aisle. Keep calm. Think. Think. Her legs trembled as helplessness smothered her. How had Jeff endured this for so long? She closed her eyes, prepared for another outburst.

Nothing happened.

Her hands trembled against the shopping-cart handle, and she could hear the raggedness of her breath in her ears. Marsha opened one eye a slit and looked to the end of the aisle. She took a step forward. Then another.

A flash of color came around the corner, and Bonnie reappeared, holding the cookies against her chest. A look of confusion filled her face, and she laid the package down on a shelf as she drew nearer. "You lost me."

Marsha's chest ached holding back her tears. She opened her arms to Bonnie and embraced her. "I would never lose you, sweetheart." Marilou filled her mind. Bonnie had lost her mother only two years ago. What could she say to her that would make any sense? "I thought you wanted to be alone a minute."

The girl tightened her grip. "I don't want to be alone anymore."

Marsha held her tightly, but couldn't speak from her sadness.

Jeff heard the door bang, and he finished the slender bead of caulking before straightening his back. He could hear Bonnie jabbering to Barb about what they'd bought as she flew past the bathroom doorway, and he relaxed his shoulders. Apparently, Marsha had survived the event.

Straddling the tub as he faced the doorway, he spotted Marsha sailing past with two grocery bags. She wasn't smiling, but that didn't mean anything. After Don's death, Marsha had been more serious and, when they'd met at Daddy Frank's, she'd acted far more uptight than after they'd spent time together this past week. Since then, she'd often mentioned he brought her smiles out of hiding. He found it hard to believe. A smile looked so natural on her.

After a moment, he swung his other leg over the tub edge and strolled into the kitchen. Marsha's head was blocked behind the refrigerator door and, when she pulled back and closed it, she jumped in surprise. "You scared me."

Marsha looked edgy, and her eyes told him something he didn't want to hear, but he asked, anyway. "How did it go?"

She pressed her hand against her heart and shook her head. "Not now."

A frown tugged at his mouth, and he took a step forward. "What?"

She stepped closer and leaned toward his ear. "A problem. Resolved, but I learned so much." She stepped back and reached for a bag of potato chips, then slipped them on top of the refrigerator. "Later, okay?"

His curiosity niggled at him, but he respected her wish.

Bonnie's voice came from the front deck, and he slid open the door and stepped outside, his nostrils assailed by the odor of bug spray. He looked down at Barb on a foldout recliner. "Attacking the enemy?"

"It's the only way I can be out here." She picked up the aerosol can from the planking and waved it in the air. "Want some?"

"No. I think you've covered the area."

Barb chuckled as Bonnie pinched her nose and backed away. "Is that why you stink?"

"Bonnie!" Jeff said, trying to hold back his laugh. "You're not supposed to tell people they smell."

She looked at him wide-eyed. "But she does."

"I do," Barb said, returning the can to the floor. "I'll shower later. Okay?"

Bonnie unplugged her nose. "Okay."

Jeff drew Bonnie to his side and settled down on the plank bench of the picnic table. "Did you have fun?"

She nodded. "Look what Aunt Marsha bought me." She pointed toward Barb's recliner. He noticed a package resting on the foot. Bonnie darted across the deck and picked it up, then hurried back as she waved the carton toward him. "Markers."

"Markers." He gazed at the line of colorful tubes and managed not to cringe. Did Marsha realize the problems with markers?

Bonnie settled beside him. "She has paper I can use, and I can make pictures."

Jeff reached over her shoulder and patted the picnic table. "And this is the perfect place for you to draw."

She gazed at the table, then back at him. "Why?"

To keep you out of trouble, he wanted to say. "You can see the water and flowers and sky from here." He pointed to the landscape, praying she would accept the suggestion.

"Okay." She looked at the markers. "I have blue."

"Every color you'll need," Jeff said. "Blue, green, brown, yellow."

"Every color." She leaped from the bench and slipped inside while booming a request for paper.

Having enough of the bug spray, Jeff pulled himself from the bench and passed Bonnie in the doorway as Marsha was handing her sheets of white paper. "Draw me a picture," he said, hoping she'd be encouraged to play by herself for a while.

She gave him a quick okay and settled at the table as he turned away.

Jeff could see over the counter dividing the living room from the kitchen, and he hurried over to Marsha. "What happened at the store?"

She gazed past him toward the sliding door, then flagged him down the hall and into the back of the cottage that faced the road. A cedar bench swing sat beneath a tree, and she led him there, then patted the seat beside her.

Even more curious, Jeff studied her face, afraid of what she might say. "It was that bad?"

"Jeff, first I need to apologize to you. It's so easy to be critical until you're in the other person's shoes. It turned out okay, but I can see now what you go through every day. Every hour." She raised a tender gaze to his. "I can see how difficult it is."

"What did she do?" He shook his head. "I'm sure it was embarrassing. I know. I've had to deal with it. People either give you dirty looks or make comments. 'Don't you know how to control your kid?' 'Why don't you take parenting classes?' It's that or worse. I've been called every name in the book." His fingers locked around his knee.

Marsha slid her hand over his and rubbed his taut fingers. "It wasn't that bad."

She told him the story, and he listened, envisioning the many tantrums he'd lived through. She paused and brushed tears from her eyes.

He realized she was upset, but the tears surprised him until she continued describing her feelings and admitting what she'd learned. "I've bugged you about explaining to Bonnie about becoming a young woman, but now I see how difficult that would be. She won't want to hear it, and it will frighten her."

He nodded, reliving the agony that he'd gone through so often as he faced Bonnie's disability. "She can grow out of some of this, they say. She'll never be normal, but she can be trained to do everyday things. After her hormones settle down." He didn't believe it himself. "Maybe."

Marsha used her index finger to draw a slow line down his arm and up again. "We can hope. If the doctors and educators said it, then let's believe it's true."

He could only nod. He'd had hope and faith once, and he'd been let down too hard. How could he have hope now?

"But that's not all," Marsha said.

Her comment snapped his attention. "What else?"

This time tears pooled in her eyes and escaped. "When she came back to my aisle, she told me I'd lost her."

"You'd lost *her?*" He shook his head, trying to make sense out of that statement.

"I hadn't run after her. I'd stood in the aisle like a statue, having no idea whether to chase her, to give in and buy the stupid cookies or to sit on the floor and cry, myself."

"And she came back and said you lost her?"

Marsha gave a slow nod. "It scared her that I didn't go after her. She lost her mother once, Jeff. Or, as she sees it, her mother lost her. She didn't come back to find her." She turned in the seat and grasped his arms. "She's afraid of losing people. It's hard enough for a fully-abled child to understand the death of a parent. Can you imagine how frightening it still is for Bonnie? You should have seen her face."

She choked back a sob, and Jeff slipped his arm around her and rested her head on his shoulder. Her body trembled beneath his hand until she stilled, her voice murmuring against his shoulder.

"I remember after Don died. I felt so alone. I was frightened, too. I was an adult, but I felt betrayed by the world. Even by God."

Jeff heard his intake of breath before he controlled his shock. "You felt betrayed by God?"

She lifted her head, her eyes tear-rimmed. "It's natural. God's merciful. We're his precious children. So why does He take the ones we love—and so horribly? Like Don, such a long, excruciating death."

Her questions echoed his own. "Why, Marsha? Why?" He faltered, willing himself to calm and ask without attacking the God she loved. "That's what I want to understand."

"Read First Peter, Jeff. It's so clear. We suffer because Christ suffered for us. Peter says, even when we suffer, we're blessed because we have hope in Jesus. We are to keep our eyes turned to Him, and He will comfort us and give us strength."

Marsha glowed as she spoke, and Jeff wished he believed everything she was saying. He wanted to glow. He wanted to feel that same assurance. He wanted to understand. Read First Peter? He didn't even own a Bible.

She straightened, shifted sideways and grasped his arms. "Would you like to hear my favorite verse? The one I used as my prayer every day after Don died?" She shook her head. "Every *hour* after Don died."

His pulse tripped, watching her face enliven as she spoke. He nodded.

"'And the God of all grace, who called you to His eternal glory in Christ, after you have suffered a little while, will Himself restore you and make you strong, firm and steadfast. To Him be the power forever and ever. Amen.'" Her gaze locked with his. "Do you hear the hope and assurance? It's 1 Peter 5: 10-11." Her palms slid down his arms to his hands, and she enveloped his fists in her soft hands. "You knew God once, Jeff. You can open your heart to Him again."

"Hey!" Bonnie's voice sailed to them from the house.

The screen door banged, and Bonnie came charging across the stubbled grass, flailing a sheet of paper, the bright colors soaking through to the underside.

"What are you doing?" She stood in front of them, one hand on her hip, the other clasping her picture.

"Taking a break," Jeff said. "Aunt Marsha is working my tail off."

"Daddy, that's silly. People don't have tails. Dogs do."

He shook his head, then eyed the picture she clutched. "Let me see."

She held the paper at the corners and stuck it forward to show them.

Jeff swallowed to contain his emotion. She'd drawn three people—obviously a man, woman and child—holding hands and walking along the beach. A huge sun filled the left corner, and the rays angled down to the feet of the three people. The thought swelled in his mind.

"It's me, you and Aunt Marsha."

"It's beautiful," Jeff said, meaning it. He knew Bonnie colored well. She stayed in the lines and selected appropriate colors. The activity preoccupied her in a positive way, but, in a primitive way, Bonnie had created shapes and perspective that surprised him.

"I love it," Marsha said, studying the drawing. "I see some talent."

"It's for you," she said, handing the drawing to Marsha.

"I'll cherish it, always."

Bonnie plopped down beside her and pressed her head against Marsha's shoulder.

Marsha rested her palm on Bonnie's head. "And I'll cherish you always, too."

Jeff looked at the two beside him, reeling with emotion. Love. Faith. Hope. Cherish. He'd been so bogged down with trying to make it through each day he hardly knew the meaning of the words, but today was different. He saw real love in Marsha's eyes and hope in her voice.

If only he could hear it in his.

Chapter Seven

Marsha stood in the middle of the library, gazing at the bookshelves. The building had the look of the outdoors with its cedar interior supported by four huge cedar pillars and wide windows looking into the wooded surrounding, so appropriate for the rural setting.

"Go ahead," she said to Barb, motioning toward the fiction section. "I'm going to look for a couple things, myself."

Barb gave her a nod, set down the books she was returning on the checkout desk and headed down an aisle in search of some new reading material.

Marsha studied the book rows marked with Dewey decimal numbers and finally located the section she wanted. She walked along the row, eyeing books about child psychology and special-needs children. She slipped a book off the shelf, gazed at the index and slid it back.

As she eyed the rows and rows of books, the task seemed daunting. All she wanted was to learn more about emotionally impaired kids. What could parents do to help them through the crises? What were their educational needs? How did parents survive?

She rested her hands on her hips and studied the titles, unable to discern where to begin. Hoping Barb hadn't already finished her search for a new novel, Marsha went to the end of the aisle and scanned the checkout desk. No Barb. Good.

As she took a step back, her eyes wavered across a bank of computers near the center of the floor. Her pulse skipped. She could find something there more quickly, she hoped.

Heading toward the two computers, she stopped and made her way toward Barb. When she caught her attention, she pointed, and Barb gave her a nod. Turning back to the computer, she faltered. The only empty seat had been taken. She scanned the floor but saw no others.

As her shoulders sagged, a librarian strode to her side. "We have another computer on the porch. She pointed to the center doorway where a lovely glass enclosure afforded a view of the woods. Marsha hurried to the area and sank onto the seat. She followed the instructions and logged onto the Internet. After pulling up a search engine, she typed *emotionally impaired child* into the space and, in a moment, a long list of Web sites filled the page.

She read about IEP goals—individual education plans—and school programs for disabled children. Her gaze slipped over student eligibility, services available and resource rooms. She lifted her shoulders, feeling she was getting nowhere, then looked behind her to see if Barb appeared ready. Not yet.

Assured, she looked back at the screen. She could just tell Barb what she was doing, but her sister would, once again, remind her she was butting into business that wasn't hers. But what could she do? She wanted to know how to help Bonnie.

Jeff's face rose in her mind. How to help him.

Near the bottom of the page, a Web site spoke to her. A Parent's Perspective. *Thank you, Lord.* This might be exactly what she wanted. She clicked on the link and scanned the article, a touching insight into the plight of families dealing with special children.

Greedy to learn, she slowed and drank in the words— usually above-average intelligence, special talents that are not developed. Talents? She lingered over this section— science, music and art. Art. She'd seen a hint of that with Bonnie's drawing.

Marsha paused and reread a paragraph. *Arguing or restraining the child will only cause him to up the ante to force the parent's attention and reward, and punishment does not work and can actually escalate the problem. We pick our battles, mainly those that deal with safety issues. Instead, we seek the trigger for our child's frustration and we remove it.*

She thought about Jeff's way of handling Bonnie, which wasn't as bad as he seemed to think, according to what this parent said. He tried and succeeded more than he failed. Who was she to try to tell him how to raise his daughter? She closed her eyes, her spirits flagging. *Lord, I'm not trying to change him, but I want it to be better, and I know it can be if it's Your will.* The Lord's will. She lifted her head and took a deep breath. God will provide, she thought.

Marsha lowered her gaze again. *Give your child positive attention by helping him feel part of the family. Teach him to do simple tasks. Once he realizes he has a purpose and is valued, it will bring improvement. Do not punish, but do reward. Remember to tell him he's done a good job. He craves your attention.*

Who didn't crave attention? She craved it, too, if she

were willing to admit it. For so long, she'd given her time to Don. She never asked for anyone's attention for herself, but now life had changed and she found it easy to sink into nothingness instead of reaching out for her own rewards.

"I'm ready."

Barb's voice startled her. She closed the program and turned to face her. "Me, too."

"What were you doing?"

She faltered, not wanting to hear Barb's lecture. "Just looking up some information." She stood. "Let's go to one of the shops. I want to pick up a picture frame."

"Picture frame?"

"For Bonnie's drawing. I think she'd be excited to see it hanging on the wall. She can use some positive attention."

"Looking up some information? Interesting." Barb gave her a knowing grin. "I know. You can't help yourself."

Marsha nodded. She couldn't.

Water swished over Jeff's ankles, and he checked his rolled-up cuffs to see if they had gotten wet. He bent over and gave them another roll. "Shorts would be safer."

Marsha grinned. "A bathing suit, safer than that."

He saw a playful look on her face as she headed toward him, her arms extended, ready to give him a good push.

"Don't you dare. My wallet's in my back pocket."

"I've accidentally sent money through the washer and dryer. No problem."

Mischief sparkled in her eyes, and he changed his tack. Instead of running away, he charged forward and captured her arms beneath his.

Laughter bubbled from her throat. "I was only kidding. I wouldn't have pushed you."

"Sure. You say that now that you're captured." He drew her closer, to be safe, he told himself, yet he knew he loved the feeling of her in his arms.

She wriggled beneath his grasp, trying to get loose, but he held her even tighter, laughing. "How do you like it?"

She stopped squirming, her gaze meeting his.

Warmth spread from the pit of his stomach. How do you like it? He loved it—playful fun, a wonderful woman who cared about Bonnie, a summer's day on a beautiful Great Lake. What more could he want?

Her gaze shifted, then captured his eyes again. "It feels nice. Really nice."

The water rippled against his legs until the wake from a passing speed boat sent a foamy wave onto his pant leg. A seagull soared overhead, its shadow darkening the blue water. He couldn't speak for a moment, caught in the depths of his imagination.

He didn't know what to do, so he laughed and let her go. "I hope you learned your lesson," he said, hearing the stupid words falling from his lips. He wanted to confess he felt the same. It was nice to play and laugh. It was great to feel alive again. So why hadn't he until recently?

Marsha searched his face, then smiled, but a hint of disappointment flickered in her eyes, and he knew he'd fallen short of being honest. She turned and scanned the beach, a frown flooding her face. "Where's Bonnie?

Hearing her question surprised him. She always looked out for Bonnie and, somehow, she'd missed what had happened earlier. "She went up to the house a while ago, but I think she wants to see her picture in the frame you hung on the wall. She's very proud. She told me she wanted to play with Barb." He tilted her chin, hoping to bring back her smile. "She asked if she could go, and I know Barb *loves* to play with her." He dragged out the word *love*, longing to see her grin.

It worked. She shook her head and smiled.

"How did I miss that?"

Jeff took her hand in his and headed back to the beach. "You were thoughtful."

"I have been." Her gaze drifted toward the horizon. "Sorry."

He released her hand to slip his arm around her shoulder. "No need to be sorry. We all have our days. For the past few days, I've been worried about Bonnie."

Marsha stopped. "About what?"

The sand pulled from beneath his feet as they stood where the lake met the shore. "She needs kids to play with. She's with adults too much."

"Bonnie's better with adults, Jeff."

"Why would you say that?"

She lowered her gaze and shrugged. "It just makes sense to me."

It didn't make sense to him, but then many things didn't.

Marsha stepped ahead of him, and he looked at her footprints as the wet sand turned lighter beneath her feet when her weight pressed away the water. He took a step and watched the same pattern, dark sand turning pale with the pressure of his imprint. "Footprints in the sand," he said for no reason.

She paused, then turned and looked at their prints, her mind seeming miles away. "I love that story. I received a bookmark once with a lapel pin with three little footprints. I wonder what happened to that bookmark."

Footprints? Story? "I've never heard it."

"You're kidding. Everyone knows that story about God's relationship with us."

He shook his head, asking himself how he'd gotten into the situation of listening to a story about God. But as he listened, he had to stop her. "So let me get this straight. When the man needed God the most, he saw only one set of prints. Right?"

"Right."

"Then I'm not the only one who feels as if God walked away."

Marsha's eyes darkened, and she pressed her hand against his cheek. "No. He didn't, Jeff. He's promised to never walk away."

"Then, where was He?" Her palm felt cool against his sun-warmed cheek, and he raised his own and pressed it against hers. "Explain it."

Marsha's eyes looked so sad, Jeff's stomach twisted. Why had he spoken that way to her?

"You didn't let me finish the story. When the man asked the Lord the same question you just asked, He said something like this. 'My son, I would never leave you. When you were at your lowest, when you were in pain, you only saw one set of prints, because I was carrying you.'"

Jeff's chest tightened and he dropped his gaze and saw their footprints side by side. He fought back tears that pushed against his eyes, seeing Marsha's serious expression.

"Think about it, Jeff. You were never alone. You aren't now."

You aren't alone. Marsha's words from two days earlier flooded Jeff's mind. He dropped a cereal bowl in the dishwasher, wiped the counter and filled his coffee cup for the third time. He should switch to decaf. He'd spent the night tossing from one side of his bed to the other, sometimes reaching out to wrap his arm around his dream.

Marsha had appeared again, glowing in the sunlit beach. They talked and laughed, and then she spoke of God again. Marsha and God. They both lingered in his mind as persistent as bees around apple cider. He recalled the day he and Marilou had gone to Franklin Cider Mill. They'd bought a jug of cider along with some deep-fried doughnuts. They'd poured cups of cider and had bitten into the warm, crunchy outer crust, then had to run for their lives. The bees had swarmed in as if invited to their party.

The memory made him smile. So did Marsha, but she'd also caused him to think, and he didn't want to do that. He liked being angry at God. How else could he get even?

The stupidity of his statement knifed through him, and he leaned against the counter, grateful for the quiet moment while Bonnie was still asleep. Jeff thought of the footprint story—the angry man who'd looked at the lone set of prints and thought they were his. "I was carrying you," God had said. The words tumbled in Jeff's thoughts until he felt dizzy.

"Read your Bible," Marsha had said days earlier. "Read First Peter." They had owned a Bible—probably two, maybe even three. Marilou had read it in the morning. She'd read passages to him. But he hadn't seen one since she'd died.

Or had he?

He wandered into the living room and scoured the bookshelf beneath the window. He crouched and let his gaze run along the book titles until it stopped at a navy hardcover with gold letters. *Holy Bible.* He extended his hand, then drew it back.

Jeff stood and wandered to the wide window looking out on the lake. He'd once believed that God directed his steps. If he still believed that, he would think the Lord had planned for him to run into Marsha that day at the ice-cream shop. Had that been providence? A coincidence?

His gaze drifted back to the bookshelf. First Peter. The verse Marsha had memorized came to him in snatches—suffer, restore, strong. He tried to put the words together like a puzzle. After you have suffered, God will restore you and make you strong. If only he could feel strong. It had been so long.

A sound from the bedroom caught his attention and Jeff turned back to the kitchen. Bonnie would be up soon and wanting breakfast. As he pulled out a bowl, he heard the pat of her feet in the hall. She walked into the room with a wide yawn, rubbing her eyes with her fists.

"Good morning," Jeff said, remembering the neighbor had said Bonnie was pretty. She was pretty. He'd never noticed. Her hair had become darker than her mother's but lighter than his and her eyes were the same as Marilou's, a light brown that reminded him of sorrel. She had two small dimples that flickered when she grinned and her nose was shaped like his with a little peak at the tip.

Bonnie settled onto the chair and rested her cheek on the table.

"Please don't put your head on the table, Bonnie."

She didn't respond, and he didn't repeat it. Today, he wasn't in the mood for a fight. He poured her cereal and milk, then wandered back to the window, watching the sun dance across the ripples.

As soon as she finished eating, he knew Bonnie would be bored—the same old pattern he'd come to accept. She needed a friend, someone to relate to, and he had no idea what to do except go back home where she did have a couple of younger children who played with her.

But he didn't want to go home. Not now.

He heard Bonnie's dish clang in the sink. "What are we going to do, Daddy?"

"I don't know. How about playing with those markers Marsha bought you?"

She didn't respond but wandered out of the kitchen in search, he hoped, of the colored pens. In moments, she returned and, while he ran the vacuum and dusted, Bonnie sat at the table engrossed in her drawings.

Peace settled over Jeff with Bonnie's preoccupation. Marsha knew what she was doing when she'd bought the markers, and he'd been surprised to see Bonnie had some artistic talent. Perhaps, she had other talents he hadn't noticed but, for now, he'd be grateful for this quiet time.

Bonnie came through the doorway, carrying a drawing. "Look." She held up the picture in front of her with the tips of her fingers. "Aunt Marsha can put this in a frame, too."

Jeff eyed the beach sketch with three people sitting on the sand, making sand castles. In the background, he recognized Marsha's A-frame cottage. Three people again. She never drew one or two, always three and always Marsha.

Here it was three again, but at home? What would that bring? The summer fun would vanish. His life would slip into the usual rut, and then what? Bonnie would be heartbroken.

So would he.

Chapter Eight

Marsha slid from the car and lifted the bag of groceries from the backseat, disappointed that Jeff hadn't arrived yet. He'd promised to hang the new kitchen light fixture and replace some light-switch covers. She could have done that herself, but he'd told her not to bother. Instead, she'd added some new border along the ceiling in the bathroom. It brightened the room with the new caulking and made it look fresh and different—just the way she'd felt lately.

A breeze blew across the water and up the hill, carrying the unique scent of the lake and warm grass. Nothing smelled quite like that wonderful aroma that helped her relax and feel free. She wished it could be bottled. She'd definitely stock up so she could take it home to the city with her.

As she neared the door, another fragrance wafted her way. Cinnamon rolls. Barb's favorite. Marsha pulled open the screen door and drew in a lengthy breath of the warm spicy rolls. "Yummy," she said, eyeing the batch cooling on racks.

"I felt in the mood," Barb said, snipping the end off the tube of frosting and zigzagging it over the pastries. "I made coffee."

"Thanks." Marsha dragged her finger across the icing that dripped from the rack and stuck it in her mouth, then unloaded the groceries while Barb poured two cups of coffee.

Barb took her cup and a warm roll. "I'm going outside. No bugs today for some reason, and I'm enjoying the sun."

"Probably the breeze," Marsha said, slipping the cereal box into the cabinet. "I'll be out in a minute."

The scent of coffee mingled with the cinnamon smell and whetted Marsha's appetite. She headed into the bedroom to slip off her slacks and slide into her shorts and sandals. No sense in wasting an opportunity to get a tan.

Before heading back into the kitchen, Marsha glanced out the back window, hoping to see Jeff. She shook her head at the empty driveway but mainly at her silly ogling.

Foolishness. She'd begun to feel like a teenager, running to the telephone when it rang hoping it was the boy who starred on the basketball team, but, in this case, Marsha's hero was her brother-in-law. Or was it *former* brother-in-law now that Don was gone?

She pushed herself down the hallway and grasped the coffee-cup handle, then a gooey cinnamon bun. She took a chomp, letting the sweetness pull her from her thoughts. As she passed the table, she noticed a legal pad with Barb's writing. Curious, she stepped forward, took another bite of the bun and let her gaze drift over the words.

Night sounds always scared Lorraine. She pulled back into the shadow behind the curtain, remembering that horrible night, the lonely night when it all began.

Another sound caught her imagination, and she shifted from the dark corner to peek through the lace at the shrouded moon. The man in the moon stared down at her through his own curtain of dark clouds.

Gooseflesh pricked her arms. That horrible night clung to her thoughts, that rainy night when her clothes clung to her as if hanging onto her for fear they might be torn from her. And they were.

Marsha caught her breath and drew away from the yellow lined paper. Though the sentences were well written, poetic almost, the images frightened her. She had expected Barb to write some pitiful rambling of a woman in love or a woman scorned, but not this. This was different.

What would Barb say if she told her she'd read a page of her work?

A noise came from behind her, and Marsha jumped and spun around. Bonnie came darting into the room, holding one of her drawings in front of her like a prize.

"Look what I made," she said, as if she'd won a blue ribbon.

Marsha eyed the sketch, and, though simple, Bonnie's talent could be witnessed in her ability to create perspective and to draw recognizable details. "That's the cottage," she said, studying the contours of her chalet.

Bonnie bobbed her head. "And that's you." She pointed to a woman and man standing beside her.

Marsha recognized Jeff easily by his physique and the playful tilt of his head. "Good job. You need some real paints."

"I have real paints." She held up her markers.

"I mean, watercolors or oils." She gave second thought to oils and the damage they might cause. "Watercolors." Marsha lifted her gaze and eyed the back door. "Where's your dad?"

"He's coming." She wobbled her head and grinned. "His

cell phone rang." She took a couple of steps away before she noticed the cinnamon buns and shot toward them. "Can I have one?"

"Sure can."

She grabbed a pastry and sped outside to Barb.

Marsha took a sip of her coffee, her pulse giving a skip as she watched the door, waiting for Jeff. *Lord, tell me what's going on. I'm confused and uneasy with what's going on.*

A moment later, Jeff strode inside, slipping the cell phone into his shirt pocket. His focus settled on the buns, then lifted to Marsha.

"Have one," she said, taking another bite to steady her thoughts.

He looked so handsome today. His hair, usually neat, had been ruffled by the breeze and his tanned skin gave him a rugged look. His knit shirt clung to his chest, reminding her of his strength and masculinity. He no longer seemed the old Jeff she knew so well, but a new Jeff that had more vitality and charm, a Jeff that stirred her heart.

Marsha turned away. She felt confused and she hated the feeling.

"Sorry I'm late," Jeff said, as if he noticed something was wrong.

Jeff was right, but Marsha didn't understand what it was she struggled with. She knew it wasn't a sin to find her former brother-in-law attractive. She suspected the Lord would be pleased that they were still good friends. Friends were precious. "You don't have to apologize. You're not punching a time clock." She managed a grin.

He stepped closer and ran his finger just below her lip. "Icing," he said, showing her the white smear he'd wiped from her mouth.

The pressure of his finger lingered against her lip, and she wondered what his lips might feel like pressed against hers. Then she stopped herself. Jeff was her former brother-in-law—and his faith was shaky. No matter how much she thought of him, she could never align herself with a man who didn't have the Lord in his heart.

The thought saddened her. No one walked a Christian life by force. It had to be Jeff's will. He had to open his heart to the Holy Spirit, and all she could do was pray that it happened for him and for Bonnie. Her niece needed to have a relationship with Jesus just as her mother had.

"Coffee, too," Jeff said, returning to the kitchenette to pour himself a cup. He ambled back and sat on a stool against the counter that divided the kitchen from the living room. "You're quiet."

"Enjoying the cinnamon bun," she said, not wanting to mention her curiosity about Barb's writing and definitely not wanting to tell him about her emotional roller coaster.

"My friend called and is coming up for the Fourth."

Marsha twitched. A friend? Male or female? "Someone's coming up for the holiday?"

"For a week. He'll be up on Sunday before the Fourth. He's bringing his daughter. I thought she'd be company for Bonnie and give you and Barb a break."

He's bringing his daughter. A man. Her shoulders relaxed, replaced by shame that she'd felt a twinge of jealousy. She couldn't believe she'd become so attached to Jeff. "That's nice, but you know Bonnie is no problem for us."

"You've both been good sports, but she really needs kids her own age. Lindsey is twelve. That's a good fit."

Marsha recalled reading in the library that disabled kids

didn't always relate well to kids without disabilities. She hoped that wasn't true. "Your friend's wife can't make it?"

Jeff's head drooped. "He's divorced. Nasty situation. His wife had an affair. What could be worse?"

Was death worse? Marsha only shook her head, not sure how to determine the answer to his question. "We'll have to plan something special when he's here." We'll. She cringed at being so blatant.

"Al's never been here so it should be fun. He's bringing his clubs so we'll probably golf."

"Golf?" Disappointment poked her. "You can leave the girls here."

"We'll probably take them in the cart. They should enjoy that."

"They might. I've never golfed. I suppose it's fun."

"You should take lessons. I know there are lots of women's leagues. Nice company for you."

Nice company in a women's league. What about nice company with Jeff? Loneliness made its unpleasant way into her thoughts. If Jeff had a friend on the island, she needed to keep herself busy doing something. Barb had seemed to loosen up. Maybe she and Barb could pass the time together. It would be good for them.

Jeff climbed on the step stool and began taking down the old ceiling light fixture. His mind wandered, wondering why Marsha had seemed so quiet during lunch. Something was bothering her, and he had no clue as to what. He'd apologized for being late, but he had believed her when she'd said that wasn't a problem. They hadn't set a specific time so he really had no need to apologize. But something was in the air.

Bonnie had behaved well at the table. He wondered if it had been because Marsha had suggested buying her some watercolors to replace the markers. Bonnie did seem to have talent and, when she was drawing, she seemed like any other child—no tantrums and no whining. She spent long periods of time concentrating on her pictures, and Jeff felt a tremendous relief and much gratefulness to Marsha, who'd had the idea to purchase the markers to begin with.

Bonnie's absorption with the markers had caused him to think. When Bonnie had a purpose, when she did something that had a positive result, she seemed to concentrate and focus, something she didn't do much of the time. He needed to teach her things, jobs that would make her feel as if she had a purpose—making her own bed, helping with the dishes, things she could use in life to be independent.

Independent? Would that ever be a reality?

He removed the last screw in the fixture and eased it down from the wall. The wiring looked good, and he'd already released the circuit breaker so he detached the wires, then stepped to the floor.

Jeff heard the screen move along the track, and he glanced toward the sound.

"How are you doing?" Marsha strode to his side, eyeing the old fixture. "Dirty. I'm embarrassed."

"Don't be. You'll have a new one up there in a few minutes."

"And one with more light." She grinned, then drew her fingers through her cascade of red hair. "I think I'll take Bonnie into town to look for watercolors. I suspect they have some at the Toy Museum. They sell all kinds of things there."

He pulled the new lighting fixture from the box. "Why

don't you wait a few minutes?" He gazed at the connections, an easy five-minute job. "I'll be done in a flash."

"You want to go to the Toy Museum?"

"Not particularly, but the lighthouse is right there."

She smiled, and Jeff saw the warmth in her eyes he'd come to know. He climbed the ladder while Marsha stood nearby, in case he fell, she said. He wondered what might have happened if he'd fallen earlier when she hadn't been hearty. Jeff grinned at the question as he attached the wiring with the connectors, pulled the screwdriver from his pocket and attached the new fixture.

"How does that look?" he asked, stepping down from the step stool. He ambled to the hallway circuit box and flicked the switch. The light flashed on, and Marsha's hair glowed in the brightness. Red hair and freckles. She seemed a vision of summer.

"Great," she said. "Now I can read a recipe. Before it was only a good guess."

He laughed at her remark. "Let me wash my hands, and we can be on our way."

Marsha headed outside, and, when he'd finished, she and Bonnie were standing near the back door.

The ride to town thrilled Bonnie when a fox darted from the roadside as they approached Font Lake. She craned her neck and knelt on the backseat, staring out the window, but the fox had vanished as quickly as he'd appeared. Jeff wished his problems would fade that quickly.

They followed Main Street through town and around Paradise Bay to the far side past the sheriff's department to the Toy Museum, an old house nestled behind a wall of trees and tall grass.

Along the path into the museum, they walked through

the wildflowers and grasses where unusual displays caught Bonnie's interest. An old stump held a piece of concrete with a clock embedded into its face and a stone robin sitting on top, silly things that fit a toy store.

Inside the building, Jeff kept an eye on Bonnie as they wandered through the rooms filled with antique toys. She gawked at the unusual coin banks and wanted to hold the dolls with porcelain heads.

When Bonnie began to whine, Marsha suggested they return to the store area. Her suggestion stopped Bonnie's tantrum before it began.

"Here we go," Marsha said, showing Bonnie the watercolor tins. Marsha selected a large pad of paper and some extra brushes before making their way to the cashier.

Bonnie said thank you on her own, and Jeff felt his chest expand. He hadn't gone totally wrong with raising Bonnie.

She bounded on ahead carrying her new sketchbook and watercolors and, when they reached the road, Jeff felt moved to take Marsha's hand as he steered her to the lighthouse.

Marsha didn't resist, and he clasped her hand more firmly, weaving his fingers through hers and feeling the wonderful closeness of a woman, her perfume filling his senses.

The white structure stood at the tip of Whiskey Point near the old Coast Guard boathouse and the city hall. The lighthouse was always the first thing Jeff noticed from the car ferry as he approached the town of St. James.

Bonnie darted to the lone picnic table and plopped down the bag holding her new painting equipment. "Can I paint?"

He eyed Marsha, and she gave an agreeable shrug.

"For a while," he said. "Let me get your water."

He took the water tray and dipped water from the lake, then set it beside her. "Don't get paint on your clothes."

"Okay," she said, already organizing her brushes and paper.

"We'll be nearby," Jeff said, grasping Marsha's hand again and heading for the nearby monument that honored those lost at sea. They studied the monument talking about a sailor's life, then walked to the old Coast Guard pier and around the far side of the building. Alone, Jeff paused. "Thanks for thinking of the watercolors. I always wonder where you get such good ideas."

"I read some articles at the library about emotionally impaired children."

He drew back. He knew she cared about Bonnie, but he had no idea she'd taken time to read articles about her disability. Her effort touched him. "You're a good woman, Marsha. A wonderful person."

She gazed at him, her eyes searching his, and he leaned forward and brushed his mouth against her warm lips. He startled himself by his action, but he'd wanted to do it for so long.

Marsha's hand flew to her mouth and her face flushed.

Disappointment charged through him. "I'm sorry, Marsha. I don't know why I did that, except it seemed right."

Her hand dropped, but the surprised look remained on her face. "I'm not angry, Jeff, just…"

She faltered, as if not knowing what to say, and he didn't know what to say, either, except to tell her the truth. She seemed to fill his mind and his dreams. Yet, it seemed out of place. She'd always been Marsha, his sister-in-law, but now it was different, and he couldn't seem to keep a grip on his emotions.

"Please forgive me. I won't do it again." He didn't want to say that, but it came out.

Marsha's expression shifted from surprise to a frown. "I'm not angry. Really."

She wasn't angry, but she'd been startled. He'd been stupid to kiss her, even a small kiss. She'd accepted his hugs and hand-holding, but a kiss was too intimate. He had no right without making sure that she would be willing.

He stepped away from the building and headed back to the picnic table, wishing he hadn't been so presumptuous. He needed to control himself and, if that meant staying away from Marsha, then so be it. If he saw her as he'd been doing, he feared he would kiss her again, but this time fully, a long lingering kiss that had already happened in his dreams.

Chapter Nine

Marsha stared at the telephone. She wanted to call Jeff and tell him she'd loved his kiss, but she couldn't allow herself to be romantically involved with a man unsure of his faith. She believed if Jeff would only open his heart, the Holy Spirit would nest inside and relieve his bitterness and frustration.

But she stopped herself. She'd already told herself over and over that forcing Jeff to church, manipulating him to say he believed, was not the answer. If he really cared about her, and she knew she cared about him, he had to allow his heart to accept the truth. She could not use her will to force his decision. She wanted to trust Jeff, to know that he'd chosen the Lord of his own free will.

Two days had passed since the kiss and Jeff had only called once to say he was busy and wouldn't be over. She'd heard the tension in his voice and she wished she could back up time and replay the kiss so she would have responded differently.

But how could it have been different?

Barb sat outside at the picnic table, this time writing her novel instead of reading one.

Marsha longed to sneak another peek at what she'd written. Barb's story had created word pictures that settled in Marsha's mind and wouldn't budge. Why that kind of dark story? She pulled herself from the sofa and slid open the screen door.

The sun felt warm against her skin, but a lake breeze spun the flavors of the air past her, leaving her feeling refreshed. A cottage could mellow a person. It certainly had Barb.

She closed the screen and sat beside Barb on the picnic-table bench facing away from her. "How's the writing going?"

"Good. I'm surprised it's coming so easily."

"What's it about?" Marsha's chest tightened.

"A woman with problems."

Leaning back, Marsha glimpsed at the page. "What kind of problems?"

"You know. Problems. Issues. We all have them."

Her back pressed against the sharp edge of the table. "I guess we do." Jeff's face filled her mind.

Barb shifted and turned over the legal pad so Marsha couldn't see the work. "I've been concerned about something."

Jeff. Marsha knew she would notice. "Concerned?"

"About Bonnie."

Marsha felt her eyes widen. "Bonnie?"

"Why are you surprised? You've been concerned about her, yourself. I'm agreeing with you."

The comment threw Marsha for a loop. "You convinced me to back off, and I did. So what happened to change your mind?"

Barb pulled one leg over the bench and straddled it.

"Observing her. Thinking about that neighbor who told her she was pretty."

"She is pretty if she learned to take care of herself. It won't be long and—" .

"That's what I mean," Barb said, her arm flailing outward as if she were at a loss for words. "To take care of herself."

"I'd hoped to influence her a little—teach her some grooming, but I'm not sure—"

Barb scowled. "I'm not talking about that kind of taking care of herself. I mean, protecting herself."

"Protecting herself? Why would you say that?"

"Because it happens." Barb lifted her pop can and took a drink.

Marsha recalled Bonnie's naiveté. "I know she needs social skills, and she needs to look more—"

"You don't get the picture, Marsha."

She studied her sister's face.."I guess I don't."

"Protect herself from men. Boys. They take advantage of girls as they blossom, especially ones who can't defend themselves."

Marsha drew back. "Why would you even think that? I can't imagine anyone hurting Bonnie in that way, Barb. They can see she's not—"

"That's just the kind they do hurt. Kids who are shy or different. Don't think she's safe from anyone. Some people can't be trusted, and it's difficult to know the difference."

Her remark jolted Marsha. "I suppose someone might try to take advantage, but Jeff keeps a good eye on her. She's never too far away from him." Marsha had always felt more concerned about the impression Bonnie made in public. She pictured Bonnie's messy hair, her bangs usually hanging in her eyes and her unkempt clothing. Barb's fear seemed such a stretch. "I know Jeff's trying to do his best, but Bonnie needs to learn about grooming and keeping her clothes neat. She's capable of doing that. She just needs guidance."

"You think that's her only problem?"

"Jeff tries to teach her those things, but—"

Barb plonked her drink on the table and leaned closer to Marsha. "Jeff has a job. He sends Bonnie to school. She's vulnerable at school. I've heard all kinds of horror stories of things that happen to kids at school."

"I know some kids make fun of her, but she's in a special program. The special-ed teacher doesn't let her go off alone."

Barb shrugged. "Let's hope."

Marsha didn't respond.

Barb slipped her other leg over the bench. "If anything happens, remember I warned you."

Marsha studied Barb's taut expression. "What brought this on? That neighbor hasn't been in the picture for over a week and a half. Why did you think about that now?"

"It's been on my mind. I didn't want to…"

"Want to what?" Marsha's face tightened with a scowl.

"Want to start anything." She swung her arm away from her body. "Start something like this. You asking me why I'm concerned. I just am."

"Okay. Let's not argue about it." She rose and stood there, not knowing what to do or say. Finally, she stepped off the porch and headed for the beach. Barb's worry had left her with an unpleasant edginess.

Jeff stood behind Bonnie at the kitchen table and watched her paint with the new watercolors. He couldn't help but gawk at what she'd drawn. Somewhere she'd learned about shadow and light, learned about blending colors by washing them with lighter or darker shades, techniques he couldn't imagine where she'd gotten.

"That's beautiful, Bon. I think you've found your calling."

"Calling?" She gazed up at him, her eyes filled with question. "Are you calling Aunt Marsha?"

He winced, knowing he'd confused her by spending so much time with Marsha and then pulling away again. He'd done it before, but now he avoided her for a different reason. This time a reason in his heart. He'd lost control of his emotions, and spending time with her made it all the harder.

Her reaction to the kiss hadn't been what he'd expected. What had he expected? His head swam with questions and answers, but none made sense. The island, the summer sky, the newness of being together, it led people to behave differently. Those sunny feelings would fade just as they did in winter. Today his heart felt like winter.

And Bonnie, he'd been unfair to her. She needed his attention. Instead, his mind and dreams were focused on Marsha.

"Are you calling, Daddy?"

Bonnie's persistent question echoed in his thoughts.

"Maybe later." Jeff turned away and wandered into the living room, then aimed for the sliding door to the deck. He strolled outside, his gaze scanning the beach. What was Marsha doing today?

Bracing his arms against the railing, Jeff drew in a lengthy breath. Rain had fallen during the night and today the flowers and wild grasses glistened with droplets not yet burned off by the sun. A sparkling day. He wished he could feel the same sparkle.

Marsha. He felt a bond to her. Yet she apparently

didn't feel it. If she hadn't been upset by the kiss, as she'd said and, if it had nothing to do with Bonnie, then what was it?

He'd assumed his edginess had caused their distance when she'd started nagging about talking with Bonnie, and he still needed to do that. He'd avoided it more than he avoided cleaning windows. The reason seemed clear. He felt inadequate. What did he know about womanhood? A son he could have talked with, but a daughter?

Reality struck him. He needed a woman, a mother figure for Bonnie, yet he'd rejected Marsha's help. She would have been willing to give Bonnie some feminine pointers, but he'd snapped at her too often. Now she never said a thing.

So that led him back to the same question. If Bonnie or the kiss wasn't the problem, then what was? Why had Marsha withdrawn? He'd come on too strong, he guessed. She wasn't ready for romance, and—

Neither was he, he'd told himself. Marilou had only been gone a little more than two years. Two long years. She would want him to find love again.

Love? Was it love he felt for Marsha, or was it familiarity and comfort? She stirred him. He thought of her all the time when they weren't together. He dreamed of her at night. He couldn't escape her and, yet, here he was trying to hide.

Foolish.

Jeff turned and entered the house, settling into a chair and leaning back his head. If Marsha weren't on the island at the same time he was, what would he be doing now? Moping the way he was today? He'd be sightseeing, swimming with Bonnie, maybe even fishing, although he'd have to put the bait on the hook. Bonnie would probably need help with that. Not Marsha. If Marsha went fishing, she'd want to be in charge…though she'd been true to her word. She'd backed off lately.

So what was it?

He lowered his head, his fingers twiddling in his lap. Here he was with quiet time while Bonnie was preoccupied, time he could be reading or…or what? His gaze drifted to the bookshelf and settled again on the navy book with gold letters. Holy Bible.

Was that it? Was it his faith that kept her backing away? He knew Marsha thought her faith could move mountains as the Bible said, but she'd never pushed him. She'd encouraged him to read some chapters. What was it? First something. First Peter.

He ambled to the shelf and grasped the book in his hands, then settled down again, tracing the gold letters with his fingertip. How often had he seen Marilou sitting at breakfast or in the evening reading from the Bible? He'd been a believer, too, but he hadn't delved into God's Word as she had.

Truth be told, he still believed or he wouldn't be fighting God. He wouldn't be trying to get even. The whole idea seemed ludicrous. How could anyone get even with God? The Lord could snap him in half with a breath.

So why hadn't He?

Jeff pictured himself bungling along, trying to be father and mother, trying to earn a living and still make time for Bonnie. He'd let his own life crumble to dust. Ashes to ashes. Dust to dust. A ragged breath escaped him. He wasn't dead yet. Marilou had died. So why was he living a ghost life?

He turned the Bible over in his hands, lifted the cover and closed it again. First Peter. How could one book of the Bible make a difference to someone who'd given up on God?

Fingering the pages, he looked at the gold letters on the navy leather before he flipped open the cover. First Peter. New Testament, he said to himself, remembering that much. In moments, he found the spot and scanned the opening chapter. Words popped out at him, places he'd never heard of— Galatia, Cappadocia, Bithynia. The Bible seemed to be for people who'd vanished from the earth. He lived in the United States. Michigan. He'd never seen that listed in the Bible.

His foolishness disgusted him. Marsha had asked him to read First Peter. If he cared for her as much as his heart told him, he could respect her request. What was he afraid of?

Jeff lowered his eyes and read the next line. *Grace and peace be yours in abundance.* He snorted at the words. Peace in abundance? He hadn't had peace for longer than he could remember. *In His great mercy He has given us new birth into a living hope through the resurrection of Jesus Christ from the dead.* Living hope. What was that? He scanned the paragraph until his eyes settled on a sentence that nailed him to the seat.

In this you greatly rejoice, though now for a little while you may have had to suffer grief in all kinds of trials. These have come so that your faith—of greater worth than gold, which perishes even though refined by fire— may be proved genuine.

He'd failed miserably. He hadn't proved his faith genuine. He'd given up at the first defeat. The day stood out in his mind as vivid as if it were yesterday. A few weeks after Marilou had died, he'd let down his guard. Before that, he'd been staunch, determined he would survive, determined he would be a good father no matter what. Yet like a defeated warrior, he'd dropped his shield and inserted the arrow into his own chest.

Jeff closed the Bible, unable to read further. He'd become a failure by his own doing.

"Daddy."

He set the Bible on the lamp table and headed for Bonnie. "What, sweetie?"

"Can we go back to the lighthouse so I can paint a better picture?"

"You mean, the one by the toy shop?"

She nodded. "With Aunt Marsha."

He ran his hands through his hair, then slipped them into his pockets, feeling overwhelmed. "How about a different lighthouse?"

"With Aunt Marsha?"

"Maybe she's busy."

"She's not. Call her."

Marsha swiped the dust cloth across the table and wandered to the dropleaf table, crouching to dust the legs, then rose to run the cloth over the top. She'd dusted yesterday, and she could see no dust, but it gave her something constructive to do. She felt useless sitting around on a Saturday when she should be enjoying the island, but somehow the joy had drifted.

Barb sat outside, writing as if she'd found her life's purpose and, when Marsha had asked if she could read some of the book, Barb had said no. The response had smarted, but Marsha realized the novel meant more to Barb than she could even fathom.

Jeff had faded from her life again. She knew it wasn't his friend keeping him busy. The man and his daughter weren't due to arrive until next Sunday.

The clock seemed to inch its way through the hours.

Morning had nearly passed with no plans for the day. She'd tried to relax, but it didn't happen. Her neck craned each time she heard a noise, and she found herself running to the window like someone's pet to see if the owner had come home.

Enough, she thought, striding to the kitchen and tossing the dust cloth beneath the sink. She charged into her bedroom and slipped on a bathing suit. At least she could enjoy the water. The day seemed perfect with a gentle breeze and a bright sun.

She grabbed a towel and marched onto the deck. "I'm going for a swim."

"It's a nice day for it," Barb said, glancing away from her legal pad, her hand covering the writing.

Marsha descended two steps when the telephone's ring sailed through the screen. Her body jerked and she turned to climb the stairs and dart into the house. Instead, she stopped herself. "Get that, will you?"

Barb gave her a look, as if to say *you know it's for you,* but Marsha didn't care. She pushed her feet through the sand and, as she reached the beach, Barb's voice flew from the deck. "It's Jeff."

"Tell him I'm swimming." She dropped her towel on the lawn recliner and bounded into the cold water. Her skin prickled with gooseflesh, but she wasn't going to stop. She'd been sitting by the phone, wondering what was wrong this time, and she'd had enough of waiting.

She reached waist high, then dived into the water, paddling until her body adjusted to the temperature. Finally, the water felt balmy, and she dug her hands into the small waves and headed out where the color changed to a deeper blue.

When she rolled onto her back and looked toward the house, Barb had vanished from the porch, and she knew she'd made her statement. She wasn't sitting around waiting to be entertained by Jeff. Who needed him, anyway?

The question felt empty and self-pitying. Bonnie needed him desperately and, if Marsha were willing to admit it, she needed him, too.

Chapter Ten

Bonnie's fists beat against the table, and Jeff clenched his teeth. She'd done so well he'd been startled today when she threw another tantrum. Just like old times. His spirit sank as he stood in the doorway and watched her.

"Bonnie, Aunt Marsha is busy. I can't make her be home when I call."

"She's swimming, you said," she screamed.

"Yes. That means she's in the water and not in her house."

"I want to go there."

So do I, he thought as he struggled to remain calm. "Are you hungry? Maybe she'll be back in the house if we eat something and then try again."

Bonnie kicked at the chair legs, and he wanted to shake her into submission, but he couldn't do that. He loved her and he understood her scenes were part of her illness, but living with her outbursts hanging over his head had taken its toll. Keeping his cool was getting harder and harder.

Jeff ignored her kicking and went to the refrigerator. His appetite had disappeared with her display, but he needed to do something. Jeff studied the choices and pulled out a package of ham, a head of lettuce and a loaf of bread.

The kicking noises stopped as he removed two whole-wheat slices from the package and retied the end. He sensed Bonnie was watching him as he pulled out slices of ham from the cellophane and folded them on top of the bread.

"What about me?"

He turned around as if surprised. "You? I didn't think you were hungry."

"I am."

He slid the bread wrapper along the counter. "Get out your slices, okay?"

Bonnie sat there, confused, he assumed. He'd always made her sandwiches, but, now that he thought about it, the time had come for Bonnie to take on some responsibility. She was nearly twelve and she needed to learn some simple tasks. He'd sheltered her way too much.

Jeff glanced at her over his shoulder, and she finally hoisted herself from the chair with a dramatic huff, untied the bread sleeve and pulled out the two pieces.

"Here you go." He handed her two slices of meat, knowing he should have told her to wash her hands, but her cooperation was going too well and the command would probably arouse another fit of temper.

Showing her, he draped the slices on his bread, and Bonnie did the same.

He tore a hunk of rinsed lettuce from the head and handed her a couple of leaves. She placed them on the meat without direction.

"Want some mustard or mayo?" He waited for her to answer.

"Mayo."

"Could you get the jar, and I'll get the knife."

Bonnie strutted to the refrigerator and pulled out the jar. As he watched her return, he sensed a look of pride on her face. He'd never given her the opportunity to make her own sandwich. The fact startled him. He'd been treating her like a baby and not the young woman she was becoming. How did he expect her to change if he didn't change with her?

When he returned the other items to the fridge, he grasped two drinks and flipped open the pop lids, then handed one to Bonnie. They walked together to the table, sitting across from each other, eating as if the tantrum had never happened. He blinked his eyes, making certain this scenario had been real and not a dream. He wished he'd realized this long ago, but it had taken Marsha to make him aware that his daughter was no longer a child, despite her childlike behavior.

As he ate, he made a decision. He wouldn't call Marsha. It was too easy for her to ignore him. After he'd cleaned up and before Bonnie could begin to nag, Jeff told her what they would do. "Let's go to Aunt Marsha's. She's probably done swimming by now."

"Yeah!" Bonnie jumped from the table and gathered her paints and sketchbook before he could get his thoughts together.

Tension knotted his arms as he drove to Marsha's cottage. All she could do was snub him or say she was busy. The idea of being rebuffed set him on edge. Yet he'd done the same to her by not calling for the past three days.

When he pulled into her driveway, he'd barely shifted into park before Bonnie unlatched her seat belt and darted into the house. He stood next to his car feeling like an outsider looking for a handout. He'd caused the distance himself. He needed to decide what to do and stick to it.

Standing outside the door a moment, Jeff listened to the reception Bonnie received. Barb commented on Bonnie's latest drawing, but he couldn't hear Marsha's voice. He strolled around the side of the A-frame. The deck was empty, and he looked down to the beach. The tall grass blocked the view. Instead of guessing, Jeff strolled down the sandy path and, as he neared the bottom, he could see Marsha stretched out on a recliner.

"Hey," he said as his feet hit the sand.

She opened her eyes, squinted against the sun, and sat up, grasping sunglasses to cover her eyes. "Hello."

Her *hello* had a careful tone, and he wished she'd left off the glasses so he could see the look in her eyes. "Barb said you were swimming."

"I was." She swung her legs over the edge of the chair and pulled her towel over them. "Barb mentioned you'd called."

"Bonnie wanted to go back to the lighthouse, but I thought about taking her down to the south end of the island to the Beaver Head Light. I'd hoped you'd like to come along." He thought about a picnic, but the delay had ruined that idea.

"I'm not dressed." She waved her hand over her towel.

"I noticed." He managed a smile, hoping it looked natural, but the conversation seemed far from that. "Can I sit?" He motioned to the space on the recliner.

She shifted a few inches, and he sat beside her, fearing the chair might tip if he put his full weight on the webbing. He felt uneasy, but he wanted to be close to her.

"I guess I was uncomfortable that I'd kissed you, Marsha. It was easy to see that it upset you, and—"

"I told you the kiss didn't upset me."

Her voice sounded timid, and he tilted his head to see

her face. Take off those glasses, he wanted to say, but didn't. "But you withdrew from me, not physically, but I sensed it."

She looked down and fingered the towel, making pleats with the edge. "It's a lot of things. The kiss was lovely."

Lovely? She sure hadn't let him know that.

"But it doesn't seem right, and I'm confused."

That made two of them. She confused him much of the time. "Confused about what?"

She gave a shrug. "What this all means, I guess. I'm not sure what you're thinking and I certainly don't know what I'm thinking—except this seems too much like a summer roma—"

The word faded, but he figured she'd started to say *romance* and was embarrassed calling their friendship that.

"It's a longtime friendship. Isn't that what we've said?" he said.

"Not if you kiss me."

This time he lowered his head. She was right, but that was what he'd wanted to do. He recalled the soft touch of her warm lips even for the brief moment that it lasted. He nodded. "You're right."

"I don't think either of us is ready for anything but friendship." She pulled off her sunglasses, and he could finally see her eyes.

The questioning look twisted through his thoughts. He didn't know what he felt, but whatever it was, it felt right and good. He didn't want to lose her friendship, but he yearned for more, and the situation chafed in his thoughts until he felt raw. "I like you, Marsha. I care about you. I don't want to do anything that will ruin what we have.... Whatever it is."

Her gaze penetrated his. "I don't, either. Can we have fun? Can we—" She seemed to struggle with her thoughts. "Can we go on as special friends until we have time to sort out what's happened?"

"That's what I want." He slipped his hand over hers, rubbing his thumb across the soft skin between her thumb and index finger.

"Is this just a summer fling? How did things change between us?"

Her questions shot through his brain and weighted his mind. "We're not the same, anymore. We're single. We weren't years ago. I never would have cheated on Marilou and I know you were dedicated to Don, but—" He hesitated to speak his thoughts. "But I always found you attractive."

"Sometimes I thought Marilou should have married Don. They were so suited to each other, but I loved her and I know she loved me."

"For better or worse," Marsha said, releasing a ragged breath. "We never know when we say those vows exactly what that means until the worst happens. Then we have to cling to those vows and to the Lord." She lifted her gaze. "I always cleaved to God's promises."

Jeff felt the prickle of admission wanting to come out. He'd read those few words in the Bible. Now he knew exactly what Marsha meant. "We suffer a while, knowing things will get better and the trials strengthen faith."

Her head snapped toward him with a questioning expression. "That's right. If everything turned out the way we expected or wanted, we'd have heaven on earth. Sin destroyed that, so we live with sin, which means we have problems and disappointments, but, through it all, we know that heaven is there waiting for us when everything will be perfect. God planned for the fall."

That threw him. "What do you mean, He planned for the fall? He could have stopped it?"

"Do you want Bonnie to love you because she chooses to or because she has no choice?"

Jeff drew back, trying to understand where she was going with the question. "You know the answer."

"God feels the same way. He gave us free will. We can make choices. Sometimes we make bad ones, but, when He made us in His image, He knew He also needed a plan to give us heaven no matter which choices we make. So He gave us Jesus to die for our sins so that we might have eternal life—that perfect world He'd wanted us to have all along—if we accept Him."

"You make it sound so easy."

"It is when you put it in His hands."

He leaned back and watched the waves pulsate to shore. In the distance, a large freighter headed toward Chicago. The ship's captain knew his course, yet he prepared for emergencies. Maybe that was what God had done.

"Look at that, Bonnie," Marsha said as they climbed from the car. Two women sat in folding chairs on the concrete parking lot with canvases resting on their knees, one with her paints on a small folding table and the other on an upside-down milk carton.

"They're painting." Bonnie gathered her sketchbook and paints while Jeff hauled a lawn chair from the car trunk.

Marsha noticed he hadn't thought to bring a table for her paints and she stood a moment, hoping to get creative, but, before an idea came, Bonnie had already engaged the two women. One of the ladies shifted her palette to the edge of her table and made room for Bonnie.

Jeff hurried over to the woman, and Marsha could tell he was apologizing. When she joined him, the woman had already insisted she had plenty of room.

The lady obviously realized that Bonnie was not a typical child, yet seemed to treat her as if she were.

"See my pictures?" Bonnie said, shoving her sketchbook toward the woman.

Jeff tried to intervene, but the lady took time to look at the paintings and praised Bonnie. The girl glowed with pride, then settled into her chair and set up her paints. Jeff returned to the car and brought back the small jar of water he'd thought to bring along.

Marsha stood behind Bonnie watching her sketch the lighthouse with a pencil, but Marsha's mind was filled with what had happened earlier. Jeff had surprised her with his comments about faith, and she wondered if he had actually looked at the Bible as she'd suggested. She didn't want to make a big deal out of it, so she'd kept the question silent, but she suspected he might have.

She shifted her attention to the lighthouse, following the yellow stone to the glass dome at the top and the clear blue sky above. *Thank you, Lord.* If Jeff had read even a little, it was a beginning. An important beginning.

Marsha felt Jeff standing beside her, his arm hanging at his side so close to her, if she reached out she could touch his hand. Recently, she'd felt comfortable holding his hand. The kiss had been a different matter. She couldn't get involved with Jeff more than she'd done already unless he was a true believer. It wouldn't work.

It might not work, anyway, she realized. She had no idea

what it was that drew her to Jeff. She felt comfortable with him. He'd known her when life had been different, and that made their friendship so much deeper than if she'd just met him at church or on a blind date.

Blind date. What a silly phrase. She'd had a few friends, especially happily married women at church, try to hook her up with nephews or in-laws or neighbors. She'd always said she wasn't ready, but now she wondered if that had changed. Perhaps that was why her heart seemed to thunder when Jeff came around. Everyone liked a little special attention, and Jeff had certainly given her that.

Jeff gave her arm a poke and tilted his head toward the lighthouse. "Walk?"

She nodded.

"We'll be back in a few minutes," Jeff said, leaning over Bonnie. "Will you be okay for a while?"

"Uh-huh." She didn't look up.

"We'll keep an eye on her," the other woman who had her paints on the milk crate said.

Jeff said thanks, then clasped Marsha's hand and led her across the parking lot to the lighthouse. "Want to go inside?"

She nodded but her thoughts stayed back with Bonnie. She found it amazing how her niece had taken to painting. She'd become a different person, much quieter and purposeful. "I'm so happy to see Bonnie having fun with the drawing."

"Thanks for coming up with the idea. I wasn't aware she had a talent like that, and it dawned on me today that I've been treating her like a child instead of a preteen." He told her about having Bonnie help prepare her lunch, but he avoided relating he'd been motivated by the tantrum. "I have to do that more often."

"Kids who feel part of the family are better behaved.

She has been acting more grown-up. I noticed it since she's started drawing. I think she feels some pride in her ability." She'd run out of air on the last sentence. The climb to the top of the lighthouse was on a tedious circular staircase that seemed unending.

Near the top, Jeff paused to look out a window over the parking lot. Marsha squeezed beside him to catch the view. Bonnie looked like a speck nestled between the two older women, and she was concentrating so hard on her drawing it made Marsha smile.

At the very top, Marsha stood at the metal railing and gazed at the view—water, trees and the parking lot. Jeff closed the distance between them and slid his arm around her waist.

"Beautiful day," she said, giving him a smile.

"Beautiful woman," he said.

The look in his eyes made her weak. "We'd better get back down," she said, not responding to his comment.

He gave her waist a squeeze, then released her, and they made their way to the ground, much easier than the climb up.

With no chairs, Marsha sat on the grass in the shade of the lighthouse, and Jeff settled beside her. Bonnie sat only a short distance away, and Marsha knew they would be patient and wait until she was ready to go. Anything else could cause an uproar and today seemed too nice to let that happen. Anyway, they weren't in a hurry.

Jeff pulled a blade of grass from the ground and ran his fingernail down the middle, dividing it in two. "I was thinking it might be fun to do something. Just the two of us." He tossed the shredded blade and looked at her. "What do you think?"

"Like what?"

He shrugged. "Maybe a sunset boat cruise. A cruiser in port takes tourists out on different trips—to see the sunset and to visit some of the outer islands. You've seen her in port. *Island Time.* I figured the sunset cruise might be fun."

"It would be cheaper to look at it from the beach."

He chuckled. "But not as nice. We could have dinner first. Do you think Barb would watch Bonnie?"

"You'd have to ask." Her pulse skipped at the thought of a sunset cruise with Jeff. She needed to keep her distance, not put herself into a romantic situation, but she couldn't make herself say no.

"I will when we get back."

Marsha pulled her gaze from his and saw Bonnie heading their way. She'd left her paints behind, but she carried the sketchbook. "Look," she said, holding up a good likeness of the yellow stone lighthouse.

"Good job," Jeff said, patting the grass beside him.

Bonnie sat and leaned against him. "I'm hungry."

"We'll head back, then."

"Can I come here tomorrow?"

"You want to come back *here?*"

"Nancy and Celia said the lighthouse is prettier in the morning with the sun on it."

"Nancy and Celia?" Jeff chuckled.

"The old ladies. That's their names."

Jeff looked at Marsha and rolled his eyes. "I hope you didn't call them old ladies."

"I did, but they already know. They told me."

Jeff released a lengthy breath and shook his head.

"Aunt Marsha can come, too," Bonnie said, totally oblivious to Jeff's concern that she'd been rude to the women.

Marsha saw Jeff ready to reprimand Bonnie, and she cut in. "I can't come in the morning. I want to go to church."

"Church?" Bonnie scowled and looked at Jeff with questioning eyes. "Why don't we go to church?"

Jeff cringed, and Marsha had a mixture of emotion—sorry for his discomfort but pleased Bonnie had asked.

"We just don't," Jeff said.

He didn't look at Marsha, and she sensed his uneasiness.

"Mommy took me to Sunday school and church, and you went to church, too."

"Yes, I used to go. I don't, anymore."

"Why?"

Marsha held her breath.

"Because, Bonnie, and don't ask any more questions."

Bonnie didn't let Jeff's stern tone dissuade her. "I want to go tomorrow."

The frown on Jeff's face deepened.

"I'll take her," Marsha said, longing for him to go, too, but fearing, if she pushed it, he would deprive Bonnie of the opportunity.

He shrugged. "You can go with Aunt Marsha if you want."

"Okay." Bonnie put her hand on her hip and grinned up at him. "And then we can come back to the lighthouse."

Chapter Eleven

Marsha stepped from the shower and grasped the bath towel to dry herself. She couldn't believe she'd accepted a date with Jeff. A friendly date, she kept reminding herself.

This morning she'd been disappointed. She'd driven to Jeff's to pick up Bonnie for church, and she'd prayed that he would go with them, but he hadn't. He'd waved to her and Barb from the doorway as Bonnie, who'd looked surprisingly timid, had walked to her car, neatly dressed and carrying a Bible under her arm. Marsha wondered if the Bible had been Bonnie's idea or Jeff's.

Marsha had leaned out the window. "We'll be at Beaver Island Christian Church on Kenwabikise Lane."

He'd lifted his hand as if he understood, then had faded from view while Marsha's hope had dipped like a boat on rough seas.

When the brick-colored church with its white shutters had come into view, Marsha had sent up a prayer, fearing Bonnie's behavior, but she'd handled the service well and had asked for help finding the Bible verses. Both Marsha and Barb had let her know how proud they'd been and, when they'd returned after church, Marsha had followed Bonnie inside to tell Jeff how well things had gone, but he'd only said thanks and reminded her he'd pick her up at seven for dinner. She sensed his distance. Tonight she wanted to know why.

Dinner at seven. Marsha's stomach did a tumble as she wiped the steam from the mirror, then draped the towel over the bar. Her skin looked rosy from the hot water and probably from the sun she'd gotten while tanning on the beach in the early afternoon.

Jeff had convinced Bonnie they'd go to the lighthouse another day, but Marsha wished he'd agreed and would have invited her to go along so she could find out what was bugging him. She didn't understand him at times.

Marsha moisturized, then slipped on her robe and added lotion to her face. So far at forty-two, she'd escaped the typical aging wrinkles, and she figured the daily face cream had kept her looking young. Young. She rolled her eyes at herself in the mirror. Forty-two wasn't young, anymore.

With age on her mind, she recalled that Jeff was a couple years younger than she was. Men of forty were usually interested in women much younger not older. She heaved a sigh and forced the thought from her mind.

By six-thirty, Marsha was ready to don the only dress she'd brought to the island. Dating hadn't even been a vague notion when she'd packed. Dating. The whole idea set her on edge. Dinner with a friend. That was all it was.

She slid the rust-colored sheath over her head. The simple rounded neckline looked plain so she added a gold necklace with an orange fire opal that sparkled shades of coral and red. Don had bought it for her on their only cruise, a trip to Mexico. They'd dreamed of many trips together, but nothing so romantic had occurred again before his illness. Putting on a pair of gold earrings and tucking her slightly damp hair behind her ears, Marsha wandered into the living room and onto the porch to let the sun dry her hair.

"Thanks for watching Bonnie," she said when Barb finally looked up from her writing.

"You're welcome. I need a break from this, anyway. My hand is getting cramped."

"Silly we didn't bring the laptop, but then who would have known my sister would become a novelist while we were gone?"

Barb gave a grunt and erased Marsha's comment with her hand. "I'm just scribbling words, but I'm enjoying it more than I ever imagined. It's good for me."

Though fearing she was treading dangerous ground, Marsha said it, anyway. "Good in what way?"

Barb's brow flickered with a frown, then she shrugged. "To see if I have a talent."

Marsha knew the novel meant more than that. Her sister seemed to have shifted from reading novels to writing one with the same energy. The idea amazed her and definitely aroused her curiosity.

Jeff's voice sounded from the back of the house.

"You're early," Marsha said.

"I know. Bonnie couldn't wait."

She grinned. "It's not a problem. I'm ready."

"I see that." He scanned her from head to toe. "You look amazing."

She eyed his dark pants and beige sports jacket over

a cream-colored shirt. "Thanks. You don't look bad yourself."

His eyes sparkled as his mouth curved into a smile. "We'll knock 'em dead at Nina's."

Nina's. She hadn't eaten there in such a long time, and the image of their mixed-berry cobbler rose in her mind. Her appetite heightened a notch as she anticipated their dinner.

While Jeff strode to the deck to talk with Barb, Marsha went to her room to grab a wrap. She suspected the cruise could get cool in the evening. When she stepped into the hallway, Jeff caught her arm and steered her out the back door. "You must have told Barb about Bonnie's helping to make her lunch."

"I did. Why?"

"She said she'd let Bonnie help her make spaghetti." He chuckled. "I don't think she knows what she's asking for. A sandwich and spaghetti are way different."

"You might be surprised."

He opened the passenger door. "I might be."

Marsha's thoughts headed back to Jeff's silence this morning—not silence, exactly, but his avoidance of talking about church. Questions filled her mind and, knowing she could ruin a perfectly good evening, she plowed ahead, anyway. "What was up this morning?"

"This morning?" He glanced at her, a frown marring his good looks."

"After church. You seemed uneasy. I hope you aren't angry that I volunteered to take Bonnie with me. You could have said no."

The frown eased. "I would have if I were set against it. I suppose she deserves to learn about God like I did when I was a kid."

"I'm glad you feel that way."

He clung to the steering wheel and didn't add anything to his comment.

His silence didn't deter her. "Then, what was it?"

"Nothing, really."

"Jeff, you just told me yesterday that you wanted to be friends—good friends, you said. How can we be friends when you can't be honest?" She gripped her handbag, fearing that she might set him off, but she had to make her point.

"I am being honest. What do you want me to say?"

"The truth? What's troubling you."

The fingers of his right hand balled into a fist. "Marsha, don't make something out of nothing. I was just feeling…I don't know…guilty, I guess. I should have taken Bonnie to church. What if she'd acted up?"

"She didn't. She was very much a young lady today."

"But what if?"

She laid her hand on his fist. "Jeff, don't look for problems when they're not there. You've lived so long dealing with Bonnie's disability that you've forgotten that she can grow out of some of her behaviors."

His fingers uncurled beneath her hand and he slipped them over hers with a squeeze. "You're right. I'd given up hope, I suppose."

She lowered her hand and shifted beneath her seat belt to look at him more directly. "I'm not trying to make you feel guilty. I'm proud of what Bonnie's done in these past few weeks, and I admire you so much for being a good father and doing what you could to teach her all the things you have."

"But I've made a lot of mistakes. I—"

"Mistakes are to learn from. Dwell on what's working now. You've done a great thing by beginning to teach her how to be self-sufficient. That's a huge step."

He nodded. "I know."

"And don't beat yourself when she backslides, because she will, but persistence and patience is the key, I think. She needs to learn that she's a young woman now and not a little girl."

"That's what you've been trying to tell me all along, I think."

Marsha nodded, but realized that was only part of it. Her mind slipped into the lingering thought created by Barb. Her sister's fears had stayed with her and Marsha had begun to wonder whether Bonnie could ever be faced with the danger of a predator. How could she be protected? She looked at Jeff's face, finally relaxing, and didn't want to bring up that particular fear today. She'd caused him enough tension for one evening.

Jeff slowed the car and turned left, heading toward the restaurant. In a few moments, the white-sided sprawling building came into sight—Beaver Island Lodge & Nina's, the sign said. Jeff pulled into a parking space and turned off the ignition, then twisted to face her. "I'm sorry I'm so dim-witted, Marsha."

She pressed her index finger against his lips. "Shh! You're no more dim-witted than anyone. Sometimes we're too close to see a problem or its solution. You know, the old 'can't see the forest for the trees.'"

Jeff kissed her finger.

The soft touch lingered when she drew it away. "Ready?"

He grinned, then walked around to open her door and led her into the building, pausing at the dining-room entrance.

The maître d' lifted two menus from beneath the stand. "Inside or on the patio?"

Jeff looked at her, and she shrugged, wanting him to decide.

"Inside by a window if that's okay?" He gave her a questioning look and she nodded.

The maître d' guided them to the table and presented them with menus. Marsha sat for a moment and looked out the window at the lowering sun glinting against the turquoise water rolling toward the sandy beach. She raised her eyes and saw Jeff watching her. "It's a beautiful day."

"And as I've said not long ago, you're a beautiful woman."

She drew in a breath and lowered her gaze. "You say things like that all the time. You embarrass me."

"Why? You just told me to be truthful, and I am."

"But—" She stumbled over the thoughts running through her head. I'm not supposed to be beautiful to you. I'm your friend. I'm only Marsha. Plain, old Marsha that you've known forever.

He gave her a look that she couldn't read and opened his menu.

Marsha did the same, perusing the wonderful entrées. Fish, steaks and chicken dishes. She chose the chicken breast sautéed in a special cream sauce, fearing she wouldn't have room for her favorite dessert.

When the waitress took their orders, Marsha turned her attention to Jeff. He looked so good in his sport jacket. She'd rarely seen him in dress clothes. Island life seemed to bring out the khakis or jeans—casual, comfortable garments that fit his calm demeanor.

"Speaking of beautiful," she said, garnering courage, "you look very handsome tonight."

He slipped his hand over hers. "Anything for a special friend."

Marsha heard an undertone of playfulness in his voice and she harked back to their early talk about sticking to their friendship. He confused her, at times, and the inflection of his voice rattled her.

"It's nice to be alone, for a change," Jeff said, breaking the silence.

"It is."

"Instead of hiding behind buildings."

Marsha grinned, picturing them hidden behind the old Coast Guard boathouse. "Or climbing a lighthouse."

He nodded. "Kids change lives. Marriages can lose the romance when the house is filled with kids."

Or when kids have problems. "I wouldn't know about that."

His smile faded. "I didn't mean to—"

"It was our choice, Jeff. You didn't offend me. We decided to wait." She drew in a deep breath. "And then we waited too long. God had other plans for us."

He squeezed her hand. "Let's just enjoy dinner."

Marsha saw the serious look in his eyes and wished they'd never fallen into the topic. His comment about marriage losing its romance made her wonder. Had the stress of Bonnie affected his and Marilou's relationship? If it had, he'd remained a faithful husband. She felt confident in that, and it gave her a new admiration for Jeff. Sometimes it was too easy to walk away from marriage. It wasn't what God expected. Until death us do part. For better or worse. She'd said it herself.

During dinner, the conversation stayed on everyday things and, when the delicious meal came to a close, Jeff wouldn't say no to buying her dessert. They finally agreed to share her favorite mixed-berry cobbler à la mode.

"Sorry," Jeff said as his fork clanged against hers.

Marsha grinned and lashed toward him, her fork a foil as they pretended to engage in a fencing match over the dessert. Embarrassed at her exuberance, she felt heat rising in her cheeks.

"Ignore the other customers." He brushed his fingers along her cheek. "They might envy our having fun."

She shook her head and delved into the serving of berries and vanilla ice cream, enjoying the sweet-tart flavor.

Jeff took the last bite, then placed his fork on the plate and glanced at his watch. "We need to get moving." He caught the waitress's eye and motioned for the bill.

During the short ride to the marina, Jeff talked about his friend's visit. "Captain Weede does outer-island cruises, too. I wonder if Al and his daughter might like to go. Bonnie would enjoy a cruise."

"I've never been to the outer islands," Marsha said, hoping for an invitation, but none came. She squelched the disappointment before it overtook her. "Since your friend is coming—and his daughter—I was thinking that I might take Bonnie to get her haircut. I'd like Bonnie to—" Meddling again. She stopped herself from saying more, but Jeff took over, saving her the problem.

"She needs a haircut. Her bangs drive me crazy. They're always in her eyes and, when her hair gets tangled, she throws a fit when I try to help her with the snarls. It's a battle every time we're trying to go somewhere."

"I'll call East Wind Spa and make an appointment. I could use a trim, myself."

Marsha relaxed her shoulders and sent up a thank you

to the Lord. She'd worked hard to avoid meddling with Jeff's way of handling Bonnie, and somehow he'd begun to accept her advice. That was all she wanted, to help without interfering.

The marina had quieted as evening approached. Most boaters had settled in for the night and were enjoying dinner somewhere, Marsha guessed, but the cruiser *Island Time* was boarding. Jeff took her arm and walked beside her up the gangway.

A breeze drifted over the water, and she slipped a beige sweater over her shoulders, glad she'd brought it along. Jeff led her to an empty bench along the side so they could have an unobstructed view of the sunset. The golden ball had lowered in the sky while coral and lavender streaks already painted the darkening clouds.

Jeff slid his arm around her shoulder. "Cold?"

"Not now," she said, capturing his hand beneath hers and loving the feel of his closeness.

Marsha felt good having a friend so dear to her, someone who knew her past trials and someone who seemed patient with her flaws—more patient than she was sometimes.

She turned her gaze from the water to Jeff's face. "I'm glad you invited me. It's nice to get away, and I've never done a cruise like this."

"I haven't, either, so it's something new we can share."

We can share. The words sounded so warm and hopeful. Sharing. She'd had no one to share things with for too long and, now that Jeff had appeared in her life again, she realized she wanted to start living again. But the idea of meeting new men and dating still left her cold. Jeff was different. Totally different. He'd become a wonderful companion who made her feel whole again.

Hearing herself sent out a warning. She knew what God would have her do. An unequal yoke was not His will, and she sensed that Jeff wasn't going to budge from his self-imposed distance from God.

An unwanted sadness washed over her. She rubbed his hand beneath hers—as if the action might create an opening, a place for the Holy Spirit to enter and begin work in his heart.

The pier appeared to move, and Marsha realized they'd begun to leave the port. The lap of the lake against the hull sent up a rhythmic sound and the breeze blew stronger, sending a chill down her back.

Jeff pulled her closer as if sensing her chill. "You're quiet."

"Enjoying the ride," she said, somewhat the truth, but also far from the thoughts that rankled her.

They leaned back, both quiet in their own thoughts, and felt the hum of the engine against the seat. The hum, the waves, the sound of the breeze created a lulling tune in Marsha's mind.

"Look," Jeff said, breaking the silence.

She focused as he pointed to the horizon. They both rose and leaned against the railing, witnessing a glorious sunset display against the slate-blue sky—a buttercup center with petals of orange to coral to magenta and the outer edges melding into deep violet.

Marsha drew in a breath, filled with longing. She looked into Jeff's eyes and sensed he was feeling the same. His gaze drifted to her mouth, and she felt her heart skip, wishing she hadn't reacted so uneasily to Jeff's kiss. At this moment, she longed to feel his mouth on hers, to—

"Amazing, isn't it?" she whispered, to waylay her yearning.

He drew her in front of him and wrapped his arms around her, drawing her into the warmth of his body. She felt his chin rest on the top of her head, then the tender pressure of his lips on her hair. *Oh, Lord, why does it have to be this way? Make him love You, Father.* The prayer flew upward from her heart, but reality weighted her chest. God didn't make anyone love him. He gave them a choice.

She knew she had to stand guard over her heart, but, at this moment, Marsha didn't want to be anywhere else in the world.

Chapter Twelve

Jeff checked his watch. He'd promised Marsha he'd drop off Bonnie for their girls' day out. She'd offered to pick her up, but he thought he could save her the trip. Anyway, he'd wanted to head into town to do some shopping while he had time alone. Though he hated to say it, things were always easier without Bonnie.

"Bonnie."

He stood in the doorway, wondering where she'd gone. In a moment, she came charging up the hill, her bare feet digging into the sand.

"Get some shoes on, please," he said as she bounded to the deck.

"Where are we going?"

"Aunt Marsha's. It's girls' day out."

Bonnie's nose wrinkled. "Aunt Marsha's not a girl. She's a woman."

"So are you, almost." The admission gave him a punch. He had so much to do to change his attitude about Bonnie's capabilities and to change Bonnie's expectations from a child's to a teenager's. Marsha had proven the more he expected from Bonnie, the more she was able to accomplish. "*Girls' day out* is just a phrase. It means you're going to do lady things."

"What kind of lady things?"

"I told you. You're going shopping and to the salon."

"Salon?"

"Put your shoes on, please, and we'll talk about it on the way. You're going to be late."

She stood a moment, belligerence growing on her face.

"I can call Aunt Marsha and tell her you don't want to spend the day with her."

"Aunt Marsha?" Her arms relaxed.

He nodded, finding himself wanting to pray the way he used to. Somehow putting his frustrations into a prayer had always seemed a release. He figured if he couldn't handle it, someone bigger could. But then that required faith in God, and he wasn't sure he wanted to deal with that.

Bonnie didn't say anything more. She trudged into her room and came out with a pair of sandals dangling in her fingers.

He knelt down to put them on her, then stopped himself.

"While you put those on, I'll get some things ready."

She eyed him a moment, then sat and began putting on the shoes.

When he returned, she'd completed the job with no argument. One battle avoided. He handed her the hairbrush. "Would you get out the tangles? I always pull your hair, and you could do it better."

She stared at the brush, then took it, apparently agreeing that controlling the brush herself made more sense. Though the job wasn't perfect, she looked neater. Jeff had seen to it that she'd taken a bath in the morning and washed her hair. He stood back watching her and seeing her as a young lady for the first time. She'd shot up overnight, and he'd just realized Bonnie had grown to over five feet tall. She was only a few inches shorter than Marsha.

At Marsha's, Bonnie lingered in the car longer than usual. Most of the time, Jeff hadn't unlatched his seat belt and Bonnie had already unhooked hers and was scampering to the door. He opened the driver's door and paused. "Is something wrong?"

"Girls' day? I've never done that."

"It's fun, Bonnie." His heart clenched in his chest. She was right. Without a mother and with his own mother deceased, she'd never experienced that. Marilou's parents lived in Oregon and, after Marilou's death, it was hard to stay connected. They sent birthday and Christmas gifts, but they hadn't seen each other. Too much to handle, he guessed.

Bonnie thought a moment, then climbed from the car and headed inside at a much slower pace than usual.

Jeff caught up with her and held the door. He watched her from behind as she ambled into the cottage with a kind of timidity he rarely saw in her.

Marsha looked up from the living room and smiled. "I'm just about ready." She leaned down and buckled her sandals.

"Aunt Marsha?" Bonnie sidled toward her and sat beside her on the edge of the sofa.

"What, sweetie?"

"What's the words I'm supposed to say to Jesus?"

"Words to Jesus?"

"You know at night when I go to bed."

Marsha slipped her arm around Bonnie's shoulders.

"You can say any words you want, because you're talking with Him."

"But He's not there."

An understanding grin filled Marsha's face. "Sure he is. He's right here with us. We just can't see Him."

Bonnie's head swiveled from side to side as if searching the room. "Is he a ghost?"

"Not a ghost. He's God. God the Son, and He has power to be with us without letting us see Him, but He's still here as sure as I am."

Jeff listened to the conversation as guilt rose. He'd never spoken to Bonnie about Jesus since Marilou had died. When she was young, she'd gone to church with them, but it had become difficult after she'd gotten older. Most of the time after that they'd taken turns rather than take a chance on one of her tantrums.

"So I can just talk like I talk with you?"

"Right. You can tell Him your problems and ask Him to help you. You can thank Him for the good things in your life." She looked at Jeff and grinned, but he saw a flicker of question as if she wondered if he minded her talking about Jesus to Bonnie. "Good things, like your daddy."

"Okay, and I can say thank you for you."

"You can." Marsha gave her a hug, then rose. "Are you ready to have some fun?"

Bonnie gave a shrug, and Marsha's gaze darted to Jeff with a questioning look.

Jeff gave her a half grin, not knowing how to explain. "She's never had a girls' day out so…"

Marsha nodded as if she understood.

"We're going shopping together, and I'm getting my hair cut."

"You are?" Bonnie's eyes widened. "Why?"

"Because it's getting too long. It's cooler in the summer when it's shorter."

Bonnie's fingers reached to the tips of her hair hanging over her shoulders. "It's cooler?"

"It sure is, and easier to take care of. Not so many tangles."

She gave Jeff a hasty look as if expecting him to comment, but he didn't. He could read Marsha's psychology and he thought maybe it would work.

Jeff watched as she continued to finger her hair as she and Marsha headed outside. He followed and patted Bonnie's door as she closed it. "Be good and have fun."

She only grinned, and Marsha chuckled. "My mom always said that to me and, for a joke, I always told her everything fun was illegal."

The comment went over Bonnie's head, but Jeff chuckled and waved as they backed out. He headed for his car, then stopped. He hadn't said hi to Barb and she'd been so good to put up with Bonnie so often. He changed his course and strode back inside.

Barb sat on the sofa, but, instead of reading a book, she had a legal pad on her lap. She looked up as he approached and gave him a nod. "You're missing out on the shopping spree."

"Yes. Thankfully."

Barb gestured for him to sit, but he didn't plan to stay. "Working on your novel?"

"Bad news gets around fast."

He sat where she'd motioned. "Marsha said it was quite good."

Her face blanched, and Jeff realized too late he'd said something wrong.

"Marsha's never read my book."

Realizing he'd goofed, Jeff's pulse tripped. "Maybe I didn't hear her right, or she might have guessed you have talent."

Barb gave a single nod. "I'm learning." She picked up a thick, large hardcover book and tapped it. "I'm reading how to write a novel. I had no idea there are so many rules."

"Rules? I didn't know that, either. I figured people just wrote a book."

She gave a half grin. "Like me. I'm trying. It's a catharsis."

Catharsis? That made him wonder. "I'm heading into town to pick up some groceries." And do some thinking. He still had the business situation to handle. "Need anything?"

"No, but thanks for asking." Barb laid the paper on the sofa beside her and leaned back. "Do you mind if I say something?"

He felt his forehead stretch upward. Say something? "No. Go right ahead."

"I don't know if Marsha's said anything to you, but I'm concerned about Bonnie. I know it's not my business, and I'll begin to sound like Marsha, butting into your life."

He grinned at that. "She's doing better."

"I'm glad." Her mouth bent to a crooked smile. "I'm concerned about Bonnie's physical maturity."

Whoa! "Bonnie's what?" Jeff asked. "What do you mean?"

As she spoke, Jeff noticed the depth of her concern. She talked about predators and Bonnie's safety. Had something like this happened to her? He shook his head, trying to make sense out of what she said. Did he have to live in fear every moment Bonnie was out of his sight?

"I've startled you," Barb said, leaning forward. "I don't mean to. I just know what can happen, and I hope you'll make sure she understands what's right and wrong when it comes to being a young lady."

"It's hard for a man to know what it's like being a young woman, Barb. I've just realized that Bonnie is becoming a teen. I still see her as my little girl. I think Marsha's had the same concern."

Barb shook her head. "Marsha's more concerned that she acts and dresses her age. I don't think she realizes the danger, either."

Danger? "I'll give what you said a lot of thought, Barb. I know you mean well and your concern is real. It's just a bit shocking to hear it. I've been in the dark, and I suppose that's stupid."

"Not stupid. Just trusting."

"Thanks for being candid."

"You're welcome, and I hope you don't think I'm being out of order."

"Not at all. I needed to hear this."

She studied his face a moment, then nodded. "I didn't mean to keep you."

"I'm glad you talked with me." He rose and took a step toward the door. "I really mean it. I'd never have considered that. It's something to think about."

He darted from the house, wanting to escape the whole idea. His little girl…his daughter being harmed by someone. Had he been stupid? He'd heard of men conning girls into cars, but disabled children? He drew in a ragged breath. He needed Marsha's wisdom.

Marsha. He'd pushed her away, and now he wanted to drag her into his mess. Is that all he was doing? When it came to being with Marsha, could Bonnie's needs be his motivation? He delved into his thoughts. No. It couldn't be the only reason. He'd had to fight his instincts to kiss her on the cruise three days earlier. She'd looked so beautiful, so loving, and he realized that all his talk about friendship was trying to convince himself where his heart was headed.

He settled into the driver's seat and turned on the ignition, letting the air-conditioning take over and cool down his thoughts. He needed to get a grip on himself when it came to Marsha and Bonnie. He needed help, and he was finally admitting it.

Marsha turned in the salon chair to face Bonnie. "What do you think?" She looked at the floor, seeing her curls coiled below her feet, and the fact startled her. She hadn't cut her hair in years. She turned back to the mirror and eyed herself.

Bonnie frowned. "It's different."

Marsha swung back. "But do you like it?"

Touching Marsha's newly shorn hair, Bonnie nodded. "It looks pretty. Is it cooler?"

"For sure."

Bonnie looked in the mirror at her own straggling long hair, then looked at the sea of cuttings beneath Marsha's chair.

Noticing Bonnie's curiosity, Marsha added an enticement. "I think I'll go and buy something new to wear to go along with my haircut."

"New clothes?" Bonnie's eyes grew wider.

"To celebrate." Today, she did feel like celebrating. A new Marsha looked back at her, feeling younger and more adventuresome than she had in many years. The long hair was always a reminder of the same Marsha who'd dealt with so much grief. This face looked happier and calmer.

"Can I have my hair cut and get some new clothes, too?"

Marsha caught her relieved sigh before it escaped and smiled instead. "Why not? That would be fun. We can both celebrate."

Bonnie didn't stop to reconsider her action. She slid into the chair and looked at the cosmetologist. "Shorter, please."

The *please* lifted Marsha's heart. Bonnie had begun to practice good manners more and more, and that had been a big change. Marsha stood behind her, smiling and talking, "oohing" and "aahing," to evade any possible negative reactions. The more hair the woman cut, the more Bonnie's face looked worried, but Marsha, acting as cheerleader, brought a smile back. When the beautician had finished and held up the mirror, Bonnie looked at the back of her hair and smiled. "Now we can celebrate."

"You look amazing. Just lovely." Her hair did look wonderful, easy to care for and so summery. She looked older, and the cut enhanced the lovely lines of her features. Her brown eyes were Jeff's, expressive and with that playful twinkle when she was having fun and she had his classic features. Only her mouth echoed Marilou's full lips and charming smile. Bonnie hadn't smiled as much a couple of weeks earlier, yet Marsha was seeing it more often now. She thanked God for the change. "Let's go shopping."

Bonnie bounded from the seat, glancing in every mirror as she made her way to the desk where Marsha paid the bill. Then they stepped into the island sunshine.

"Let's try the Boat-tique." The shop had become the department store of the island, and she was sure she could find something cute there to please Bonnie. Anything to make her happy and to celebrate the haircuts.

"You look like a young lady, Bonnie," she said as she continued driving down Donegal Bay Road to Main Street.

Bonnie studied her. "You look like a lady, too, but older."

Marsha chuckled at her honesty. Much older, she thought. She parked and headed inside the building close to the yacht dock. Inside the boutique, she stopped a clerk and learned they had a Teen Corner. Not having been here for a while, she'd forgotten what the shop had to offer.

Bouncing along beside her, Bonnie seemed thrilled with her new look and, when she saw the clothes, she began pulling garments from the racks.

"Wait a minute," Marsha said, trying to control her tone, but not wanting Bonnie to create a mess. "First, what size are you?" she eyed Bonnie's slender frame, trying to calculate.

As she feared, Bonnie shrugged her shoulders.

Marsha returned the items to the rack and guided her to the larger sizes. "Let's try a three, and let's look at them one at a time."

Bonnie dived into the clothing again as Marsha tried sweetly to control her exuberance.

"I like this one," Bonnie said, holding up jeans with embroidery along the leg, "and this, too."

She'd pulled out a skirt, too short for Marsha's taste. "That's beige and will get dirty. How about this one?" She spotted a cute, longer denim skirt with a flowery trim along the hem and a similar flower on the back pocket.

Bonnie seemed to like that one, and, as she reached for another, Marsha redirected her to the tops. Marsha spotted a top that had similar flowers to the denim skirt and matched Bonnie's eye color perfectly. Bonnie clutched another top to her chest that worked with the jeans, and Marsha gave an approving nod, grateful that she'd avoided any of Bonnie's outbursts.

"Now it's my turn," Marsha said, carrying Bonnie's choices to the women's section. She found a camel-colored T-shirt with a beige-and-orange trim, then gathered a couple of other knit tops and eyed a crinkle crepe skirt in a floral print that befitted summer on an island.

Summer on an island. Now who was poetic? She knew her motivation. If she and Jeff had another evening out, she'd have something new to wear.

She'd guessed well on Bonnie's size. Bonnie looked so different in the outfits, and she posed in front of the mirror until Marsha had to put an end to it by promising her an ice cream from Daddy Frank's. She purchased their choices, wondering what Jeff would think of his daughter's new look.

As they headed to the car, Barb's worries slammed into her mind. Seeing Bonnie with her haircut and in the more grown-up clothes made her realize that Barb could be right. She needed to talk with Jeff. Bonnie needed to be told not to go with strangers. Sometimes her niece was so forward, talking to people in stores and on the street without a care. Someone needed to give her guidance.

Anxious, she tossed the packages into the backseat and made sure Bonnie was buckled in before heading to Daddy Frank's, and then back to face Jeff.

Chapter Thirteen

Bonnie bounded into the room with a shopping bag from Beaver Boat-tique and a haircut that knocked Jeff backward. He'd never imagined a cut could change his little girl into a near teenager within hours. He opened his arms, and she bounded into them bubbling about an ice-cream cone, the shopping and the haircut.

When he lifted his gaze, his heart stood still. Marsha had appeared in the doorway, a halo of red curls ending before her shoulders. He liked the new look, yet he somehow missed those copper tendrils that had often hung in wispy strands escaping from behind her well-shaped ears.

"Look at the two of you," he said, not knowing what else to say. Barb's words echoed in his head and took the edge off Bonnie's new, grown-up look. "Where's my little girl?"

"I'm right here," Bonnie said, pointing to herself. "I just got my hair cut."

He gave her a bear hug, his eyes captured by Marsha standing so near, then forced himself to ask about Bonnie's shopping bag.

"I must owe you a fortune," he said to Marsha as Bonnie pulled items from the bag and let them drop to the floor. "Hold on there, Kemo Sabe." He caught a skirt decorated with flowers before it hit the floor. "These are brand new. You should take care of them."

"I'm sorry," she said, trying to gather the two that had landed on the floor. "Look at what Aunt Marsha bought me."

He settled onto the sofa as Bonnie showed him each garment and promised a fashion show, but he held her off for a moment and focused on Marsha.

"You owe me nothing," she said, motioning to the garments. "They're an early birthday gift."

"No. Not so many things." He shook his head.

"It was my pleasure."

He rose, feeling mesmerized. "Let me look at you." He walked around her, amazed at how the haircut added a new sparkle to her eyes. "You look like a new woman."

"I feel like one. Kind of a strange feeling."

"Not strange." He touched her soft curls. "Amazing." He let his hand shift to her cheek, hoping she saw in his eyes what he felt in his heart.

He could no longer continue the friendship game with Marsha when he wanted a relationship. The admission sizzled through his veins. He'd have to say something and pray...hope that she felt the same.

"I look amazing, too," Bonnie said, sliding in front of him.

He knelt beside her and touched her hair to curb her jealousy, something he'd never noticed before. "You do look amazing."

Bonnie grinned. "I know."

Marsha laughed with him, and he gave Bonnie another hug.

"So what did you buy?" he asked Marsha.

"They're in the car. Just a couple of things."

"She bought a pretty skirt with flowers," Bonnie said.

He gazed at Bonnie and saw a new look in her eyes. His daughter talking about clothes. That was astounding. Usually she threw on anything, garments with patterns and colors that didn't match. "I'll have to see that."

"Get the bag, Aunt Marsha."

Marsha shook her head. "Later. I have to get home." She took a step backward. "Have fun."

Jeff followed her to the door and touched her arm. "Hang on a minute," he whispered, then turned to face Bonnie. "Would you take your new clothes into the bedroom and hang them up, please?"

Her nose curled for an instant, but then she gave him a halfhearted grin. She gathered the garments and carried them into her room. When he turned back to Marsha, a scowl settled on her face. He pushed open the door wider and motioned her outside.

"I'm serious, Jeff. I don't want you to pay for the clothes. It was my—"

"That's not it."

The frown shifted to concern. "Is something wrong?"

"No. Something's right."

"Right?"

"I hope so." He slipped his arm around her shoulder and ambled to the car, a knot in his throat. "This is difficult."

Marsha faltered and her expression turned to alarm. "Something is wrong, Jeff."

He shook his head and rested a hand on each of her shoulders. "It's only wrong if you don't feel like I do."

"About what?"

His heart jolted against his chest. "Us."

"Us?" She gazed at him a long time. "You know how I feel about you, Jeff. You've been like a gift to me. I came here thinking I'd sit at the cottage, do a few things around the place and maybe go back to a few of my favorite places. Nothing special. You've made my time here special."

He searched her eyes, seeing a glint of something more, but he didn't want to second-guess. He drew in a breath and forced out the question. "Is this only a friendship, Marsha?"

Her eyes widened. "Is this only…"

His hands left her shoulders and moved upward to her cheeks. They felt warm against his cool hands.

"Friendship?" She closed her eyes and he felt her jaw tense.

"Or is it more?" he asked, longing to hear her say it had grown beyond friendship.

Her eyes opened. "Do you want an honest answer?"

No, he thought not, from the look in her eyes, but he needed to know. "Yes, be honest."

"If I speak from my heart, yes, it's more than friendship. If I speak from my good sense, it's no."

"What does that mean?"

"We've only spent a few weeks together and it's just too fast to be realistic. It's like a shipboard rom—"

"Marsha." He clasped her shoulders and drew her closer. "It's not as if we've just met. We have a history together."

Tears rimmed her eyes. "But history doesn't mean a commitment, Jeff. You mean so much to me. You and Bonnie, but—"

"But, what? You can't give us a chance?"

She looked at him with the saddest eyes he'd ever seen.

"Then, I misread things, Marsha. I'd really thought—"

"You haven't misread things."

Tears rolled down her cheeks, and she raised her arms and wrapped them around his neck, a paradox between her words and what he saw in her eyes. "I can't trust my heart right now and I have things to deal with."

"Is it me, Marsha? Is there something wrong with me?"

She only looked at him.

"Is it Bonnie?"

"I love Bonnie."

"Then…" It had to be something about him.

"Let's be patient, okay?"

"Patient?" He'd been struggling to control his feelings for the past couple of weeks. He felt as if God—fate—had led him to Marsha. Had he only deluded himself? His mind spiraled out of control. He'd never felt more unsure, more confused.

"Please."

Her plaintive voice reached him, and he nodded, unable to deal with it all right now. He needed to think.

She slipped into the car and waved goodbye through the open window.

"I'll call you later," he said as she drove off.

Jeff stood outside a moment, pondering what she'd said. Her look, her words and her actions didn't mesh. She said one thing, but her arms around his neck and her eyes said more. Had he done something to upset her? He thought back, remembering his talk with Barb. He mentioned her book and—

That was it. Barb had been upset and now she'd probably confronted Marsha. He'd botched that up badly.

He looked at the empty driveway while loneliness wove through his chest, the same feeling he'd experienced when he thought about returning down state. Maybe Marsha was right. Could he make himself stick to a friendship? That was priceless, but he'd thought friendship made a solid foundation for a relationship. He could only surmise that wasn't to be.

Marsha waited the rest of the day for Jeff's call, and it never came. She felt anguish over their discussion. How could she tell him the problem was his lack of faith along with her general guilt? He'd told her not to feel it, but she did. She couldn't hurt Bonnie, who'd grown so close to her. What if they began dating for real and then their relationship fell apart? What would happen then? She'd feel estranged from Bonnie. The longer she waited, the more certain she became that she'd ended their relationship before it had begun.

Finally, the next morning, after a rotten sleep, Jeff phoned her and asked if she could drop by and talk. Talk? They'd talked yesterday and it had been a disaster. Now she paced again, trying not to let Barb notice her concern.

A while back, they had come to an understanding, a confusing agreement but one they'd both accepted. They would be good friends. Why hadn't they stuck with the arrangement? Somehow, their hearts had sailed on a course of their own and become tossed like flotsam in the wake of the problems they faced.

She needed to be strong. She'd read God's Word each night, rereading the passages in 2 Corinthians 6 that said, *Do not be yoked together with unbelievers. For what do righteousness and wickedness have in common? Or what fellowship can light have with darkness?* The final question said it all. *What does a believer have in common with an unbeliever?*

Yet, as much as she knew those were God's words, she thought about the things she had in common with Jeff. They'd shared a past—both laughter and tears. They'd been bound together as family and, in bad times, she'd found strength in Jeff's company during Don's illness. She loved Bonnie and cared so much about her. And she knew that Jeff had believed once.

She shook her head. Did God really mean it? Couldn't her faith influence him? Couldn't their relationship bring him back to the Lord? God certainly meant she should not get involved with someone who'd never know the Triune God—Father, Son and Holy Spirit. Jeff knew God. He'd just taken a back step. Back *steps*, she reminded herself.

Twisting God's Word for her purpose took the wind out of her. The Bible said what it said no matter how she tried to make it different. She closed her eyes a moment, asking the Lord to take away the problem, to open Jeff's heart again, to let His light shine into Jeff's darkness even if hers couldn't.

Marsha finally quit staring out the window and settled on a recliner on the deck. Barb had returned to her place on the sofa, combining writing with reading a novel. She'd said she'd come to a dry spot in her work and thought she'd take a break, but Marsha sensed something else was wrong. Barb's earlier change of heart had shifted to her more disagreeable, quiet demeanor, and Marsha hadn't been able to figure out why.

When the screen door sounded, Marsha looked up expecting to see Bonnie or Jeff, but Barb stood there with a scowl on her face.

"What's wrong?" Marsha asked, fearing that she was facing a blowup.

"I've decided to say something before I create a mountain out of a molehill." She slid the door closed and sank onto the picnic bench, leaning her back against the table.

"What?"

"Have you read my book?"

Marsha's already agitated pulse kicked up a notch. Her back stiffened, and she wanted to lie so badly, but she knew she couldn't. "I looked at a page a week ago, after you'd just begun to write. When I asked you about looking at it, you said no so I never looked again."

"It wasn't your place to look at it, at all."

"I know. I promise that was all. I saw the one page. The story looked interesting, and I wanted to read more."

Barb's head lowered, and she looked stressed.

"I'm sorry, Barb. I didn't even think."

Barb's head bobbed as if that was a given.

"How did you know?" Marsha asked.

"Jeff. He mentioned it accidentally. I saw the look on his face. He didn't realize he'd made a mistake. I just let it drop."

Jeff. She'd forgotten she'd mentioned Barb's writing to him. She should have told him not to say anything, but that in itself was wrong. It meant she knew she'd done something inappropriate. She'd put her nose in Barb's business again. "I'm so sorry."

"It's okay." She rose and slid open the screen door.

"It's not okay."

She shrugged and went inside while Marsha sat there. Would she ever learn that she didn't have to be in charge of everything? "I'm making an effort, Lord," she said to herself, and she really had been. But now she wanted to talk with Jeff again about Barb's concerns.

She shouldn't.

"Hi, Bonnie." She heard Barb's voice through the screen.

Bonnie came through the doorway, wearing a new top with an old pair of pants.

"You look very nice," Marsha said.

Bonnie leaned over and kissed Marsha's cheek. "Thank you for the presents."

"You're very welcome." She looked behind her through the screen into the house shadows. "Where's your dad?"

"He's here."

As the words left her, Jeff came walking around the side of the house. "I figured I'd catch you out here, sunning." He motioned to the beach. "Bonnie brought her suit with her. Do you mind if she swims?"

"Alone?"

"No, we can go down and watch her."

She studied his face, seeing no sign of his thoughts, yet hoping they might resolve the tension. "Sure."

Bonnie reached over to pull off her top, and Marsha was startled for a moment until she realized that Bonnie had worn the bathing suit underneath her clothes. "I'm smart, Daddy said."

"You are." She stood and picked up Bonnie's clothes from the deck floor, then looked at Jeff. "Go ahead down, and I'll be there in a minute. I have to get another chair."

Jeff lifted a chair into the air. "I brought one from the back."

He'd brought one for her. Her heart lifted. She managed a grin, then called to Barb where they'd be and followed him down to the beach, but, as her heel dug into the sand, her grin faded to worry. Would this be the Dear Jane letter that she'd begun to consider?

Realizing she had been the master of ambivalence, Marsha couldn't blame Jeff, but she wanted more. Time? Assurance from God? She didn't know what she wanted, but she knew that Jeff had filled a hole inside her, and she didn't want to be empty again.

Jeff opened the chair and flagged her to take whichever seat she preferred. She sat on the beach chair, leaving the recliner for him. Being edgy, she didn't feel in the mood to lean back and apparently he didn't, either. He sat on the edge of the recliner and faced her.

She looked at Bonnie splashing in the water and waited for him to say what was on his mind, but he only looked at her.

"First, I know I've done something to upset you, and I want to apologize. I was talking with Barb after you left for the haircuts, and I mentioned how you'd said her novel was pretty good. I could tell she was upset. Apparently, she didn't know you'd seen it."

Marsha nodded. "She told me what you'd said."

"I'm really sorry. I had no idea. I was trying to compliment her. I realize that's what's upset you."

Marsha's heart sank. She wanted to scream "It's your lack of faith, Jeff," but she couldn't. If he really wanted to take their friendship to another level, he might pretend to believe or it might force him to church for her. That was not what she wanted. She wanted him to go to church for his relationship with God. She could only pray.

"It's okay, Jeff. I didn't ask you not to say anything. I shouldn't have been looking at her story without her permission. You know me. I bungle into things that I don't have the right to."

"You're doing better." He gave her a frail grin.

"Thanks. I'm really trying to watch myself. And I've been praying about it."

"Tell God thanks for me, would you?"

Tell Him yourself. It was that attitude she couldn't live with. She let the thought slip away and, instead, prayed that one day he would tell the Lord thank you on his own.

Silence hung between them, and her gaze drifted to the water again where she spotted Bonnie dog-paddling. She wanted to be a good swimmer so badly, but Marsha hoped she wouldn't go too far out into the water without one of them in with her.

"Be careful, Bon," Jeff called as if reading her mind.

She watched his shoulders raise as he drew in a breath, then he turned back to her.

"Barb mentioned something that has me concerned."

"Barb?" She tried to imagine what her sister had said.

"She talked to me about predators and, now that I look at Bonnie with the haircut and the new clothes, it just smacked me between the eyes. Why have I been so unaware?"

Predators? Barb had told him. Her heart softened at the desperate look on his face. "You're Bonnie's daddy. You don't think of her as reaching womanhood. She's still your little girl."

He shook his head. "Yes, but, if I opened my eyes, there's reality staring me in the face—too obvious for me to miss."

His focus shifted to the water, and Marsha's followed, seeing Bonnie bob up and down as each wave rolled in. "I know."

"And that's what you've been saying. But predators? She's disabled. Am I stupid?" He slapped his hand against his jaw and shook his head. "Yet, I read the paper.

I hear about people doing things to little children, doing things to people with handicaps. I just didn't want to believe it."

"Neither did I." She plucked at a loose thread on the chair. "Barb talked to me a while ago, and I was so tied up in wanting her to act and look like a teenager that I missed the whole idea, myself." She leaned forward and grasped his hands. "We have to give this to the Lord, Jeff."

As the words left her mouth, she drew back, realizing she could lay it at Jesus' feet, but he couldn't. That was what God's Word meant. How could they work together from such different points of view?

He nodded and didn't rebuff her comment. Her heart skipped, wondering if he'd heard her. Her plea went heavenward again for the Holy Spirit to intervene.

"I have to be more careful," Jeff said, "and I can't be so trusting." He motioned down the beach. "Like that neighbor of mine. He might have been perfectly innocent, just trying to compliment a child he knew had a disability, but maybe not. How do I know?"

"You don't, but you can't be wary of everyone. Just use good sense." She wanted to support him, but, mostly, she wanted to talk about them. She wanted to have her concern fade away. She wanted to be in his strong arms. For now, she found her refuge in the Lord.

Jeff released a ragged sigh, and his gaze shifted to Bonnie. Finally, he looked down at his feet and pushed the sole of his shoe into the sand. "Footprints in the sand." He lifted his gaze. "Right now I want to see only one set."

Marsha's heart lifted to the sky. Was this a beginning? *Thank you, Lord.* She couldn't speak for the emotion that filled her.

Jeff nodded toward the water, and Marsha saw Bonnie heading back in their direction. "I suppose we better drop the subject before Miss Nosey hears something." He leaned closer with a whisper. "I'm seeing a little jealousy in her. Have you noticed?"

Marsha shook her head. "Only a little, and that's natural. She's daddy's little girl." The words took her back. "I was daddy's little girl even when I was in my twenties. It's not age."

"Did you see me?" Water dripped from Bonnie when she reached them. "Come out and swim."

"Not today. We have company coming this weekend, and I have lots to do." He tousled her wet hair. "*We* have lots to do. We have to clean the guest rooms."

"Yuck," she said.

"Don't you want company?"

She shrugged. "Can Aunt Marsha come over on Sunday when they come over?"

Marsha shook her head. "Your daddy needs time to visit with his friend. Anyway, I have to go to church and take care of some things around here."

"I have to go to church, too," Bonnie said.

"Not this Sunday," Marsha said. "You have to be home for the company."

Jeff shook his head. "They won't be here until later in the afternoon. She can go if she wants."

"Are you sure?"

"Positive." He rose and held out his hand to help her rise and, once she was up, he grabbed the chair. "It's time I get busy."

Marsha should have been happy that he'd agreed for Bonnie to go to church, but she'd so longed to hear him say he would join them. She hated the distance between them. Instead of keeping things status quo, she felt as if they'd tumbled down a hill in opposite directions. The closeness she loved had vanished.

Jeff looked out the window and, as soon as Marsha pulled up, he called Bonnie. He opened the door and gave a wave. Bonnie had chosen her new skirt for church, and Jeff eyed his daughter again, still amazed at the new haircut and up-to-date clothing style.

Before Marsha came to the door, he walked outside with Bonnie. He'd made a decision during the night and, this morning, though uneasy, he forced himself to follow through.

"Good morning," he said, leaning through the passenger window. "Where's Barb?

"Not feeling well this morning."

"Too bad," he said, opening the passenger door while Bonnie slipped between him and the car.

"You look so nice," Marsha said, motioning to Bonnie's new outfit.

She grinned and started to climb into the front seat, but Jeff stopped her. "Let's put you in the back, Bon. I'm going with you."

Marsha's smile morphed to wide-eyed surprise. "You are?"

He slipped into the seat and closed the door. "I figured I should be a good example for my daughter."

"That's right, Daddy," Bonnie said from the back. "Parents have to be good examples."

Marsha's mouth had closed, yet she still had that deer-in-the-headlights look on her face.

"Since I'm going with you, I could drive if you'd prefer," Jeff said, wondering if he needed to flag his hand in front of her eyes to get her attention.

"No, this is fine," she said finally, backing from the driveway, then heading back toward town.

He really should have picked her up, but the decision to go with them had wavered in his head until she'd arrived. The closer they came to the church, the more his muscles knotted. Before he'd gone to bed, he'd read more of First Peter and, once again, the message had smacked him between the eyes. He couldn't remember the exact words, but the ideas clung in his thoughts. Be self-controlled; set your hope fully on the grace of Jesus. Grace? What was grace? Mercy? Pardon? A reprieve? *My grace is sufficient for you, for My power is made perfect in weakness.* He'd quoted a verse. Where had that come from?

"Thinking?"

Marsha's voice jarred him out of his thoughts. "I guess." He knew, but how could he tell her the words that had rattled him. God's power could be used in his weakness. That was grace. God could forgive and show His love to the sinner. *Grace.* The word washed over him.

"You know, I'm really happy you decided to come."

"Don't expect much. I'm here for Bonnie." The words left his mouth, and he immediately asked himself why he said something so ridiculous. He'd just thought those powerful words and now he'd ridiculed them. He'd only succeeded to hurt Marsha. Faith meant so much to her, and he saw the results of her faith in the way she lived.

"I shouldn't have said that. I'm going to church for me, too," he admitted.

She glanced at him, her expression filled with confusion. Then, her jaw relaxed and she turned her attention to the road.

At Back Road, she made a left and, in a short distance, she pulled into the church parking lot. "I guess this is it." His voice sounded like a scared man sitting in the first seat of a roller coaster.

Marsha didn't say a word. She opened the driver-side door and climbed out, then stood in front of the car waiting for him and Bonnie to unlatch their belts and join her. She hit the remote followed by the soft beep as the doors locked.

They entered the center door into the wide foyer with the sanctuary on the right and the fellowship hall on the left. Marsha guided Bonnie to the Sunday-school room, and he stood waiting, his body twitching with nerves.

When she returned, his hand trembled as he grasped Marsha's elbow and walked beside her down the aisle. The morning sun sent shimmers of color from the stained-glass windows—the Paschal Lamb, all kinds of biblical scenes showing stories he remembered so well—and it took him back to times with Marilou when they'd gone to church with such high hopes.

But that was the past, and today he also had new hopes. Hopes to get his life back together, to be a better father for Bonnie, to…to what? To be with Marsha. She'd asked him to be patient. Patient, for what? If she was that indecisive about their relationship, maybe it was hopeless.

Marsha had already become part of his life, and he couldn't imagine what it would be like if he returned home and they drifted apart again.

Marsha shifted into a pew, and he followed. He tried to concentrate, but he kept returning to Marsha.

He couldn't remember when the distance between them had happened. They'd been so close during Don's illness, and, after his funeral, he'd still called and dropped by. Marilou had invited her to dinner a few times, but she'd seemed uneasy, like the proverbial third wheel. He hadn't known how to make it better.

Things had changed when Marilou had died. He'd decided to die with her. Yes, he'd kept going—work, chores, Bonnie. But life, real life, had vanished and he'd wallowed in his own grief. Then grief had turned to bitterness and anger. Lately, he'd realized that wasn't the way to live.

The verses he'd read in 1 Peter 2 that dealt with suffering stuck in his mind like the clutch of his first 1977 junker. The verses wouldn't leave him. They asked what kind of credit should a person get if he received punishment for doing something wrong. But, if the person suffered for doing good and he withstood the punishment, then God looked favorably on him. He'd read further and the Bible said this was an example for everyone to follow just as Christ had suffered for the world.

If God had expected him to earn credit for tolerating sorrow, Jeff knew he'd failed. He hadn't earned one iota of credit. He'd fallen so short he couldn't imagine how God could forgive him. Yet he knew the Bible said, over and over, people are forgiven by the blood of Jesus. Why couldn't he accept that and stop fighting the truth he knew in his heart?

Jeff sensed Marsha looking at him. He turned toward her and managed a grin.

Her face brightened, and she reached over and grasped his hand—hers so soft and small he felt overwhelmed. Did his coming to church mean that much to her?

She gave his hand another squeeze, and he knew the answer.

It did.

His mind whirled as things fell into place. Had this been the problem all along? He couldn't believe it had taken him so long to realize what had kept them apart.

Chapter Fourteen

Marsha turned onto Donegal Bay Road. "What time did you say your friend's coming?"

"Late afternoon."

She nodded, wanting him to talk about church, but he'd said nothing. Marsha had struggled following the worship service. Her heart soared, knowing that Jeff had been sitting beside her. Yet something frightened her. She sensed he'd decided to attend worship with the speed of a brush fire, and she wondered if the Holy Spirit had worked the change or if he had figured out why she'd been afraid to move ahead with their relationship.

Instead of questioning, she'd bowed her head and thanked God for whatever reason he'd decided to come. When God was at work, she had no right to question. She hoped something had happened during the service to help Jeff feel more comfortable and open to accepting the faith he once knew.

She longed to ask, but she fought the urge. "Did you enjoy Sunday school, Bonnie?"

"Yes."

"Good. What did you learn?" She felt guilty quizzing her niece, but it was better than prying information from Jeff.

"I learned Jesus is my best friend." She stuck her arm as far over the back of their seat as she could while restrained in her seat belt. "We made this."

She dangled a card-stock bookmark adorned with a piece of colorful yarn from her finger.

Jeff took the craft from her and showed Marsha. The likeness of Jesus had been photocopied to the card stock with the words *my best friend* below. Bonnie had colored it with markers, and Marsha figured she could have done something far more artistic if she'd created the whole picture herself.

"Very nice," Marsha said, keeping her opinion to herself.

He didn't comment and handed it back to Bonnie.

"I think I'll take Al fishing while he's here," Jeff said as if her earlier question were still part of their conversation.

"That would be nice. If you want to leave the girls at the house just let me know."

"Thanks. They may want to go, but I'll check."

The conversation felt strained and Marsha was almost relieved when she turned onto the stretch of road along the water and saw Jeff's house ahead of her.

When she turned into the driveway, she felt at a loss for words. "Have a nice day," she said, stepping out of his car, sounding mundane in light of their recent talk.

"You, too." Jeff waved and Bonnie stood beside him, looking a little lost.

Climbing into her car, Marsha hoped that the situation with Al and his daughter would be fun for Bonnie. She backed from the driveway and drove the familiar trip back home, her thoughts shifting to Barb.

Barb had looked fine the night before and had no complaints, so her sudden not-feeling-well excuse sat heavily on Marsha's mind. Barb had been quieter since she'd learned Marsha had read her novel opening. She'd apologized. What more could she do? Now she was honestly tired of Barb's concern about what she'd done. It wasn't as if she had planned to steal her story idea or anything.

She pulled into her driveway and headed for the house, her mind a flurry of issues. She expected Jeff to be busy with his friend, and even her offers to sit with the girls had been tossed off with a thanks, but—

But what? She'd keep herself busy just as she would have to do once she returned home. Though her hopes had been that she and Jeff would continue to be friends—there was that word again—she suspected that would fade as quickly as dew in the morning.

When she stepped inside, Barb was lying on the sofa reading a novel. She lowered the book and peered at Marsha over the edge. "You're back early. I figured you'd go out to lunch."

Marsha dropped her purse into the chair and strutted to the sliding-door screen. "His friend comes today. He wanted to do some laundry before he arrives."

Barb didn't comment, but in a moment, she placed a bookmark between the pages and sat up.

A rain cloud billowed over the lake, shadowed with slate-colored streaks. They had escaped the rain most every day since their arrival. She hoped it didn't rain for Al's visit. The island could be dreary in bad weather since most of the activities were outdoors.

She turned into the room. "Hungry?"

Barb shook her head. "My appetite has been bad for a few days."

Once again, Marsha hadn't noticed. She passed Barb and opened the refrigerator, then closed it again, aware that she had missed something. She turned to face Barb. "Something's wrong."

It wasn't a question. She couldn't believe she'd been so unaware. Not feeling well had been an excuse to arouse conversation. She'd let it slip by this morning as she'd almost done again.

She sank into the chair and looked at Barb's stressed face. "What's wrong?"

Barb flinched at her question, and Marsha knew this was something serious. Had Jeff said something to her? Her heart kicked, then skipped a beat. "What is it?"

"I should have told you this a long time ago. I don't know why I didn't."

Get on with it, Marsha screamed in her head. "Just tell me. What did Jeff say?"

Barb's face washed with disbelief. "This isn't about you, Marsha. It's about me."

The sting of her words smarted through Marsha's conscience. Not everything was about her. Why would she even think such a thing? "I'm sorry, Barb. I'm edgy today. Please. I'm listening."

"This began when I felt so angry at you for looking at my novel."

"But I apolo—"

"It has nothing to do with an apology. It made me realize that you couldn't be blamed for something you didn't know."

Marsha gripped the arm of the chair but remained silent. She too often talked when she should listen.

"The story is a release for me. Something that happened to me so long ago and has stayed inside me like an aching boil that could never burst because it would only poison me more."

"What happened?" Her mind flew back to their past. Barb had changed somewhere in time from a typical teenager to a withdrawn wallflower, but Marsha couldn't remember exactly when it had happened.

Her sister's face twisted as if she'd lost control, but then she closed her eyes a moment and seemed to calm.

Marsha thought about the novel. What had she read? Something about a rainy night. She dug into her memory. A flash of paragraph crept from her mind. Her clothes clung to her as if hanging on to her for fear they might be torn from her. And they were. She'd never remembered that happening to Barb.

She leaned forward, closing the distance between them. "Your writing has given you a release." She repeated her sister's words, hoping to motivate her to talk.

She nodded. "The story's not the same as mine, but the emotion is. The fear is. The guilt is."

Guilt? Fear? She clung to her sister's words.

"I—"a ragged breath shot from Barb's lungs and seemed to rattle her bones "—I was molested when I was thirteen."

"You were what?" Marsha forced her legs to move forward. She sank onto the sofa close to her sister. "Barb. No. By who?"

"Our neighbor." Her voice was a whisper.

"Which neighbor?" Her mind tore into her memory, reconstructing her neighborhood and the people who lived there.

"Mr. Buehl."

Buehl? The name meant nothing until she recalled the small house at the end of the street with the mousy woman and the tall, angular man who lived there. "They had a son? Clinton?"

Barb nodded.

"Was it Clinton who did this?"

"No. His father." She closed her eyes. "The first time it happened he came over to borrow something when no one was home but me."

The first time. Marsha's shoulders knotted. "Did he rape you?"

"No, but he might as well have. He touched my body and kissed me on the mouth. It was disgusting."

"What did you do?"

"I was scared to death. I was only thirteen. I thought I'd done something to make him think it was okay. I pulled away, but I can still feel his slimy mouth pushing against mine and his big hands bruising my skin."

"Oh, Barb." All the questions Marsha had had over the years dissipated into understanding. Barb's reaction to being touched unexpectedly. Her distrust of men. Her lack of sociability. It all tumbled into the open like a puzzle that tipped over and lay exposed to be put together with careful hands. "I'm heartbroken. I'm so sorry that I wasn't supportive when you needed help. I didn't know."

"I kept it hidden, especially when it happened again. He must have followed me sometimes. Remember the vacant lot near the corner? I took a shortcut one evening from a school event, and he caught me there. He exposed himself. It made me sick."

"Why didn't you tell anyone? Why did you hold it inside?"

She fell against the sofa cushion. "Mom was so sick then. How could I burden the family with that problem?"

Marsha pressed her hand to her chest. "What about me? You could have told me."

"I didn't think you'd understand and, if you did, you'd have told Mom. I thought it would end, but it didn't. I finally avoided going anywhere at night and I didn't answer the door when I was home alone with Mom or when she was in the hospital. You were out on dates or working your job at the pharmacy. I felt so alone."

The tears Marsha had been fighting gave way and rolled down her cheeks in a steady stream. She'd been so wrapped up in her own life she'd missed something drastic that had affected her sister. How could she have been so unaware?

Barb wrapped her arm around Marsha's shoulder. "It should be me crying, Marsha, not you, but then I've shed enough tears for both of us."

"I'm sorry for blubbering. I'm just startled and so angry at myself. I should have figured it out. You changed so much. One day you stopped laughing. You didn't participate in anything. You volunteered to care for Mom. Why didn't I see it?"

"Because you were a teenager wanting to live your life to the fullest. I never blamed you, but I just couldn't tell anyone. It was too painful and frightening."

Marsha wiped her eyes with her fist, then rose and grabbed a tissue to blow her nose. "So what made you tell me now?"

"I've already told you." She motioned to her legal pad. "The writing. It's been a release. I guess you call it a catharsis. Putting it on paper, giving it to a character and allowing her to struggle and grieve took the pain from me. As I wrote, I realized I was innocent. I should have told someone to get the man off the streets. I wonder how many other girls he hurt in that way."

"How awful. They moved, didn't they?"

"It was the best day of my life. When I saw the moving van pull away, I felt released from prison, yet I kept the bars closed. I put up the barricade to protect myself. I wasn't going to take any more chances on being hurt again."

"So you never dated. You never married. You never had children, and all because of that horrible man."

She shook her head. "No, because I didn't do anything about it. I knew I should, but I'd allowed it to happen more than once, more than twice, and I figured people would think I was lying or making it up or only the Lord knows what went on in my mind. I was ashamed. I felt dirty."

Barb's concern for Bonnie fell into place. "You're as white as snow, Barb. God knows the truth. You were never guilty, and it was never your fault, and now I see why you've talked about predators and why you fear for Bonnie. It was all too real to you."

"Way too real."

Marsha opened her arms, and Barb rose and fell into her embrace. This time Barb's tears wet Marsha's shoulders, tears she should have shared so many years ago, but at least now, they were out and shed. *Lord, heal her wound and open new doors for Barb.*

"Great shot," Jeff said, watching Al's ball hit just short of the green.

Then Jeff strode forward and stood on the tee, lined up his drive and did a practice swing, hoping to leave his hook behind and at least get somewhere near the end of the fairway. He swung back, and, as his arms moved forward, Bonnie let out a yell, and he pulled the shot, clipping the end of the club, and landed the ball seventy-five yards ahead of him. He barely passed the women's tee.

"Bonnie, please don't yell when we're hitting the ball."

Al chuckled. "Good excuse for fluffin' the shot."

Jeff managed to smile, but he'd struggled throughout the game to concentrate. Bringing the girls had been a mistake.

Since they'd arrived, Jeff had had second thoughts about Al bringing Lindsey, but it was too late now. Jeff had been startled when Al's daughter had arrived, wearing the shortest shorts he'd ever seen and a skimpy top that seemed too revealing for a girl of twelve. She'd looked at Bonnie as if she were an alien, and it troubled him. He feared Marsha was right again. Regular kids and Bonnie might not mix.

Today Lindsey had dressed in something similar while Bonnie wore her jeans and a T-shirt. He'd noticed Lindsey rolling her eyes at things Bonnie said and hoped that Al had explained to her that Bonnie had a disability. He hated making excuses for his daughter. He loved her, but sometimes life seemed so unfair, and then he detested feeling that way. He couldn't win.

He jammed his club into the bag, climbed into the cart and drove the few feet up the fairway. When he stepped out, Bonnie slipped into the driver's seat.

"Can I drive, Daddy?"

"Let me make this shot, and then we'll talk about it." He didn't need a tantrum now, and he feared one would be coming. He grabbed his three wood and lined up the ball, then swung. It hit the green about two hundred yards ahead, and he breathed again.

"Good one," Al called from his cart.

Jeff noticed he'd let Lindsey in the driver's seat, so how

could he say no to Bonnie, but he had to. "Bonnie, it's against the law. You have to be older."

"But Lindsey's driving." She swung her hand toward Al's cart and gripped the steering wheel tighter.

He stared at her, knowing his argument would fly over her head. "She's breaking the law."

"I don't care about the law," she screamed.

He wished he could clamp his hand over her mouth, and he sent a desperate look to Al, but he could see Lindsey wasn't planning to budge. She sat behind the steering wheel with her father next to her, her face brimming with belligerence.

Oh, Lord, give me the words. The prayer startled him. It was like the old prayers he used to say so naturally. His pulse pitched along his veins. "Bonnie, I do care about the law. Do you think Aunt Marsha would allow you to do something illegal?"

She looked at him with narrowed eyes, but he saw a flicker of consideration in them, and he kept going.

"You told me Jesus is your best friend and He tells us to do what is right. So let's do what Jesus wants us to do. We need to follow the laws."

One hand slipped from the steering wheel, but she didn't move. He could see she was thinking and, finally, she scooted over and let him sit behind the wheel.

He heard Lindsey mutter something derogatory under her breath, but he ignored it and said a thank you to the sky, then headed toward the ninth hole.

"I don't like that girl," Bonnie said as he drove. "She calls me names."

"But we don't do that, right? We do what's good. She has problems, too, Bonnie and I'll tell you about it later."

His comment apparently made her curious, because she smiled at him and, when he climbed from the cart, she asked if she could pull his club from his golf bag, and he agreed.

She stood beside the cart as he walked to the tee, and he felt grateful that she'd grown up so much in the last few weeks.

Al's ball went into the rough, and Jeff stood on the tee eyeing the last hole. The course had been a tough one, with narrow tree-shrouded fairways and tall grasses that reminded him of a Scottish course. He lined up the ball and drove it over the tall grass onto the flat fairway.

Al strutted to his side and shook his hand. "Good shot, and I'm sorry about Lindsey. She's with her mother most of the time, and she lets her get away with too much. Then I take her for a few days, and I'm the bad guy so…" He gave a feeble shrug. "I crumble under the pressure. I'd like to see her be more like Bonnie."

Jeff smiled, thinking if Al really understood he would never have made that statement, but it still gave him a feeling of pride. "She has her problems, but she's a good girl."

They finished the last hole with Al one stroke up on Jeff. "Not a bad game," Jeff said. "If I wouldn't have bungled that one shot, who knows?"

They shook hands and drove the carts back to the exit, but Jeff's mind kept drifting back to his prayer. He'd prayed, and God had answered. Some people might say it was a coincidence that Bonnie had cooperated, but Marsha would say it was God, and he wanted to think it had been, too.

They climbed into the car and stopped for lunch in town. When the girls finished, they went outside to look at the boats in the marina, and he leaned back finishing the last of his soft drink.

"How's life?" Al asked when they were alone. "Better than mine, I hope."

Jeff sensed he wanted to talk, and so he didn't answer the question. "Things are bad for you?"

"Competition constantly. Divorce isn't what God wants, Jeff. I'm so sorry Angie wanted out of the marriage. I don't think she's any happier, either. Like I said, Lindsey wears her out and she gives in. Then, when she's with me and I try to control her, I'm the bad guy. Who wants to spend every other weekend with a daughter and be the bad guy? But I have to do something."

"Sounds tough." He thought of all he'd learned about Bonnie. "I think kids want to be loved and, if they feel on shaky ground, they act up for attention. If we don't reward the bad by making a big deal out of it, but really reward the good, then they catch on."

Al's eyebrows lifted. "Good psychology. Where'd you get your major?"

Jeff grinned. "From Marsha."

"Marsha?" Al's eyebrows shot upward even higher.

"That's another story. One other thing I've noticed is that Bonnie behaves better when she has expectations. I'm trying to let her help more and have been complimenting her. I have expectations and she knows, if she follows them, she will get positive attention. And she has talent. She's very artistic. Marsha saw that, and it's so great to see her draw for an hour without being bored."

Al nodded. "Some good things to think about, Jeff, but let's get back to this Marsha. Who is she?"

Jeff felt heat rise up his neck. "She's my former sister-in-law. My late brother, Don's, wife."

Al's forehead wrinkled. "Don died."

"Yes, years ago. The four of us had been close and Marilou and I spent a lot of time with Marsha while Don was sick, but we drifted, and now we've stumbled over each other again." He told him the journey they'd taken since arriving on the island, and Jeff felt good saying the things aloud and getting them out in the open.

"And you're calling this a friendship?" A silly grin lingered on Al's face.

Jeff shrugged. "It's been difficult. I feel bad taking time away from Bonnie. She needs so much, and then Marsha and I both felt guilty at first as if—"

"You were cheating on your spouses."

"Right. How did you guess?"

"Because I feel the same way. I've tried to date, and it seems so shallow. The women are attractive and willing, but it just doesn't sit well. I still feel connected to Angie in some ways, or maybe it's that I haven't found a real woman. You know, one that is more than a beautiful body, but one with depth of character and one that really wants me for me."

Jeff only nodded. Finding the right woman who made him feel complete again had been only a dream—something he'd never expected to happen—and then she appeared. Marsha, of all people. Marsha with her red hair and freckles. Marsha with her wisdom and determination. He loved every bit of it.

Jeff drew himself from his thoughts. "Would you like to meet her?"

"Marsha?"

"Yes. She's still here. She volunteered to take the girls off our hands while we go fishing. In fact, she offered to take them today, and I said no." He saw Al's wide-eyed expression. "Bad decision, I guess."

"Probably." Al laughed. "Anyway, yes. I'd love to meet her. I'm surprised I haven't already."

"Me, too, but I've been confused. I'm trying to convince myself this can't go anywhere, or maybe I'm trying to agree with Marsha, who seems to say it can't, but lately, I'm thinking we're both very wrong."

Chapter Fifteen

Marsha laughed as Barb and the two younger girls raced through the waves. She called it a race, but Bonnie couldn't race. She was doing her best with her dog paddle. Marsha knew Barb was holding back so the girls had half a chance. Barb had been on the swim team at school in junior high until she'd dropped out, and now Marsha understood why she'd done that. It had never made sense before. Every time she thought of Barb's silent pain, she hurt inside.

She slipped on a beach cover and sat on the recliner. She expected Jeff and Al to return soon from their fishing trip, and she didn't want to be caught in the water.

Al seemed like a nice man, but Marsha wondered why Al had stared at her when they'd first met. It had made her nervous, and she'd hoped the look wasn't a come-on, but later, he'd spent time talking with Barb, which had really surprised her. It gave Marsha a lift to see her socializing.

Looking across the bay, Marsha watched another freighter making its long trek to Chicago. Most of them were headed to the large port there. The sun glinted off the small whitecaps that rolled in, and, when the girls stopped their racing, they enjoyed the challenge of the frothy waves. They bounced near the shore and laughed as the larger ones knocked them from their feet.

Barb headed back to the beach, looking happier than she had in a long time, and Marsha could only imagine that lifting the burden from her shoulders had made a difference. They hadn't talked about it anymore, but the news had given Marsha a brand new understanding of her sister and the sorrow she bore in silence.

"I've had enough," Barb said, settling into a beach chair. "I'll dry off for a minute. Then I'm getting dressed." She threw a towel over her lap and stretched out her legs.

Curious, Marsha couldn't hold back her question. "What do you think of Al?"

"He seems like a nice man, but I worry about his daughter. She's headed for trouble. She's too grown up for twelve years of age."

"I was thinking the same." She glanced above the tall grasses toward the top of the hill. "They should be here soon."

"You're probably right." Barb craned her neck toward the cottage. "I'm going up. I don't want to be caught in my bathing suit." She stood, wrapped the large towel around her waist and headed up the hill.

Marsha leaned back, letting her mind drift while she watched the girls. She missed Jeff. He'd called a couple of times, once to let her know the girls would go golfing with him yesterday and then later, when Jeff had said they'd take her up on the offer to watch them while he and Al fished today. Apparently, golfing with the girls in tow hadn't gone that well.

She realized it had only been three days, but the special time, the sharing time, they hadn't had that even on Sunday.

She'd had no chance to find out what he thought about church, positive or negative. Nothing. Al had been standing nearby when he'd dropped off the girls, and it made talking about anything personal too difficult. She liked Al, but—

"Daddy!"

Marsha sat up and glanced over her shoulder when she heard Bonnie's cry. She hadn't seen Jeff and Al coming down the path because the tall shrubs and grass blocked her view.

"Hi," Jeff said, moving to her side and squeezing her shoulder. "How'd it go?"

"Fine. No problems." Not totally accurate though. She smiled at Al, unable to tell Jeff the total truth. Lindsey had called Bonnie a retard, and Bonnie had gotten teary eyed. Marsha had let the girl know how she felt, then felt badly for being so angry. The girl had looked surprised, but had finally said she was sorry. From her expression, Marsha figured she didn't really feel sorry, but at least she'd apologized. That was a step in the right direction.

"Let's go," Jeff called, beckoning the girls from the water. "We're going to Daddy Frank's for lunch. Guess who picked the spot?"

Marsha waited, hoping to hear an invitation to join them, but she didn't.

Bonnie bounded from the water with Lindsey following behind as if she didn't want to respond to Jeff's call but knew she'd better.

Jeff guided Bonnie toward Marsha. "Thank Aunt Marsha for letting you stay here."

Bonnie leaned down and gave Marsha a wet hug. "Thank you."

"You're welcome," she said, feeling the chill of the icy water she'd convinced herself earlier wasn't too cold.

"We'll talk later." He rested his hand on Bonnie's back and followed Lindsey and Al up the path while Marsha watched them go, feeling as if she'd had sand kicked in her face.

After she figured they'd gone, she climbed the hill and went to her room. She dressed and tried to swallow some fruit, but it stuck in her throat. What had she expected? Somehow, in her delusional world, she'd thought Jeff cared for her enough to have her fit into his life—even as a friend. She'd tried to quash her feelings for so long, but she'd finally given up and faced the truth. She'd begun to fall in love. It had nothing to do with purpose or being needed. She'd finally understood this was a totally selfish motive. She wanted to love and be loved again. It was that simple.

Simple? How could she put that word in the same sentence with her and Jeff? Nothing was simple. The situation reeked of complications. They'd been in-laws; his life was devoted to Bonnie; he'd lost his personal relationship with the Lord. She'd pushed him away because of that. She'd given up on romance. She'd let caregiving be her focus; she'd invited Barb to live with her, and Barb had given up her apartment and moved in. Even if she and Jeff had fallen in love, what could she do now? Oh, by the way Barb, I'm marrying Jeff so get out now that you've just settled in.

Her stomach twisted with confusion as she eyed Barb sitting in her favorite spot, writing again on the yellow legal pad.

"I'm going back down to get some sun," Marsha said, grabbing a magazine.

"Would you like to read some of my novel?"

Marsha's pulse tripped. "I'd love to, if you don't mind."

Her sister reached down and handed her a thick legal pad. "Here's the beginning."

Marsha took the stack of paper and held it to her chest. "This means a lot to me, Barb."

"It means a lot to me, too."

Tears prickled in Marsha's eyes for Barb and for her own misery. She opened the door and made her way down to the beach. A breeze ruffled the pages when she lifted the pad to her lap, and she began at the beginning.

The sun warmed her arms, but her body felt chilled from the sadness in the words her sister had written. In this story, a young woman had been attacked and brutally hurt by a predator who continued to stalk her.

She turned the pages. Chapter one. Chapter two. Chapter three.

Holding her breath, Marsha contemplated what she'd read. She didn't know anything about writing, but this was good. Barb had brought this woman to life and created emotions that raced from the paper to her fingers as she turned the yellow pages as fast as her eyes could take in the story.

"Barb said you were here."

Marsha jumped, hearing Jeff's voice. "What are you doing here? I thought you had plans."

"I skipped lunch. Al said he'd take the girls to town. He dropped me off."

She searched his face, wondering if something was wrong. "Any particular reason?"

"I've missed you."

She caught her breath. "I've missed you."

"I'm glad." He looked behind him and drew the chair up to the recliner. "I wanted to tell you a couple of things."

She searched his eyes, fearing what he had to say.

He gave her a knowing look. "So much has happened. I don't know where to begin."

Her shoulders knotted and she felt a frown settle on her face.

"First, you were right about regular kids and disabled. Lindsey and Bonnie are like oil and water. Nothing in common, and I don't like some of the things she says or her looks. I wouldn't have let Bonnie go today except, when Al is there, Lindsey seems to behave."

Relief washed over her. One more thing she didn't have to tell him.

"She rolls her eyes and says things that hurt Bonnie's feelings."

Marsha nodded. Like retard, she told herself. "She's spoiled."

"I understand how those things happen, and Al feels badly but it's not good." He grasped her hand and wove his fingers through hers. "The other thing I want to tell you is that I prayed yesterday. It happened as naturally as breathing."

A prayer answered. Marsha swallowed back her emotion. "I'm glad. It's a door opening."

"A door that's been closed too long."

"You've been reading the Bible, haven't you?"

He gave her a sly grin and nodded. "Curious, I suppose, about the verses you mentioned, and they hit home. They made me think, especially how I was cheating Bonnie, later how I was cheating myself."

With gratefulness flying to heaven, she placed her palm over his hands. "That warms my heart. I can't tell you how much."

"And I want to talk about another door that's been closed too long."

She looked into his eyes and felt weak.

"Let's take a walk." He rose and held out his hand.

Marsha grasped it, hope spiraling through her. When she stood, Jeff wove his fingers through hers. She strode beside him along the sand, her thoughts shifting to the footprints they'd talked about, what seemed so long ago.

As they walked, he released her hand and slipped his arm around her waist. He didn't say anything, but she sensed he was struggling. She recognized the look in his eyes, and now anticipated what he might say.

"Ready?"

She lifted her gaze to his, hoping she was right. "I've been ready for a while now."

He drew her closer to his side. "You know this is about us."

She looked into his tender gaze. "I hoped so."

Jeff stopped and turned her toward him. "We've been kidding ourselves about this friendship thing. I know we've both struggled with guilty feelings and questions as to motivation. I've asked myself, how does she really feel?"

"And I asked myself how does *he* really feel?" she added.

"I know, now, you've been concerned about my lack of faith, and I think that's what's been holding you back."

She nodded, trying to control the tears pooling in her eyes. "What you said today makes all the difference."

He brushed away the tears from her cheek. "I've always admired you, Marsha. Your strength and courage. Your stamina and spirit. You could find humor in the worst situations and make me laugh. Your wisdom. Your love for Bonnie." He tilted her chin upward. "I think our relationship has gone far beyond friendship."

"So do I."

"So what do we do about it?"

She searched his eyes, and he gave her the answer without words. His mouth lowered to hers and, instead of fighting the emotion, she drank in the sweetness. She wrapped her arms around his neck, feeling her heart beat against his chest, his body trembling against hers.

They stood alone, bound in each other's arms, the sound of the waves lapping against the shore, a gull dipping toward the water as their only witness, and it was all she wanted.

She drew back to catch her breath and felt like a young girl with her first love. With no words to say, she tiptoed to meet his mouth again, lingering in the joy of the experience and the giving that she'd withheld for so long.

He eased back and gazed into her eyes. "You've made me so happy. I know this is new, but I trust my heart. I trust what's happened to me these past four weeks. I don't think meeting here was a coincidence. I believe it was God-guided."

Marsha's heart sang with his admission, and she sent up a prayer of thanksgiving for what God had done for them, but she felt herself hesitate. "I trust my heart, too, but we need time, Jeff. I hope you agree."

"Time?"

"We're caught up in these wonderful feelings of wholeness, but we don't want to hurt anyone. We need to go home and see how it works there in real time, not summer time."

He put a palm on each side of her face. "Do you think this is a summer romance? It's not for me, Marsha. I know the difference. I've been alone for two years. I've tried to date women, but it's empty. The feelings I had for them can't compare to anything I've experienced with you on the island."

"I know." Her chest ached with the worries that tumbled through her mind. "But there's Barb. She just moved in with me. What can I say to her?"

"Tell her the truth."

"Yes, but…I've learned some things recently. She's trusted me with some horrible experiences from her past, and I don't want to make her feel she's in the way. Not today. Not while we're here." She saw disappointment in his eyes and she wanted to scream at the situation, but even Bonnie seemed to be growing out of her tantrums, and she couldn't give way to her frustration. "I'm not doubting my feelings. I'm just asking you to give us time before we say anything. Let Barb get used to the idea of seeing you around when we get back home."

He held her at arm's length and gave her a faint smile. "My Marsha. She's still taking care of people."

His comment stabbed her. She didn't feel free to tell him Barb's secret, but he had to understand. "Trust me just a little more, Jeff. Please."

He closed his eyes and drew her into his embrace. "I trust you. You can have your time, but I'm disappointed. Tomorrow's the Fourth. I want to put your name up in lights. I want to sing this revelation from the housetops."

So did she, but she had responsibilities. She needed to explain things to Barb, first. She needed to— What? Her excuse sounded so shallow, even to her.

Jeff had to hogtie Bonnie to get her ready for the town's festivities, and it made him laugh. Both girls seemed excited over the morning Fourth of July activities. He'd explained the events were a full day with the parades, skydivers, a carnival and fireworks at the end of the day. They didn't celebrate the Fourth nearly as fully in the big cities downstate.

"Let's hurry," he said, prodding Bonnie to finish combing her hair. "Aunt Marsha is ready and wants to get a good spot for the parade."

Aunt Marsha. Bonnie adored her, and so did he, but she'd knocked the wind out of his sails yesterday when he'd admitted his feelings. The words *I love you* had nearly fallen from his lips and, with her caution to wait, he was grateful he'd controlled himself. But no matter what he called it, Jeff knew he had fallen in love—the proverbial head-over-heels kind that almost made him feel giddy.

Lindsey fussed over her hair and makeup, which upset Bonnie. She wanted eye shadow and lipstick, too, but Jeff took her aside and tried to explain Lindsey was older. Even then, he wasn't happy about seeing the girl decked out like one of the floats they would see in the parade.

Finally, with threats of staying home from the celebration, Bonnie gave in, but her mouth curved down to a miserable look, and he hoped it would fade by the time they arrived at Marsha's.

Al packed the trunk with chairs while Jeff gathered his contribution to the picnic and, once loaded, they made the short trip to Marsha's. He wanted to tell Al what had happened after his talk with Marsha—get his advice—but he decided not to dwell on it. He only hoped that Marsha hadn't let their discussion ruin the day.

His fears were lifted when he pulled up to the A-frame. Barb and Marsha were at the door, ready to load her trunk. Jeff jumped from the driver's seat. "Can we fit everything in one car? Parking could be a problem. I think we can put the four smallest people into the backseat."

He saw Barb pat her hips, and he chuckled. "You can sit in front with Al. He'll have to drive."

She shrugged and Marsha smiled as she handed him a picnic hamper. "We have more chairs and a large Thermos of lemonade. That should do it."

Al grasped the chairs from Barb while Jeff carried the box. In minutes, the trunk was packed and so was the car. He and Marsha squeezed together—pure pleasure for him—while the girls scrunched into the rest of the seat. He was grateful the trip was short. They found a space on Donegal Bay Road near Main Street and, with everyone lugging something, they walked to a grassy spot across from the Shamrock Restaurant and opened the folding chairs while the girls spread a blanket on the grass.

The day was perfect and, as Jeff watched, near noon he saw a band gathering on the stage. Christian music filled the air, songs he didn't know, but he clapped his hands and tapped his toe. When his gaze drifted to Marsha, she smiled, but he thought he saw something questioning in her eyes.

"Are you okay?" he asked.

"Perfect. The day's beautiful and the company is even better."

Her comment reassured him. Maybe they could get through these trials. She'd said Barb had confessed something to her, something important from the way she'd talked, and he had to respect that. Still, her hesitation bothered him. He feared this might be only an excuse. She'd been single for four years. For him, it had only been two. Yet, she hadn't mentioned dating or seeking company, and he knew that Don's illness had dealt a horrible blow to romance in their lives. Yet, she'd remained a devoted wife, showing him love and caring for him to the end.

What did Jeff expect? Sometimes he seemed to second-guess too many things. He needed to let things happen and not push them. If Marsha loved him, he would know soon enough. She'd asked for time, not a lifetime.

Marsha gave him a questioning look, and he managed

a smile, then focused on the band's message of salvation, which, until recently, he'd forced from his life.

She motioned to the picnic basket and, as they listened, she passed out the plates and laid the food in containers on the blanket. Marsha had even thought to bring a jar of peanut butter, just in case.

When they were eating, Jeff noticed a couple of teenage boys hanging around, and he saw Lindsey looking at them. He needed to keep tabs on her or caution Al, but he hated to put a damper on everyone's fun. He'd be alert himself.

Jeff's thoughts shifted to Lindsey's behavior, and he surprised himself feeling proud of Bonnie. He couldn't believe how well she'd behaved since Al had arrived. She'd had one temper tantrum at the golf course, but other than that, she hadn't caused an uproar, and he was grateful. Marsha had said sometimes kids grow out of it, and maybe so. What he had noticed was she'd gotten moodier and cried more easily. He wondered if Lindsey had triggered that problem.

Tap dancers were followed by a community choir singing "God Bless America" and "You're a Grand Old Flag." People in the crowd lifted their small American flags and waved them. Marsha sang along with the choir, and pride filled Jeff's chest hearing her excellent voice.

"Look!" Bonnie called as the choir left the stage.

Jeff stared into the sky as jets flew over in formation. Then they all gasped when a biplane appeared next doing loop-the-loops and, finally, the skydivers glided through the air.

"Wow!" Lindsey yelled, and Bonnie followed suit. Lindsey rose and Bonnie followed, moving behind the chairs. Jeff glanced over his shoulder, and they had their eyes aimed at the sky so he relaxed.

When the show ended, Jeff looked again, and the girls were leaning against someone's car, watching as the parade came down Main Street—floats and music, bicycles decorated with colorful plastic ribbons—each one extolling the theme, the beauty of Beaver Island.

Thinking about Bonnie, he turned again, but this time he didn't see either of the girls. He bounded from his chair. "I'll be back in a minute," he whispered to Marsha and made his way through the crowd, anxiety knotting his stomach.

He looked both ways along the street and finally spotted Lindsey. The girls had moved down a few vehicles and were leaning against a truck with the teenagers he'd seen earlier. Lindsey was nestled beside one of the boys and the other had his arm around Bonnie with his arm too close to her chest.

Fire rose in him, and he sent up a prayer as he charged forward. "There you are," he said, controlling his hands from balling into fists. "Girls, come back to our spot." He waved them away. Lindsey muttered a comment, and Bonnie looked confused.

As the girls moved aside, Jeff closed in on the boys. "These girls are underage and off-limits, boys. If I see you near them again, I'll have to do something I'd rather not do."

The boys gave him a smirk and swaggered away, making an obscene gesture. He caught up with the girls and stopped them. "This is between you and me, Lindsey. I don't want to ruin your dad's day, but one more time, and he'll have to know."

She rolled her eyes, and Bonnie touched his arm, her expression telling him she didn't know why he was angry. Tonight, he needed to tell her about boys. The whole idea ⸺ ⸺ his throat.

⸺ ⸺ ve him a quizzical look, but he just shook his

head, and she didn't ask. Lindsey gave him an occasional frown, but, when the parade ended and the carnival began, she stuck by them as they eyed the activities—a dunk-the-celebrity tank, a huge plastic trampoline castle, games for the kids and even cotton candy.

"What happened?" Marsha asked as they trailed behind the others.

"Bonnie and Lindsey were with two boys down the road a ways."

She arched an eyebrow, and he stopped her before she said anything. "I'll talk with her tonight. I promise."

Marsha shook her head. "I worry," she said, weaving her fingers through his. She lifted their hands so he could see them bound together. "You don't mind, do you?"

"Do you have to ask?" He squeezed her fingers, pleased that she'd taken action. He'd longed to put his arm around her earlier, but Barb had been nearby, and he'd promised Marsha time.

Time. Time on my hands. The old song lyrics wove through his mind.

Bonnie apparently had noticed their contact and waited for him. When he reached her, she latched on to his other hand. Jealousy. He'd never imagined it would happen, although he'd already seen inklings of it. But it confused him. Bonnie loved Marsha and had been the one to instigate getting together so often. He sent up a prayer, amazed at how easy it felt after so long evading the Lord.

As the evening darkened, they gathered back at their spots on the grass to watch the boat parade, then the time came for the fireworks.

He caught Bonnie's eye and pointed to the south side of Paradise Bay across from Whiskey Point.

With darkness over them, all eyes turned toward the sky, all except his. In the dimness, he studied Marsha's face, longing to tell the world how he felt about her and wondering how he could let a day go past without holding her in his arms.

Barb and Al were deep in conversation as they'd been from nearly the moment they'd been introduced. He wondered what topic had been so interesting, what had drawn them together.

The fireworks began with everyone glued to the bursts of color, the spirals that hissed as they descended, the secondary bursts that glowed like golden chrysanthemums in a forest-green garden.

Jeff grasped Marsha's hand and gave it a tug. When she looked at him, he tilted his head toward the street. "For a minute," he whispered, beckoning her to follow.

They rose, unnoticed it seemed, and slipped away while a boom reverberated into the sky with the "oohs" and "aahs" of the crowd.

"We can't do this," Marsha whispered, tugging against his hand.

"Sure we can. Just for a minute."

He felt like a kid trying to sneak his first kiss. In fact, he hated having to hide his feelings and he hoped Marsha resolved the situation soon. He wanted to understand, but he didn't. Jeff wanted to shout his feelings from the rooftops.

He drew her away from the crowd and up Donegal Bay Road to his car. He leaned his back against it, letting the vehicle block them from view, and drew her into his arms. "I can't be with you without holding you for a moment."

She tossed her head as if she couldn't believe him, but she didn't struggle when he tightened his embrace.

"I feel like I'm doing something wrong," she said into his ear.

"Wrong? How can this be wrong?" He lowered his mouth to hers, feeling the tender touch of her soft lips. She released a tiny moan that charged to his heart. He couldn't believe he felt as he did. His life, so empty and weighted with problems, had suddenly burst into a wonderful new experience, more wonderful than the fireworks display.

She drew back, lifted her hand and pressed it against his cheek. "You are everything I've ever dreamed of…and more."

He wanted to tell her about his dreams. She'd appeared in them so often, sometimes dressed in that pale blue color that she'd worn when he'd first arrived—a color as soft as a morning sky.

Jeff brushed his lips against hers, tasting the sweetness of her mouth and drawing in the scent of her fragrance. He released a breath, ragged yet filled with deep pleasure.

"We should get back," she said, slipping her fingers through his again. "They'll notice we're gone, and Bonnie will be frightened."

He nodded, wanting to stay there forever in the privacy of the night, wanting to talk about his dreams and his hopes, wanting so much. Yet her words hit home. Bonnie became frightened over so many things, and it took Marsha to remind him. His daughter needed so much.

He wove his fingers through hers and strolled back to the group and, as they settled, he grinned at his foolish worries. Bonnie hadn't missed him. Her eyes were aimed at the sky, mesmerized by the glinting fireworks, just as he'd been captivated by the fireworks in his heart.

But his fireworks had dimmed. How could he convince Marsha loving him wasn't wrong? It was a gift from God, a God who offered him grace. Tonight, he knew the meaning of the word.

Chapter Sixteen

"Where'd you go last night during the fireworks?" Barb asked at breakfast.

Marsha wanted to dodge her question. She couldn't lie to her, but she didn't want to tell her everything yet. Not now. "Jeff wanted to talk. With everyone around, it's been difficult." That was true. Mostly.

Barb nodded. "You two seem close."

"We are. We've shared a lot in our past. I suppose it's comfortable to be with someone who watched it all happen with me and understands the pain because he's had his own."

"Is it getting serious?"

Marsha frowned, and she wanted to bolt from the room so as not to answer. She shrugged. "We've never spoken of love." That was the truth.

"I hate to see you make a mistake."

Barb's words startled her. "A mistake?"

"You've been Marsha the caregiver for so long, and it's easy to creep back into the habit, even when you're trying not to do it. Bonnie needs you, and now Jeff seems to need you. Is that what the draw is?"

Marsha felt her face sag into a deeper frown. "Barb, I don't—"

"I could be wrong, but the relationship has happened so fast. I watched you change these past weeks. It's been like a tractor whose brakes failed on a hill. It just comes barreling down, smashing everything in its path."

"Smashing everything? I'm not smashing into anything, Barb. I—" Was she worried about their living arrangements? Could that be it or was it a real concern?

Barb held up her hand. "You don't need to explain to me. I just wanted to tell you what I've been thinking. I don't want to see Bonnie hurt."

"Neither do I. I wouldn't hurt her for the world."

"She's so attached to you and, if the romance is a flash in the pan, then what? You'd hurt a child who is already hurting."

Marsha stared at the floor. Bonnie. She'd wondered the same, but her emotions had kept her self-focused instead of thinking of her niece. "I appreciate your honesty." She managed to get that out.

Barb let the matter drop, but Marsha couldn't. Maybe Barb was wrong. Maybe it wasn't a fleeting relationship. Maybe it could go somewhere if she could let go of her worries.

But Bonnie. She couldn't allow the child to be hurt by her and Jeff's actions.

The telephone jarred her thoughts.

Barb answered and Marsha heard her laugh. "I'll check. Just a minute." She covered the receiver with her hand. "They want us to go sightseeing. Protar's House, Cable Bay—Al wants to see the footbridge where the Wildwood Inn was—and then the girls want to climb the sand dunes."

Hearing Barb say *us*, Marsha contained the surprise in her voice. "That's fine. When?"

Barb finished the conversation, then meandered back to the kitchen table. "I'm up for it, all but the dunes. They can drop me back here." She eyed her watch. "They'll be here in a half hour or so."

Marsha looked down at her denim shorts and T-shirt and decided to change. She stacked her dishes in the sink, grabbed her final cup of coffee and headed to her room.

Alone, she sank on the bed, amazed at Barb. Confessing her secret had turned her into a new person, all except her pessimism. But Marsha couldn't dismiss it. Bonnie had made great progress, too, but how would Marsha's relationship with Jeff affect her niece?

She closed her eyes, thinking of her feelings for Jeff. Were they sincere? Could they be long-term? Forever? She'd asked herself the question numerous times. Still, she'd always come up with the same answer. Her feelings for Jeff were real.

She thought back to how she'd messed up with her desire for purpose. She'd insisted Barb move in with her; she'd nosed her way into Jeff's business with Bonnie; and she'd even had to struggle not to crowd Jeff with her faith. God had proved He could do the job without her. She cringed. What made her think she had her hand on the reins of anyone's life?

After slipping out of her shorts, Marsha tugged on her capri pants, light blue with pink-and-white embroidery at the hem. She found a blue-and-white top that looked nice and pulled that over her head, then grasped a comb and dragged it through her new short hair. She loved the shorter style. It made her feel different, just as Jeff's entrance into her life had made her feel brand new. So why did she feel torn by indecision?

Marsha took a last look in the mirror, then laid the brush on her dresser, grasped her sandals and carried them into the living room.

Barb came out of her bedroom a few minutes later, her hair pulled back, blush on her cheeks and a tint to her lips. She looked good, and Marsha thought she'd even lost some weight since she'd been on the island.

For this occasion, they took two cars. Al drove Marsha's with Barb and Lindsey, and Marsha rode with Jeff and Bonnie. For the long ride, comfort won out over camaraderie.

When they reached Cable Bay, they headed across the expanse of white sand and wild grasses. Jeff lagged behind and wove his fingers through her. She felt miserable sneaking around behind everyone, and she was sure Jeff had been disappointed in her. She couldn't help but think of Barb's earlier comments. Was their relationship a fantasy, and how would it affect Bonnie if it ended? The questions crushed her joy.

With Bonnie on her mind, she turned to Jeff, recalling Bonnie's incident the evening before. She hoped Jeff had followed through with his promise. "How'd the talk go?"

He shrugged. "Okay, I guess. I don't know if she totally understood what I was saying, but she listened."

"A little at a time." She gave his hand a squeeze. "I'm glad you talked with her."

They reached the shore where the foamy waves dashed against the sand. The concrete piers from the old Wildwood Inn's foundation could still be seen. Marsha stood back, watching the girls run along the beach, releasing some of their unquenchable energy. Lindsey had softened a little, and Bonnie didn't seem to have her feelings hurt so often. That was a relief.

Marsha poked a marsh marigold with the toe of her sandal, thinking about returning home and whether things would really fall into place as Jeff had suggested.

Marriage. Was that the direction he was headed? She sensed from his actions he meant making a commitment. If it happened, what would their families say? Jeff's family was gone, but she still had parents and cousins. Would they think she'd used Jeff to try to fill Don's shoes? It was far from the truth. They were brothers, but different in so many ways she'd come to realize. Then her nagging thoughts rose again.

Jeff had wandered back to Al. Jeff looked so good standing beside Al, his strong arms gesturing toward the ruins. "This inn was built back when James Strang ruled the island. He declared himself king."

"What?" Al took a back-step. "A king? Are you kidding?"

Barb stood nearby listening as if it were the first time she'd heard the story.

"No. It used to be a tough place to live, but the murder and mayhem ended in the mideighteenth century."

"Murder and mayhem?" Al's eyes widened.

"James Strang arrived on the island and chased off most of the Irish population—my ancestors included. Only a few brave souls stayed here to witness Strang proclaiming himself king."

Al shook his head in seeming disbelief. "What happened?"

"Some of his disgruntled followers assassinated him, and Strang's group started leaving, so the Irishmen returned to reclaim their land, including the Sullivans." He tapped his chest. "That's my family."

Marsha grinned at the pride she saw in Jeff's face.

"I didn't realize you had historic connections to the island," Al said, giving him a pat on the back.

Distracted, Marsha tuned out the history lesson since she'd heard it so often. Instead, she watched the easygoing interaction between Jeff and Al and realized she'd been jealous of Jeff's friendship with Al. Just as Bonnie had begun to show a little jealousy of her time with Jeff. Marsha had bungled into their lives and she'd allowed Bonnie to latch on to her without considering the repercussions. What if she and Jeff couldn't be more than friends when they returned home?

Why did she feel this way? Unsure of Jeff? Unsure of herself? None of that made any sense. She'd botched things up good. The quicker she returned home, the better they'd all be. Then she would know what would happen between them.

The men seemed to have their fill of Cable Bay, and they headed back to the cars and drove the bumpy roads to Protar's House, a simple log cabin where the man with a hidden past had doctored the residents with his potions free of charge. While Al found it intriguing, the girls wandered outside and asked every few minutes if they were going to the sand dunes. Marsha began to feel the same way, and she gave Jeff a private poke and suggested they leave.

They returned to Donegal Bay Road, but, when they approached the A-frame, Barb apparently decided to go along to Mount Pisgah, because Al flagged them on. Marsha sat dumbfounded as they headed to Lakeview Road. Her sister had become one surprise after another.

They parked at the base of the seven-hundred-and-thirty-foot sand dune, and the girls scampered from the cars, tore off their shoes and charged up the hill about two yards before the sand slipped from beneath their feet.

"This is too hard," Bonnie yelled.

"Take it slow." Jeff took a running start and passed the girls by a few feet, then halted and laughed. "So much for that."

Marsha tried to dislodge her worries watching Jeff charge on ahead, and finding her sandals impeding her climb, she tossed them below and pushed her way upward, her legs aching as she approached Jeff. When she tumbled into his arms, he laughed at her before kissing her on the nose.

She felt herself wince, not from the kiss but from her weighty thoughts and not wanting to make a display. She hated doubting her feelings about Jeff. If she could open her heart and not hide it from the others, the situation could be wonderful.

Jeff noticed her expression and faltered.

"I'm sorry." Her head and heart tangled as her feet and legs had knotted in the sand. "I—" She gestured to the others below them.

"I understand," he said, tousling her hair and shooting her a playful look.

His playfulness distracted her, and she pretended to reach for him, but, instead, gave him a sneaky push. His feet slipped out from under him, and he plopped onto the sand.

"Daddy fell," Bonnie called, pointing to them from below and making a valiant effort to climb the dune, but, no matter how hard she tried, she lagged behind Lindsey.

Marsha looked beyond the girls. "I thought Al was coming up here."

Jeff gave a one-shoulder shrug. "He decided to stay back with Barb, I guess."

She shifted her gaze and saw Barb and Al sitting on a grassy area to the side of the sand dune. Her curiosity itched to know what they were talking about, but she realized too late that, while she was looking at Barb, Jeff had begun his attack. He captured her ankles and gave them a little tug. Marsha tumbled to the ground beside him, their laughter sailing downward.

Barb looked up with a wide smile and pointed at them sitting in the sand.

Marsha waved back, unable to harness her curiosity as she watched Barb and Al. The distraction seemed wonderful. She clambered to her feet and forced her legs to push forward to the top.

Breathless, she gave the magnificent view a sweeping look. It made it worth the climb. In the distance, she saw High Island and others dotting the water. "Look," she said, pointing toward the rolling water. "It's beautiful."

Jeff slipped his arm around her waist and tilted her chin upward. "I like what I'm looking at right here."

She felt the roll of his muscles beneath her arm as he drew her closer. "Me, too."

Without caring about who might be watching or her stressful thoughts this time, Marsha leaned into Jeff's kiss.

He drew back, and his eyes glistened. "I've never kissed anyone on the top of a sand dune until now."

"Me, neither," she said, "and at forty-two, I doubt if it will ever happen again." She gave him a teasing look. "You do remember that I'm older than you?"

"I remember." He tweaked her cheek. "I like older women."

She gave him another prankish shove, but this time he was prepared and held his ground. He nabbed her and drew her into his arms. "We're on top of the world."

She looked into his glowing eyes and sadness flattened her spirit. She had no words to respond. She would feel on top of the world if she could dig herself out of the pit of fear. Where was her faith? Right now Jeff's seemed greater than hers.

Marsha looked down the sand dune, then heavenward. *Lord, how can the top of the world feel like the pits?*

Jeff snuggled her closer. Today had been wonderful, yet she'd allowed herself to sink into the doldrums of concern. Where was her trust?

Marsha stood in the shower, feeling sand in her hair and those little particles that wouldn't brush away covering her body. The grit prickled beneath her feet in the shower before it finally washed down the drain. She stepped from the enclosure and towel dried her body, then found another towel to wrap around her hair.

The day had been exhilarating, except for Barb's comments twisting in her mind. As many times as she'd been to the island, Marsha had never climbed Mount Pisgah, and she had to admit, she'd felt like a girl again, laughing and playing with Jeff. He'd opened doors she'd never dreamed possible.

Marsha dressed, then headed to the living room and sank into a chair. She tossed one of her legs over the arm. "I'm tired. Sand-dune climbing takes a lot of energy."

Barb nodded, but a look came into her eyes that gave Marsha an unwelcome sensation.

"Something wrong?" Marsha asked.

"No, but I've made a decision, and I hope it doesn't upset you."

"What decision?" Her chest felt tight.

"I'm leaving on Saturday when Al goes home. He lives in Birmingham so it's not too far from the house."

Marsha dropped her legs from the chair arm and straightened. "Why are you leaving?"

Barb's shoulder twitched. "I'd be more comfortable at home. I've had some fun here, but I need time by myself."

Time by herself. Marsha didn't like the sound of that and wondered what had triggered that idea. Al came to mind. Had he said something to hurt Barb's feelings? She dropped that train of thought. If he had, Barb wouldn't be riding back with him.

Marsha tried to control her expression, but she knew Barb saw the mixture of confusion and concern on her face. "I really don't understand why you're running off."

"To be honest, I want to look for an apartment. I'm more content living by myself. This setup really hasn't worked out."

"Have I done something, Barb?" She held her breath, fearing what she would hear. Was it her relationship with Jeff?

"You've done nothing. Really." She gave her a faint smile. "Once again, this isn't about you. It's about me."

Marsha felt the sting again.

Barb looked into her eyes, her expression more direct than Marsha had experienced in the past months. "No matter how I try to get rid of the feeling, I think of myself as the poor spinster sister needing a place to live. I think that's why my attitude has been so bad lately. I know you don't think that way, but I do. I need to have my own life and my own things. I made a mistake moving in, and I'm sorry I messed things up for you."

"You never messed up anything. I messed with your life, trying to mold you into someone I thought you should be. You set me straight on that, and I'm the one who made a mess."

"I appreciate that, Marsha, really. I love you. It's nothing to do with loving you."

While her heart tugged with emotion, Marsha rose and opened her arms to Barb. "I love you, too."

Barb stepped into her embrace. "I know you do, but I really want to go.

"I can't stop you, but I'll miss you."

Barb grasped Marsha's shoulders with a telling smile. "I don't think so. You're having a good time, and that's important to me." She released her and strode to the kitchen.

"Thanks, and it's been extra fun having you join us for the outings."

"So we're both happy then."

Happy? Was she?

Barb opened the refrigerator and pulled out an orange pop. "Want one?"

"How about some of that lemonade."

Barb poured a glass, then carried it to Marsha.

She took the drink from her sister, still feeling unsettled. "Are you sure you're not upset about Jeff?"

"Jeff? How many times do I have to tell you? It's me, Marsha. I watched you and Jeff earlier today, and I haven't seen you this happy in a long time. Maybe I'm wrong about your relationship."

"I feel as if it's meant to be, Barb. I'm so content with Jeff. I worried about his faith, and the Lord took care of that."

"And I think the Lord's taking care of you, too. Forget what I said earlier. After seeing you together this afternoon, I've had second thoughts. Who am I to know anything about love?"

"Barb, you love—"

"Romantic love."

Marsha didn't know how to respond.

"Let's not be so serious. God's in charge—not you or me."

Tension fell from Marsha's shoulders, and she chuckled. For once, it wasn't only her trying to be in charge.

Barb shifted to the sliding door and looked outside. "Storm clouds."

Marsha rose and stood behind her, eyeing the dark cumulus clouds that hovered over the lake. Barb's decision hung over her as dreary as the heavy sky. Though her sister denied anything being wrong, Marsha sensed something more going on, something that charged through her as unpleasant as a lightning bolt.

"This is a rotten day for you to leave," Jeff said as Al packed his gear.

"I'd rather get back today and have Sunday to get ready for work. Anyway, Lindsey's mother expects her back today. They're having some kind of a family party on Sunday."

"And Barb's leaving, too." He searched Al's face, hoping to make sense out of it. "I'm surprised."

Al shrugged. "She said she'd rather get home."

Jeff worried what it meant. Was she upset about Marsha and him? Could that be it?

A sharp crack and boom of thunder shook the house, and Jeff ducked at the ear-splitting noise. "You're going on the car ferry in this weather?"

"I put it in God's hands, Jeff." He squeezed Jeff's shoulder. "I think you should do the same." He strode to the doorway. "Lindsey, are you ready?"

She yelled something back, and Al returned to his suitcase. "It's been a great time. Really."

Jeff stood there, unresponsive, trying to make sense out of Al's comment. "What do you mean I should do the same?"

Al chuckled and snapped the locks on his weekender. "This friendship thing needs to be shifted into gear. Don't dally, Jeff. That's a good-looking woman you're patty-caking with. It's so obvious how you feel about her." He slapped his shoulder. "Forget the guilt. You're both single and, if you've found someone that lights up your eyes like she does, then go for it. Put the worries you have in God's hands."

Jeff drew in a breath. "I'm trying to do that."

"Don't try, pal. Do it." He tugged his case from the bed and swung it toward the doorway. "Now, if I can get Lindsey packed, we'll be on our way."

Jeff followed him to the doorway with concern instead of feeling he'd been given a pep talk. If Al had seen Jeff's feelings so clearly, then Barb had, too, and that had to be the problem. Barb felt hurt or angry at Marsha's hiding their romance. Now how would Marsha handle that? His shoulders weighted with his irritation. They should have been open from the beginning.

Looking up from his thoughts, Jeff saw Lindsey standing in the hallway with her case beside her, chomping on gum, stretching it out of her mouth, then rolling it back in. She had planted her bored expression on her face, and Jeff prayed that Bonnie wouldn't go through that stage, but he'd seen it happening already.

Bonnie had stormed into her room after breakfast and refused to come out. He'd found her lying on her bed with her sketchbook, looking at her drawings that had gone by the wayside while Lindsey had been here.

"I'm glad they're leaving," she'd said, then rolled over and faced the wall.

Jeff saw no point in fighting a battle, and Lindsey didn't seem to care. He'd left her in her room and had visited with Al awhile until he'd made the move to leave.

"Do you want to say goodbye?" Jeff asked, peeking into Bonnie's room. She gave him a look but pulled herself off the bed and came to the doorway.

"Bye."

"Bye, Bonnie," Al said, giving her a smile.

Lindsey grunted a goodbye and headed out the door. The rain pelted her before Jeff could suggest an umbrella.

"No problem," Al said. "Thanks for the great week." He swung the suitcase over his head as if it were an umbrella and darted for his car.

In moments, they were backing out, the headlights picking up the slashes of heavy rain falling in large puddles on the hard ground.

Jeff watched them go, then returned to the living room. The quiet house seemed too silent. He longed to head for Marsha's, but she'd said the place needed to be cleaned, and she needed time to do that. More time. Why did women always want time for everything but what the man wanted?

Lowering his head, Jeff faced the truth. The statement was unfair. That wasn't the case at all and, even thinking it, made him sound like a stubborn kid, pouting because he didn't have his own way. Marsha needed to do her chores and she probably needed time to deal with Barb's leaving. He assumed she would be upset.

He walked to the front door and looked outside. "I don't see a letup. The sky's as dark as pitch," he said aloud to himself.

Jeff settled on the sofa, thinking about Al heading home in the bad weather. He prayed Barb's leaving didn't add any more strain on his own relationship with Marsha. Even with her playfulness yesterday on Mount Pisgah, she'd seemed troubled. He'd tossed the possible reasons why around until he'd finally given up. He'd never understand women. They worried about things he couldn't grasp. He had faith Marsha would realize how he and Bonnie felt about her. Then hopefully her doubts would vanish. He longed for a lifelong commitment. He could only pray that she would eventually want the same.

Another crack of lightning split the sky, and he expected Bonnie to come darting out, but she didn't. He suspected she'd fallen asleep.

He lifted his legs and stretched them the length of the sofa, then plumped the pillow and slid down, his hands resting over his head. Closing his eyes, his mind meandered from one thought to the next—Al's comments, Barb's departure, Marsha's stress, Marsha's everything. She filled his thoughts, always.

A prayer came to his mind and, as he sent it heavenward, a calm spread over him. Somehow, things would work out. He felt hope rise in his heart and relaxed against the soft pillow beneath his head.

He and Marsha...

Chapter Seventeen

Marsha watched the lightning streak the sky and couldn't help but worry about Barb and Al taking the ferry during a storm. She only hoped they'd made it across before the worst of it.

To help her ignore the storm, she cleaned the cottage and did laundry. She thought about the past weeks, about everything—Barb, Bonnie and Jeff. The last conversation she'd had with Barb had eased her mind. Barb had spoken the truth. Marsha asked herself where her faith had been. She needed to trust God. Even Jeff had said he sensed the Lord had brought them together.

Bonnie. Marsha's mind tangled with so many aspects of the child. In the short time they'd been on the island, Marsha had watched Bonnie mature. Had it been her woman's touch or just a coincidence? She didn't know, but it didn't matter. Bonnie had become a preteen, and, though she still had her disability, Marsha had faith that she could live with it. Maybe even have a productive life one day.

And Bonnie's talent. What a surprise and delight. Watching Bonnie sketch and paint for an hour or more with no anger but only pride for what she'd done, filled Marsha with more pleasure than she could have imagined.

Then Jeff. His image rose in her mind like the morning sun—bright and promising. Some people were depressed on a gloomy day. They needed the sun to energize them. Jeff had provided that for her. She worried and fretted over what it meant. Was her relationship with him based on her need as a caregiver? Was it due to an aunt's concern for her niece? Was it self-serving? Marsha shook her head.

No matter what she feared, she felt confident her feelings for Jeff were as real and huge as Lake Michigan, which dashed against the shore morning and night.

She settled onto the sofa, wishing she were with Jeff right now, but she had no desire to go out in the rain.

A crack of lightning split the sky; the sliding door rattled and the lights dimmed, then came back on again. Marsha sat nailed to the cushion fearing the worst.

Another zap zigzagged across the sky and, this time, the lights dimmed and died.

Marsha blinked into the darkness. So much for good planning. She tried to get her bearings, then rose and whacked her leg against the counter stool. She stepped away, hoping to maneuver her way around the breakfast bar and get to the kitchen.

When another flash of lightning brightened the room, she got her bearings, then edged her way forward, hoping she could find a flashlight. Foolish that she hadn't thought of it earlier with the storm carrying on like the Fourth of

July's fireworks. She felt her way around the counter and put her hand on a drawer.

She jerked it open and felt inside for the flashlight. None there. She had one in the car, but she hated to go out in the pelting rain, and she knew she had one inside. Somewhere.

As she tugged open another drawer, it tipped downward and half the utensils fell to the ground before she could catch them. She slipped the drawer onto the counter and felt inside.

Her heart lifted. Flashlight.

Marsha grasped it and pushed the On button. A dim circle of light shone on the counter. She searched in the drawer with the dying illumination and spotted batteries.

Standing in the dimness with the dying flashlight in one hand and the batteries in the other, Marsha questioned her sanity. Why was she here alone while Jeff's image filled her mind?

"Do I want to spend the rest of the evening in the dark?"

Lightning zagged across the sky again as she answered her question. Absolutely not.

She tucked the flashlight under her arm, pointed the light at the telephone, then grasped the receiver and punched in Jeff's phone number with her other hand.

When she heard his voice, her heart lifted. "Do you have electricity?"

"Electricity? Sure. What's up?"

Relief washed over her. "My lights are out here. Can I come over?"

"You don't have to ask. Are you hungry?"

With all the confusion, she'd forgotten to eat. "I am."

"I have lots of food. I'll warm it up. Now get over here, but be careful."

She hung up, and her smile reached all the way to her heart.

"Who was that?"

Jeff lowered the phone receiver and headed for the refrigerator. "Aunt Marsha. Her power's out."

"What?"

"She has no electricity."

"Is she coming here?"

"Yes. She's on her way."

"Okay," Bonnie said.

Jeff expected her to bounce from the bedroom, but she didn't. He turned back to the refrigerator and kicked himself into gear. Praising the Lord that his lights weren't out—not yet, anyway—he set the sloppy joes on the stove, turned on the burner, then pulled a package of buns from the cabinet. He sure had nothing fancy. He grabbed down a bag of chips and another of cookies. Forget gourmet when he prepared a meal.

When another lightning bolt ripped across the sky, Jeff went into the pantry cupboard and pulled out some candles. Marilou had always kept them on hand since power failure happened when people least expected it. He put the tapers into holders and set them on the counter with a book of matches, then found his flashlight and set that where he could find it.

The scent of beef and spicy sauce filled the air, and Jeff turned down the burner. He set a couple of plates with silverware on the table, listening for the sound of Marsha's car. He'd eaten earlier, but what man couldn't enjoy a snack?

Thunder rolled overhead, and, when Marsha spoke, he jumped.

"It smells great in here."

His heart zinged just hearing her voice. "I didn't hear you with all that clatter outside."

"I didn't knock." She slipped off her jacket. "What smells so good?"

"Sloppy joes," he said, feeling like the Cheshire Cat with his inane grin. "Not gourmet, but filling." He patted the chair.

She sank into it. "Where's Bonnie?"

"She's been sleeping most of the day."

"Really?" she said, dishing the meat mixture onto the bun.

Jeff set a bowl of chips on the table, then made himself a sandwich and joined her. Before he took a bite, Bonnie ambled into the room, her face creased from sleep.

"Hungry, Bon?"

Marsha's face filled with concern. "Aren't you feeling well?"

Bonnie shook her head. "My stomach feels funny."

Marsha rose. "Can I do anything for you?"

"No." She turned and headed back to her room.

Marsha crossed the kitchen and followed her into the bedroom.

Jeff waited, hearing their voices from down the hall. He rose and filled another bun with the meat. As he sat, Marsha's footsteps drew nearer. When she eyed his plate, he nodded. "Okay, I admit it. I'm eating another sandwich."

She grinned, then looked thoughtful. "Do you think she's upset because Al and Lindsey went home?" She sat again, nibbling on some chips while she watched him eat.

Jeff shook his head. "That's not it."

"Are you sure? Lindsey finally softened up a little."

"Bonnie told me today she'd be glad when Lindsey was gone."

Marsha chuckled. "Lindsey did have her moments, didn't she? Still, I almost felt sorry for Al. It's hard being a part-time parent."

"I can't even imagine." When he felt resentment sometimes, he needed to recall this moment. What would it be like to have his child only every other weekend? How difficult would that be?

Marsha didn't say anything to break his thoughts and, when he focused on her, she rose and began putting away the leftovers. "Thanks for the dinner."

He stood and pushed the chair back, hearing it scrape against the floor. He moved behind her at the counter and laid his hand on her arm. "Listen."

Marsha stood a moment as if listening, then turned to face him. "Listen to what?"

"To nothing. We're really alone."

She swung her arm toward the hallway. "What about Bonnie?"

"She's probably asleep, already. She's been like this all day. I had to force her to say goodbye to Al and Lindsey. She's been moody for the past week—off and on. Today it's on."

"I'm sorry. She's been doing so well, too."

A flash lit the sky, and Jeff glanced at the counter. "I'm prepared."

Marsha smiled. "Don was a Boy Scout. Were you?"

"Aren't all little boys?"

While she chuckled, he linked his arm in hers and pulled her closer. "Let's sit." He motioned toward the living room.

He guided her to the sofa and patted the cushion, then sat beside her.

"Do you think Bonnie's okay?" she asked.

"It's either a summer cold or too much excitement. It's hard to tell."

"And don't forget, girls do get to an age when they become moody."

He saw her searching his eyes and knew what she was going to ask.

She lowered her gaze. "I'm sorry, Jeff, but I'm concerned about Bonnie. You've seen her mature even in these past weeks, and you know what happened on the Fourth of July. It's not just her behavior—she's about to—"

"I will, Marsha. I will. I promise."

She rose and wandered to the glass door as the lightning flashed an amazing display in the distance across the dark water. "I know it's not easy," she said, gazing into the night. "It would be easier for me, but I'm not her mother…" She turned and faced him. "It's best if you talk to her about things like that."

Jeff felt his shoulders knot. "I said I will."

Marsha gave a tiny shrug and silenced.

He hated to be short with her, but Marsha had no idea how many times he'd tried to broach the subject. How could he explain to his daughter about being a woman, about the changes in her body and what it meant? He wished Marilou were alive to do it, or even his mother. He had no one on earth to count on…except the Lord, and he figured the Lord wasn't going to take over that job, either.

The silence unsettled him, and he knew he had to change the subject. He had so much to say.

He searched Marsha's shadowy face, her eyes questioning, and, for a moment, he took the easier topic, the one that made him curious. "What happened with Barb? Why did she leave?"

She exhaled a lengthy breath and plopped beside him. "She said she'd be more comfortable at home. I thought she was finally enjoying herself."

"Me, too." He traced his thoughts, trying to think of what had happened to make her decide to leave. "I hope you're not upset."

"Just curious, really."

He could see hurt, or maybe confusion, in her eyes.

"Barb told me she wants to find an apartment. She's not happy living with me."

Jeff's chest pushed against his heat. "That must hurt a little, but it does solve one of your concerns." Though he should be sympathetic for Marsha's situation, knowing that Barb had made the decision to move seemed a problem solved.

"It does, but I didn't want to bring it up today and cause hard feelings."

He rested his hand on hers, feeling the softness, then lifted it and kissed her knuckles, then her palm. "I hope you told her about us, at least. It was the perfect time."

"Barb mentioned how close you and I have become a couple of days ago, but I didn't feel ready to say anything, not after what she'd just said. I hinted, but— Maybe she knows and she's afraid of what will happen to her if…"

He drew her other hand into his and decided to speak his mind. "I know you're sensitive to Barb's situation, but I am disappointed. I really hoped you'd just be open and tell her the truth."

Marsha's eyes searched his. "I'm disappointed in myself, Jeff."

Before he could say anything, Bonnie tromped down the hallway, and he heard the bathroom door give a bang.

"Daddy!"

Bonnie's frantic cry caused them both to jump. He rushed to the bathroom door, grasped the knob, then stopped himself. "What's wrong?"

"Blood."

Blood? "Where?"

Her answer nailed him to the floor. Why hadn't he listened to Marsha? He clung to the doorknob, not knowing which way to turn. Time had run out. He wanted to kick himself.

Blood? Marsha waited while Jeff went to Bonnie as her frustration and compassion fought for first place. She'd told him over and over to explain things to Bonnie.

In minutes, Jeff came through the doorway and gave Marsha a helpless look.

"What do you want me to do?"

"Help me." He looked as if he'd been accused of a crime. Guilt spilled from his eyes, and Marsha hugged him instead of saying I told you so. How could she be angry? She didn't mind helping, but it would have been so much better if he'd done it before the fact, before Bonnie was frightened over something so natural and so much a part of a woman's life.

"Okay, but you're not escaping this fully. She'll need to talk with you, too, later."

He nodded.

"Is she in the bathroom?"

"Her bedroom now. I told her you'd be in to talk to her. I—I'm sorry. I—"

She pressed her finger over his lips. "Do you have anything in the house? She'll need pads."

He looked frantic. "I haven't cleaned out the linen closet. Maybe you'll find something there."

Marsha backed away and headed into the bathroom, recalling her first experience. Her mother had explained things to her when she was eleven, probably because she, too, had begun to blossom into a woman. Yet even knowing, she'd nearly fainted when she saw the evidence of her first menstrual experience.

Bonnie's recent moodiness settled into Marsha's mind. Though her tantrums had diminished, she'd shifted into mood swings. Why hadn't Marsha realized?

She pulled open the linen-closet door, shifting things around, hoping she'd find what she needed. Her stomach twisted for Bonnie. Now Bonnie truly had to understand what this meant and the danger she could be in, the fears that Barb had expressed so much. Jeff couldn't baby Bonnie, anymore. She needed to learn to be an adult and monitor her behavior around boys.

When Marsha moved some tissue in the back corner of the lower shelf, she relaxed. She found the package she needed, drew out a pad and placed it on the sink counter.

She needed to approach Bonnie with a quiet understanding, the kind of understanding that God gave his children when they gathered together. The experience bound people, united them in a common fellowship and, now that Bonnie had become a woman, she, too, was bound in the fellowship of womanhood. The beauty of it all covered her negative thoughts.

When she returned to the hallway, Jeff stood nearby, waiting. The silence surprised her, and she realized the storm had faded. "I'll explain what this means and how to use the pad, Jeff, but you need to be in on the rest. You need to talk with her about what it means to become mature and the dangers."

He agreed and strode to Bonnie's door. He tapped and spoke through the wooden barricade. "Bon, Aunt Marsha's here. Can she come in?"

Bonnie's voice was so soft Marsha couldn't hear her response.

He motioned to Marsha and pushed open the door.

Marsha stepped inside alone and sat on the edge of Bonnie's bed. "You want to talk, first?"

She shrugged. "Daddy said it means I'm a woman."

"Pretty close. It's something God gave us so we could have babies when we're old enough to get married, but not before."

"I'm too young to get married."

"You sure are, but He's preparing you to be a woman."

She held Bonnie in her arms and explained how to care for herself. When she'd finished, she sent Bonnie to the bathroom to take a shower.

Jeff hovered by the doorway, his face wrought with anxiety. "Thank you." He drew Marsha into his arms. "I didn't know what to do. I told you I feel so inadequate about things like this. My mother never talked with me. I learned everything from Don."

"I bet he was a good teacher."

Jeff grinned. "Actually, he was. He believed in morality and saving himself for marriage. I've always followed his lead."

"I wouldn't have thought anything else of you. You're a good man and so was Don. He would have made a good father just like you."

Jeff held her more tightly. "You're a good mom."

Gooseflesh rose on Marsha's arms, hearing the words. *Mom.* She'd never longed for motherhood, but she loved her connection with Bonnie, and she hoped Jeff was right.

She might never be a mother now, but she could certainly mother Bonnie.

"You mean everything to me," Jeff whispered in her ear.

Her pulse jumped and her mouth opened to tell him the same, but the bathroom door opened and Bonnie came out, ready for bed, looking shy and uneasy. She headed back to her room, then stopped in the doorway and looked at them.

The moment had passed. Marsha decided to save her declaration for tomorrow. No matter what else, she knew in her heart she loved Jeff.

"It's your turn," Marsha said, gesturing to the bedroom door. "The storm's passed, and I'm going home. Hopefully, the lights will be on in the morning."

"You can stay here."

Marsha shook her head. "I'll borrow your flashlight, if you don't mind, and I'll talk with you tomorrow.

He stepped toward her, but she held up her hand. This is the time for you and Bonnie. I'll see you tomorrow."

He didn't move for a moment, then closed the distance between them and kissed her gently. "I don't know what to say."

"Say good night." She gave him a quick kiss, then grabbed her coat and motioned to Bonnie's doorway. "She needs her dad."

She opened the door and stepped into the dark night without waiting for his reply.

Chapter Eighteen

Sunlight peeked through the bottom of Marsha's shade, and she covered her eyes. The storm had ended just as she prayed her personal storm would end soon. She'd made a decision last night while she'd lain in bed, thinking of Jeff and all they'd been through. How could she doubt what God had in mind for her?

She knew exactly when she'd fallen in love. His first kiss had been so brief and so unexpected it had frightened her. But that was the day she knew that Jeff was more than a friend. She'd tried to pretend otherwise, but her heart knew the truth.

Recently, she'd given God thanks so often for all He'd done for her—for the relationship she'd found with Jeff, for his new-found faith, for the love she felt for Bonnie, for opening doors between her and Barb, for the myriad blessings He'd poured over her. Now she had to act on those blessings and make things right. Sorrow rolled over her, thinking how she'd doubted, how she'd ignored God's leading.

Marsha adjusted her head to miss most of the sunshine that stretched along her pillow. She thought about her plan. She hoped Jeff wouldn't be disappointed when she told him.

As she tossed back the blankets, she shifted her feet to the edge of the bed, then slipped to the floor. She needed to get moving and call Jeff. She hoped Bonnie felt better this morning.

Marsha plodded into the kitchen and started the coffee, then dialed his phone number and her heart tripped when she heard his voice.

"How'd it go?"

"I told her how proud I was of her handling becoming a young woman and how much she's matured in her behavior."

"That's good, Jeff. That's what she needs to hear. All those positive things."

"Oh, yes, and I told her how talented she was and how happy that made me."

"I prayed about it last night, too. I hope both of us look at Bonnie with new eyes. You've made a great start with her."

"Thanks. It's taken me a while, but with your prodding, I finally did a few things right. I know last night I nearly botched things up, but you came to my rescue. Again."

"That's what I like to do. I'm a rescuer."

"You've rescued me, Marsha, and you've given me so much more. I wanted to talk about some things last night. You asked me about the truth and you startled me, but, with Bonnie, we didn't have a chance—

"We will today. I'm going to church this morning, and then we can talk about it. I have some thoughts, too."

"Should I be worried?"

"I hope not."

She heard a release of breath. "I'll check with Bonnie

and see if she wants to go to church this morning. She's still in bed."

"I'll drop by in a little while," she said, feeling as if things were finally falling into place.

"Bonnie." Jeff rapped at her bedroom door. "Are you awake?"

"Uh-huh."

"Can I come in?"

"Okay."

He turned the knob and stood in the doorway. "Do you want to go to church?"

She stretched her arms out from her sides and yawned. "Sunday school."

"Okay. Sunday school."

She nodded.

"Then, you'd better get up. I'll make breakfast."

He stepped into the hallway and closed her door. He still reeled when it struck him that his little Bonnie was starting to grow up. The change had happened before his eyes and it had taken his awareness too long to catch up.

Breakfast took only a minute to prepare. He made coffee, pulled down cereal boxes and bowls, and, by the time the coffee was ready, Bonnie had come into the kitchen, dressed in pants and a cute top.

He handed her a bowl and let her choose her cereal, and they sat together, eating while his mind struggled with what he wanted to say to her.

"You like Marsha, don't you?" he asked, knowing it was a rudimentary question but a way to begin.

Bonnie lifted her head, a piece of cereal clinging to her

lip and studied him. She lifted the napkin and wiped off the food before speaking. "I love Aunt Marsha."

"I thought you did."

"Do you love her?"

He caught his breath. "I do."

"Is she your girlfriend?" Excitement rose to her face. "Like in the movies?"

"I guess you could say that." He hid his grin.

"Will you get married?"

"That's a good possibility."

"Hooray!" she said. "Then, Aunt Marsha would be my new mom."

"She would be your stepmom. Would you like that?"

Bonnie nodded. "I miss Mom."

He couldn't respond for a moment. "I miss her, too, Bonnie."

She patted her dad's hand. "It's okay, Daddy. She's with Jesus."

"I'm sure she is." His heart melted hearing his daughter's words and filled with joy at her acceptance.

They quieted again, finishing breakfast until the back door opened and he heard Marsha's voice.

"Everyone up?" she called.

"In the kitchen." He focused on the doorway, waiting for her to appear.

She stopped and looked at him with questioning eyes.

"We're great," he said, assuring her that Bonnie seemed perfectly normal.

Marsha moved to Bonnie's side and bent over to kiss her cheek. "How are you feeling this morning?"

"Better." She gave Marsha a shy smile.

"You look good. You have rosy cheeks today."

"So do you."

Marsha chuckled. "I cheated though. Mine are from a compact."

Bonnie gave her a quizzical look, then grinned. "You're daddy's girlfriend."

Jeff wanted to sink below his chair. "Bonnie, that talk was between you and me."

"You, me and Aunt Marsha. She's supposed to know, too."

Jeff chuckled at Marsha's fiery blush. "You didn't need that compact this morning."

"I wasn't expecting to be greeted with this kind of information." Her eyes searched his. "Should I know anything else?"

"After church. Can you wait?"

"She can wait," Bonnie said. "It's time for Sunday school." She rose, set her dish in the sink and grinned. "Ready?"

Jeff wagged his head, amazed. "I think we are." The words held far more meaning than Bonnie could guess, but he hoped Marsha was as ready as he'd become.

As they headed to church, Marsha sorted through the things she wanted to talk about with Jeff. First, she was most curious about the girlfriend comment. What had he said to Bonnie? The thought made her grin.

Finding the Lord had been the greatest gift for Marsha. She wanted Jeff to know how much it meant that he'd begun to worship with her. He'd made the first big step and, each day, she noticed a difference in his faith. He prayed at meals and talked about blessings instead of luck. Daily, she praised God for the wonder.

During the service, Marsha's spirit lifted. Her closeness

to Jeff seemed right as they sat side by side, listening to God's Word.

When the pastor read the Old Testament scripture, she sat captivated by the thought. *He tends his flock like a shepherd: He gathers the lambs in his arms and carries them close to His heart; He gently leads those that have young.*

Weren't they all like young lambs, needing the shepherd to lead them as they lost their way? Jesus gathered them in His arms close to His heart.

She thought of Jesus' love and how the Lord had guided Jeff back to Him. She'd found comfort in the Lord's arms and in Jeff's strong arms. He'd held her when she'd struggled with issues and he'd cuddled her to him when her heart had overflowed with joy.

The final hymn rang to the rafters and, when the service ended, they headed toward the Sunday school to find Bonnie. She came to greet them with a new project, a cross made from Popsicle sticks that she'd painted and decorated with a flower.

Marsha held the cross while Bonnie beamed. "This is really lovely, Bon. I missed seeing your pictures. You were too busy when the company was here."

She said thank you, then skipped off to show the project to one of the Sunday-school teachers.

While they waited, Marsha couldn't resist asking about Bonnie's girlfriend comment.

Jeff grinned and told her what had happened.

Marsha felt amazed at what he told her. Last night, she'd gone home with his sweet words ringing in her ears. But marriage? He'd never mentioned marriage, but then it hadn't been Jeff but Bonnie who'd brought it up.

"I realize we haven't discussed all of this," Jeff said, wrapping his arm around her shoulder, "but I think it's time."

"We do have lots to talk about. For one, I made a decision last night, and I hope you won't be disappointed."

A scowl settled on his face. "What kind of decision?"

Marsha cleared her throat. "I think I'll go back home today."

Jeff's eyes widened. "Home? Why?"

"Barb. I need to talk with her, and I don't want to do it on the phone. I want to be open with her about us."

His scowl shifted to acceptance. "I'm happy to hear you say that, but stay today. Let's do something together. I know we'll have Bonnie with us, but it's the first day I've felt we're a *we* instead of a *you* and a *me.*"

The words thrilled her. "Okay, but I'll leave tomorrow. It'll probably take me that long to get ready, anyway."

His eyes brightened, and he slipped her hand into his and kissed her fingers. His gentle touch rushed through her with the same sweet tenderness as his kisses.

How could she ever say no?

Jeff listened to Bonnie shuffling in the bedroom, getting ready for bed. The evening had been long. He'd taken Bonnie and Marsha to the Stoney Acre Grill for dinner, and then they'd brought pie home for dessert and sat outside to watch the sunset. The hues had spread over the water like watercolors on a wet canvas, so special he thanked God for the precious moment with the two women he loved.

Jeff sat up, remembering that Marsha would leave in the morning. He wished she'd wait, but he understood. He was pleased she wanted to talk with Barb, and he'd suggested to Bonnie they could go home early, too, but she'd been disappointed so he'd dropped the subject. They'd be leaving at the end of the week, anyway.

He patted his belly, feeling full both in body and in spirit. A long time had passed since he'd felt so complete and so ready to move on. His mind stretched back to early June when he'd run into Marsha at Daddy Frank's. He could only shake his head, amazed at how the Lord guided people into the course He'd planned for them.

When Bonnie finally went to sleep, Jeff and Marsha walked outside and looked at the amazing sky.

"When I look at the millions of stars, I can't imagine how anyone can deny God," Marsha said. "They've hung in the same path forever. To create such a perfect system couldn't be a coincidence. Creation takes a mind much greater than any living being."

Jeff stepped behind her and wrapped his arms around her. "I think back and ask myself how I could have tried to deny the Lord when I knew in my heart He was there."

She nestled closer, thrilled to hear him speak with such sincerity. "We all make mistakes, Jeff. Look at how I've bungled things every step of the way with my worries and need to control."

"But you've changed, and so have I. I recall so many things I did wrong these past years. I wanted to prove to the world that I could be father and mother to Bonnie. Maybe it was to spite the Lord, I don't know. It was ridiculous. I made myself so unhappy and so resentful, and I did such a disservice to Bonnie."

"Jeff, don't say those things about—"

"No, let me say them. I was thinking last night how my attitude also messed up our relationship. You love God with your whole heart and mind, and there I was stomping around trying to be God to myself."

"But it worked out, Jeff. It's over."

"It is, and I'm so grateful. Again, I thank you for your patience, but mostly I thank God for His."

She snuggled closer to his side. "I'm sure we all try the Lord's patience too many times, but He always forgives us." She paused, thinking of her own confession. "I have something to tell you."

Beneath his furrowed brow, his questioning eyes pierced hers.

"I've been jealous."

"Jealous?" His brow lifted. "Of what?"

"Al. The way you two talked so comfortably, and I realized I created such stress between us with my worries."

Jeff brushed his cheek against her hair. "I would never let that stop me from cherishing you. We all have feelings we wish we could erase." He looked away. "The thing I need to admit just kills me."

He turned her body to face him and, in the dusky light from the living room, she saw his anguish. "I not only blamed God for Marilou's death, but also I was furious at Him for giving me a daughter with a disability. I resented Bonnie after Marilou died. I felt inadequate and totally lost. I'm ashamed of that."

Marsha rested her palms against his cheeks and looked into his pain-filled eyes. "It's been forgiven, Jeff. Despite your feelings at that time, you love Bonnie with all your heart. You couldn't have been a better father."

"Sure I could have, and I am now. I've let her meet Jesus. That's the best thing I've done besides fall in love with you."

In love with you. Emotion charged through her. Tears tripped over her lashes and washed down her cheeks as she gazed into his eyes. "And I've fallen in love with you, too. I can't believe it, but I have."

He brushed away her tears and found her mouth, waiting for him. He explored her lips, and she listened to his breathing. She felt him shudder as his arms drew her closer. He deepened the kiss, what she'd yearned for so long, and she yielded to it, giving and taking with the greatest sense of completeness she had ever known.

"I never thought I would say those words again, but I have." He kissed her eyes and the tip of her nose. "This is all real and true, not a dream."

"I love you," she whispered against his mouth.

He eased back, his eyes holding hers captive. "Marsha, I love you, and you love me. Bonnie loves us. God's brought us together. What could make us more confident? Marsha, say you'll marry me."

Her mind spun. She hadn't talked with Barb yet. His proposal happened so suddenly. What about her house? What about— She halted her silly questions. "Would you say that again? Just one more time."

His lips lingered so near hers she could feel his breath. "I love you. Will you marry me?"

"Yes." The word breathed on his lips. "Yes. Yes. Yes."

"Then, let's all go home. We have a lifetime to plan."

Marsha shifted in the chair. "So you're sure it's not my meddling?"

Barb leaned back and shook her head. "Once again, it's—"

"About you and not me." Marsha caved into the chair

cushion. Would she ever learn? "I'm sorry I asked you to move in, Barb. I didn't realize what it would do."

"It might have been wonderful, Marsha. Don't kick yourself. I'm the kind of person who just needs space right now. I went through a major change up north. Truly amazing. Talking with you opened doors I never thought would open. It's a relief, and I'll be forever grateful that spending time with you triggered my confession."

"You carried it alone too long."

Barb rubbed her neck. "I didn't even give it to the Lord. I clung to the shame as if it were a ball and chain."

"We all do that. I talk faith, but it's so easy to not act it. I pray every day that I learn to let go of things I can't change."

Thoughtful silence filled the room, and Marsha knew she still had things to say, wonderful things that hugged her thoughts.

"Ready for my surprise?"

Barb shifted her focus to her. "Why not?

"Jeff proposed." Marsha studied Barb's wavering expression as she told her about their talk.

Barb's eyes widened. "Proposed? You two worked fast after I left."

"He asked me to marry him, and I said yes."

"And this time you're positive?"

"As sure as I'm sitting here. I really think that God was at work in our lives."

Barb rose and embraced Marsha. "I'm happy for you. He's a wonderful man."

"I'm glad you like Jeff."

Barb stepped back. "And Bonnie. She's an interesting girl. In that month, I saw her change so much. I think it was your influence, Marsha."

"So does Jeff, but I think it was a lot of things. You were part of it." Marsha walked to the window and looked onto the paved street, so different from her gravel driveway on the island.

"When's the big day?"

"We haven't talked about that, but I think soon. It just feels right, and we're so much in love. We want to do everything right, and we're both so eager to be husband and wife."

Barb grinned. "You'd better make it real soon, then."

The telephone's ring cut the air.

"That's Jeff," Marsha said, heading for the phone. "He's supposed to be here by now. He called me and said he'd decided to come home, too."

She grasped the receiver and listened to the man's request. "It's for you, Barb." She held out the telephone, fighting her curiosity.

Barb grasped the receiver as if the phone always rang for her. "Sounds good. I'll be ready."

She hung up and faced Marsha. "That was Al."

"Al?" Marsha noticed the sparkle in Barb's eye. "Al?"

"He's taking me to dinner and a movie tonight."

"Really?"

Barb laughed. "You look shocked."

Marsha sank onto the nearest chair and shook her head. "You never date."

"No, I didn't, but talking to you showed me other pathways I never knew existed. I felt as if a weight lifted off my shoulders, as if I'd been washed clean and made new. An amazing feeling."

"I shouldn't be surprised," Marsha said, thinking back to the cottage. "You and Al hit it off right away."

"He's really kind. He said something about his past and his messed-up life, and I just blurted out mine. His compassion shocked me. I never expected it from anyone who didn't know me."

Marsha watched her sister's face beam. "I'm really happy. Thrilled, actually."

"It may go nowhere, but it's a start for me, with a Christian man I can trust."

A rap sounded on the door, and Jeff strode in with Bonnie and a huge bouquet of flowers.

Marsha's heart tripped.

"For you," he said, handing her the colorful blossoms.

"I love fresh flowers."

"I know." He tweaked her cheek.

"How do you know? You've never given me flowers before."

He grinned. "You told me once."

"When?" Her mind shot back to the summer, and she didn't recall flowers ever entering their conversation.

"The day you pinned a lily in Bonnie's hair."

Marsha gaped at him as she hugged the bouquet. "You're kidding. You remember that? It was so long ago."

"A wise man never forgets the important things a woman tells him."

She laughed as she crossed the room. "Let me get these into some water."

Marsha hurried from the room, grabbed a vase from the cabinet and filled it with water. She unwrapped the florist paper and quickly arranged the lovely bouquet in the vase.

When she returned, she set the vase on a table by the window, hearing Jeff talk about their trip home. When she neared him, he looked at her with expectancy in his eyes.

"The flowers are beautiful." She motioned to the arrangement.

He looked at the flowers, then to her, then Barb. "She told you already."

Seeing his disappointment, Marsha hurried forward. "I couldn't wait. I didn't know when you'd get here."

Barb rose and opened her arms. "Congratulations, Jeff. I'm happy for both of you."

"What about me?" Bonnie said, putting her hand on her hip.

"I'm happy for you, too," Barb said. "Give me a hug." She opened her arms and Bonnie ran into her embrace.

"You know the best part. I'll be your aunt Barb when your dad and Aunt Marsha get married."

"You can be my auntie Barb, and Aunt Marsha will be my new mom."

Marsha's heart skipped. "I will, and that's one of the best parts of getting married."

Jeff slipped to her side. "So, does Barb like the idea?"

"You mean, about your getting married? Yes, I do," Barb said.

Jeff chuckled. "I didn't mean—"

Marsha shook her head. "I haven't told her that yet."

"Told me what?"

He slipped his arm around Marsha's waist. "Since we're getting married, we hoped you'd stay here. You can either rent or buy—or rent with option to buy. Whatever works for you."

"You mean, I won't have to look for an apartment?" A smile lit her face.

Marsha nodded. "I'd love you to live here, Barb. I'll still be here for a while, but that old image you had of yourself doesn't mean anything now."

Jeff gave her a perplexed look. "What image?"

Barb removed her arms from Bonnie, shifted behind her and rested her hands on the girl's shoulders. "That I'm her poor spinster sister." She eyed Marsha. "One date doesn't change that, you know."

Jeff's eyebrows raised. "Date?"

Marsha gave him poke. "Al."

"Al. Well, I'll be. Good for you, Barb." He strode to her side and gave her a big hug.

When he released her, he strode to Marsha's side. "And, while we're all together, let's take care of one final bit of business."

Marsha watched a sly look grow on his face. "What kind of business?"

"This kind." He reached into his pocket and pulled out a small wrapped package.

She gazed at it, and he extended his arm. "It's for you." He closed the distance between them and placed the gift into her hand. "Open it."

Marsha's heart thundered as she accepted the present. "Is it—"

"It's a ring," Bonnie said. "It's a diamond. Open it."

"So much for surprises," Marsha said, unable to hold back her laugh, and she didn't have to. Everyone laughed with her.

Bonnie laughed, too, although Marsha guessed she had no idea why.

"Aren't you going to open it?" Bonnie asked.

Marsha gave her a tender smile and pulled the paper from the package, to reveal a white stain box. With her heart pounding, she lifted the lid. The ring took her breath away.

"It's beautiful, Jeff. Absolutely gorgeous."

He stepped beside her and lifted the ring from the velvet lining, then slipped it on her finger. The large diamond flashed fire in the morning light.

"I hope you like it," Jeff said.

"I love it," she said, gazing at the stone with tears in her eyes, "but not as much as I love you."

"Kiss her, Daddy," Bonnie said, pushing him closer to Marsha. "I see them do that on TV commercials."

Jeff grinned and pressed his lips against hers, so sweet and gentle she felt her heart soar.

"Now, me," Bonnie said.

Marsha and Jeff hurried to her side and opened their arms in one giant bear hug.

Jeff leaned into Marsha's ear. "This has made all my dreams come true."

Chapter Nineteen

July 4, one year later

"Look at that sunset." Marsha drew in a lengthy breath as she watched the colors spread across the silvery water. "I can't believe a whole year has passed and here we are again." She glanced down at her diamond, sparkling in the setting sun. They'd gotten married and rented her house to Barb. Everything had fallen into place.

"It's like time hasn't changed a thing."

Jeff drew her closer. "It's not the same."

She frowned and looked at him. "Why not?"

"Because this time you're my wife."

She shook her head. "You'd think I'd be ready for your silly comments, but you got me."

"I sure do," he said, brushing his lips across the tip of her nose, then to her mouth.

Marsha savored the kiss, knowing each gentle touch and the feel of his lips on hers. They never disappointed her.

He drew back and eyed his watch. "We should probably get down to the marina. The fireworks will start soon."

"Fireworks," Bonnie said, appearing at the doorway. "Let's go."

Marsha smiled to herself as they scampered to the car, dragging their chairs and a blanket. She wondered if she would ever grow up when it came to fireworks.

Finding a space to watch the event proved more difficult this year, having come much later. They'd missed the parades and carnival to stay at the house and enjoy the beach and the beautiful day.

Marsha didn't miss her little A-frame. Al loved it and had decided to buy it. Marsha hoped that, one day, he and Barb might set a date. He'd opened doors for Barb, and she seemed like a new woman; not new, really, but like the sister she'd known once so very long ago.

"Here's a place," Bonnie called, motioning to them.

Marsha cringed when she realized what Bonnie had done.

"I'm sorry," Marsha said to the couple who were shifting their chairs and blanket over farther on the lawn.

"No problem," the man said. "She asked us to move very politely."

Jeff tried to cover his grin. "I'll talk to her later," he whispered, then thanked the man and his family who'd made room for their chairs.

They unfolded their chairs, then Jeff helped Bonnie spread out the blanket. Tonight they'd only carried a small cooler with drinks and a bag of chips.

"It won't be long now," Jeff said, popping the top on a can. "Who wants one?"

Marsha let Bonnie take the first, and she took the next. Life had become as sweet as the drink she sipped. She couldn't deny there were moments of stress. Bonnie wasn't perfect, like today when she'd apparently asked the people to move over, but she'd changed.

The first sizzle burst into the sky followed by a boom. The night lit up with a starburst of color blossoming outward and dying into embers. The next bang lit the sky.

Marsha looked at Jeff. He'd changed, too, in a wonderful way. He'd finally been able to love her the way he'd wanted. He hadn't disappointed her. The gorgeous fireworks didn't hold a candle to the love she shared with Jeff.

He'd often told her she'd appeared in his dreams, but today, they needed no more dreams. God had blessed them with an amazing reality, a life together with His blessing.

* * * * *

*Don't miss Gail Gaymer Martin's
next Love Inspired romance,
FAMILY IN HIS HEART,
available January 2008.*

Dear Reader,

I think we all question God's purpose for allowing bad things in your life. My stepdaughter Brenda struggled with stage 4 ovarian cancer and died on September 16, 2006. She had everything to live for and she was so filled with faith. Why did this horrendous disease happen? As I struggled with this, I looked for the positives that have resulted. I've learned to appreciate my husband and our marriage much more during this time. It has changed me for the better. Brenda had been covered by prayers of family, friends and many who didn't even know her. They sent cards, gifts of money and lent a hand, far beyond our expectations. Cesar Millan, the Dog Whisperer, touched Brenda's life with a telephone call out of the goodness of his heart. How can I question why things happen?

When life tumbles around us and we begin to question God's purpose, look for the good that results. God is with us always, and remember 1 Peter 1: 7. Trials happen so that our faith may be proved genuine, and we praise Him who gave us life.

Gail Gaymer Martin

QUESTIONS FOR DISCUSSION

1. Having a purpose in life seems to be a basic struggle for Marsha. Identify your life purpose and how it has affected your life.

2. What are the dynamics of in-laws falling in love and marrying? Do you know any in-laws who've married? If so, what are the pros and cons?

3. Jeff's question was why does God allow bad things to happen? Marsha had her explanations. What are yours?

4. Have you ever felt as if God has let you down or have you felt angry at God? What caused these feelings? How did this affect your life and how was it resolved?

5. Marsha struggled with the issue of what God means by being "unequally yoked." Does this situation affect a marriage, and, if so, how?

6. Having an emotionally impaired child can be a challenge. Discuss the techniques Jeff and Marsha used with Bonnie. Which seemed most effective?

7. What does the Footprints In The Sand story mean to your life?

8. Barb's novel writing provided her a catharsis. Discuss Journaling or other methods of dealing with life issues.

9. Have you or someone in your life experienced molestation? Barb might have done things to help herself, but she didn't know how. Discuss ways to deal with this tragic situation.

10. Jeff believed God guided his steps to Marsha. Discuss times in your life when coincidence was actually God's leading.

Love Inspired®

Celebrate Love Inspired's 10th anniversary with top authors and great stories all year long!

A Mommy in Mind
by Arlene Jones

A Tiny Blessings Tale

Reporter Lori Sumner's adoption of a little girl was nearly complete when the baby's teenage mother changed her mind. And even if it meant being pitted against handsome attorney Ramon Estes, Lori was determined to fight for her child!

Steeple Hill®

REQUEST YOUR FREE BOOKS!

2 FREE INSPIRATIONAL NOVELS PLUS 2 FREE MYSTERY GIFTS

Love Inspired

YES! Please send me 2 FREE Love Inspired® novels and my 2 FREE mystery gifts. After receiving them, if I don't wish to receive any more books, I can return the shipping statement marked "cancel." If I don't cancel, I will receive 4 brand-new novels every month and be billed just $3.99 per book in the U.S., or $4.74 per book in Canada, plus 25¢ shipping and handling per book and applicable taxes, if any*. That's a savings of 20% off the cover price! I understand that accepting the 2 free books and gifts places me under no obligation to buy anything. I can always return a shipment and cancel at any time. Even if I never buy another book from Steeple Hill, the two free books and gifts are mine to keep forever.

113 IDN EF26   313 IDN EF27

Name	(PLEASE PRINT)
Address	Apt. #
City	State/Prov.	Zip/Postal Code
Signature (if under 18, a parent or guardian must sign)	

Order online at www.LoveInspiredBooks.com

Or mail to Steeple Hill Reader Service™:

IN U.S.A.: P.O. Box 1867, Buffalo, NY 14240-1867
IN CANADA: P.O. Box 609, Fort Erie, Ontario L2A 5X3

Not valid to current Love Inspired subscribers.

Want to try two free books from another series?
Call 1-800-873-8635 or visit www.morefreebooks.com

* Terms and prices subject to change without notice. NY residents add applicable sales tax. Canadian residents will be charged applicable provincial taxes and GST. This offer is limited to one order per household. All orders subject to approval. Credit or debit balances in a customer's account(s) may be offset by any other outstanding balance owed by or to the customer. Please allow 4 to 6 weeks for delivery.

LIREG07

Love Inspired

SUSPENSE
RIVETING INSPIRATIONAL ROMANCE

SECRET AGENT MINISTER
Lenora Worth

Things were not as they seemed...

The minister of Lydia Cantrell's dreams had another calling.
As his secretary, she knew the church members adored him,
but she was shocked to discover Pastor Dev Malone's past as
a Christian secret agent. Her shock turned to disbelief when
Pastor Dev revealed he'd made some enemies—
and that he and Lydia were in danger.

Available September wherever you buy books.

Steeple
Hill®

Love Inspired®

TITLES AVAILABLE NEXT MONTH

Don't miss these four stories in September

SOMEBODY'S BABY by Annie Jones
Josie Redmond had raised her twin sister's baby as her own, and now the child's father was in town seeking his son. But when Adam Burdett saw Josie with little Nathan, he discovered it wasn't just his child he was interested in.

A MOMMY IN MIND by Arlene James
A Tiny Blessings Tale

A tiny baby stole Lori Summer's heart and made her petition to adopt. Before the papers were signed, though, the teenage mother changed her mind. The teen's lawyer Ramon Estes believed in his case, but longed to get to know his opposition in a more personal way.

A TREASURE OF THE HEART by Valerie Hansen
She needed stability, so Lillie Delaney headed to her tiny hometown to find it. But everything there had changed. She turned to Pastor James Warner for guidance, only to find a handsome motorcycle riding rebel who showed her that the Lord does indeed work in very mysterious ways....

LOVE'S HEALING TOUCH by Jane Myers Perrine
In the busy hospital emergency room, Dr. Ana Ramirez admired orderly Mike Fuller's quick skills and impressive bedside manner. So she proposed a simple cup of coffee to talk about his future, never expecting to find herself wishing she were a part of it.

LICNM0807